Losing London

A Novel by
Joey Jones

ISBN: 0692778616
ISBN-13: 9780692778616

For my dad (1937-2007).
He always believed in me.
He always loved me.

Also by Joey Jones
A Bridge Apart

A Bridge Apart, the debut novel by Joey Jones, is a remarkable love story that tests the limits of trust and forgiveness...

In the quaint river town of New Bern, North Carolina, at 28 years of age the pieces of Andrew Callaway's life are all falling into place. His real estate firm is flourishing and he's engaged to be married in less than two weeks to a beautiful banker named Meredith Hastings. But when Meredith heads to Tampa, Florida—the wedding location—with her mother, fate, or maybe some human intervention, has it that Andrew happens upon Cooper McKay, the only other woman he's ever loved.

A string of shocking emails lead Andrew to question whether he can trust his fiancé, and in the midst of trying to unravel the mystery he finds himself spending time with Cooper. When Meredith catches wind of what's going on back at home, she's forced to consider calling off the wedding, which ultimately draws Andrew closer to Cooper. Andrew soon discovers he's making choices he might not be able, or even want, to untangle. As the story unfolds, the decisions that are made will drastically change the lives of everyone involved, and bind them closer together than they could have ever imagined.

Acknowledgments

*L*osing *London*, my second novel, is a dream come true. There are many people who helped make this book become a reality. First, I would like to thank God for the gift of writing. Next, I better thank my wife for supporting my new career as a novelist. She knows my faults, but she loves me anyway. My sons, Branden and Parker, make me smile and laugh often. Branden deserves my gratitude for having the guts—as a teenager—to read my first novel, *A Bridge Apart*. Parker was just born in July, and I thank God that he is healthy and amazing.

I would also like to thank my wonderful family. My parents, Joe and Patsy Jones, helped mold me into the man I've become, and I hope I leave a legacy that makes them proud. My dad now lives in Heaven, and I miss him dearly. My Mom, my breakfast partner and one of my best friends, is the most humble person I know. My brothers and sisters, DeAnn, Judy, Lee, Penny, and Richard are some of my closest friends. Their support, in many ways, is my foundation.

My editors and reviewers, Rebekah Jones, Kim Jones, Erin Haywood, Pam Gray, and Donna Matthews, are extremely talented at polishing my writing. My graphic designer, Meredith Walsh, has done an amazing job with both of my novel covers.

Lastly, I would like to thank some people who have been influential throughout my life. Some for a season, but each for a reason.

Thank you to Andrew Haywood, BJ Horne, Billy Nobles, Cathy Errick, Diane Tyndall, Gail Spain, Jan Raynor, Jeanette Towne, Josh Haywood, Josh Towne, Kenny Ford, Mitch Fortescue, Nicholas Sparks, Ray White, Richard Banks, Steve Cobb, and Steven Harrell. It is a privilege to call each of you my friend.

Losing London

1

Losing London had caused more tears to stream down Harper Adams' face than all of her previous life experiences combined. Losing James had proven to be a distant second. Losing two people she loved more than anything in the world within a one-month period was a reality she would have never imagined possible. There was, however, a difference.

Now that the initial sting of rejection had passed, she couldn't care less if she ever saw the face of her ex-husband again. Eleven months ago, James had slammed the door on his way out of their townhouse in Silver Spring, Maryland, and she hadn't heard from him since. The jerk hadn't so much as picked up the phone or even taken five minutes to drop a sympathy card in the mail.

When the mailman knocked on her door today, Thursday, June 4th, she was surprised to find him there. Most days, she found herself waving as he drove off from the row of boxes out by the road. Harper reached for the package in his hand, and as he walked to his truck in the parking lot, her hazel eyes remained fixated on the name in the top left corner: Dr. Harold Thorpe. Dr. Thorpe, a slender and overworked gentleman in his mid-sixties—twice her age—had been a close friend to her sister. In fact, he was the main reason London had moved to Emerald Isle, North Carolina two years ago.

Why in the world would he send me a package? she wondered. She had met the man many years ago, but that was about it. They'd never even had a real, adult conversation.

The 8x12 inch padded envelope felt light in her hand. Beyond curious about the contents, Harper hurried inside and dug through the drawer next to the sink, searching for a pair of scissors. "Where does all this stuff come from?" she asked an empty room as she dug through the mess.

Harper halted the search for an instant and sighed, taking a moment to study the pair of tweezers in front of her face. Where had those been yesterday when she'd spent twenty minutes hunting for them? Dumb question, she quickly realized. Next, she came across the tape dispenser that she'd needed last week. But no scissors. Out of everything in this drawer, she found it hard to believe that there wasn't a single sharp object inside.

Keys, she decided, *I'll just use a key.*

The set on the keyring jingled when she plucked them from a nail—a nail that James had tacked into the wall when they'd first moved into the townhouse after their honeymoon five years ago. A second nail, just above her spot, remained empty. Harper stood there long enough to remember what that meant. No one else had taken his place—that's exactly what *that* meant. And to be honest, she'd recently started to wonder if she would ever find a man who would be able to sweep her off her feet the way James once had. But maybe the real question was: Would any man worth a darn want to be with a twenty-nine-year-old divorced woman who had gained fifteen pounds since graduating college?

At such a silly thought, Harper turned her attention back to the package, which she had decided contained a book, and tried to shake off the ridiculous ideas running through her aching head. That, she suddenly remembered, is what she'd been doing when the doorbell rang . . . she'd been on her way to the medicine cabinet.

Harper chuckled. Finding someone she'd trust to hang his keys on that nail . . . who was she kidding? She hadn't even been on a real date since James ran off with that bimbo. Why should she even have any interest in a serious relationship at this point in her life, anyway? How could she ever trust a man again? When she had needed her husband the most, he had packed his bags and left her with an empty townhouse and two pairs of his dress shoes. Those ended up flying out of the second story window. She'd hoped to hit his car, but the taillights moved a little too quickly as she'd cocked her arm and launched each one like a football.

The key cut right through the tape. Harper then used her fingers to separate the flaps on the envelope, and she nearly fainted when she held one of the most beautiful books she'd ever seen in front of her eyes. The cover design was absolutely amazing. One she knew she would have picked up if she were browsing the local bookstore shelves for a good read. But it wasn't the silhouette of a couple sitting in an antique convertible car overlooking the ocean in the dusk that tugged at her heart. It was the name below the title.

How?

When?

These one word questions led her on a search for any clues she might be able to find immediately.

Wedged into the cream-colored pages, she noticed a single sheet of paper, barely protruding from the top of the book. Wondering if it held some answers, she found herself tugging at it with her fingertips.

Unfolding the letter, she instantly recognized the handwriting . . . London's handwriting.

2

With a Michelob Light occupying his left hand, Mitch Quinn was swaying on his porch swing in Emerald Isle. He held the beer, not because he liked the taste, but because drinking beer had become a habit. Good in some ways, bad in others. A lot of his habits had changed in the past year, like not going to church. Kenny, the pastor at one of the local churches and a good friend, dropped by his house from time to time but not once had he asked Mitch why he hadn't seen him at a single service since officiating London's funeral. *The funeral . . .* Mitch hadn't gone to that either. As Pastor Kenny stood behind the pulpit and spoke kind words about London's time on Earth—making sure to mention all the lives she'd touched along the way—Mitch had spent the morning of the graveside service alone, wrapped in an old blanket on a cold, tissue-covered wooden floor . . . wearing nothing but an unbuttoned long-sleeved dress shirt, a black tie, and a pair of Joe Cool boxers. London had given him the boxers. As loved ones gathered around the cherry oak casket to offer their condolences, the hanger on Mitch's doorknob wore his dress coat.

Funerals had never been his thing. Not that they were anyone's *thing* so to speak. Even if he didn't really know the person who had died all that well, for him, having to witness the hurt of those who did—dressed in black and attached at the arm—always seemed to gut him the same as if he had lost his best friend. This time he had.

Death, he had noticed over the years, seemed to eat at even the most put together man like a newly hatched worm carving a tunnel into the core of an innocent apple. No matter how good a person's life had been before the loss, when the person they love more than life itself dies, their world seems to erupt. The universe around them appears twice its size and at the same time they feel as though it has become ten times emptier. The causes of death, which Mitch had taken notice of while reading the morning newspaper for as long as he could remember, were as endless as the obituaries within it. Heart attacks. Cancer. Pneumonia. Strokes. Diabetes. Old age. Sadly, over a steaming latte he knew the names often went unnoticed. Faces overlooked. Eulogies unread. Until, that is, the letters in black ink pieced together a name that hits home.

For Mitch Quinn, who tossed another empty beer can onto the boards below his feet, that day had come exactly one year ago today. He'd known all along that losing London would be difficult, but never had he considered that it would drain every ounce of life from his inner confines. When his agent called to offer his condolences a few days after London's passing, then twenty words later asked the question: "When can I expect to see you back out in the field?", Mitch, without hesitation, replied with the question that still racked his mind daily: "How long does it take to get over the death of your soulmate?" The air between them grew silent for a moment. "That's when you'll see me again," Mitch concluded. Since then, he hadn't even bothered checking in with the office.

He was still mad at himself for not going to the funeral. He should have. No matter how much he hated funerals, he should have been there. It was selfish of him not to go. He knew that now, but what good did it do him? None. If anything, it made him wonder what London would think of him if she'd somehow known he hadn't been there—if she were up in Heaven watching down on him and everyone else.

At least he had sent a plant, he thought, as a cool breeze blew in off the Atlantic Ocean, just on the other side of his house. It had always been amazing to him how the salty air could whip around the house and clear his sinuses. Two days before the funeral he had spent an hour surrounded by the smell of daffodils and the sound of water dripping from the mouth of a naked statue. He'd wandered aimlessly around the fountain in the center of the local flower shop, almost certain that he would wear a circular path in the carpet before the lady ringing up customers would be able to assist him. After she finally made her way over to him, Mitch remembered how stupid he felt when he couldn't find the courage to muster up even one word. Picking out flowers that would make London smile had always come easy for him, but selecting the right piece for the uninvited occasion—that still didn't feel like reality—had seemed impossible. He was glad that the florist had finally come over, but at that moment he felt like a one-year-old. He stared at her, but he wasn't quite sure what to say, or if he even knew how to talk anymore.

"Sorry it has taken me so long to get to you," he vaguely heard her say. "My help called in sick today . . ." The lack of response and the look on Mitch's face explained to the woman that he was confused, frustrated, and angry all at the same time, which she had learned from years of experience in the floral business usually meant one of two things: divorce or death.

After a moment, she discovered the answer . . . the frown on his face told the story. Someone close, she could sense. Someone he loved deeply. Probably his wife.

Mitch attempted to mimic a smile that appeared to come naturally for her, but that week, along with the months that followed, his lips seemed to curl only one way. He hadn't anticipated his first trip out of the house since London passed going that badly. *Just ask for her help, Mitch,* he whispered inside his head, as if trying to remember how to speak the English language. That is what she was there for, right?

He stood in silence for a moment longer, and that is when he felt the tears begin to form in the corner of his eyelids. *Walk out before you start crying,* he warned himself. But before he could take even one step toward the door that jingled every time a customer walked in or out, Mitch found himself sobbing on the flower shop floor, in the presence of a woman he'd seen before but never even had a real conversation with.

Her nametag read *Cindy*, and as she hustled to the counter for a box of tissues, Mitch continued to wail. She handed him one and gently set the box on the floor beside him. Since no other customers were in the store, she flipped the sign in the window, locked the door, and pulled down the shades.

"It's okay to cry," she made sure he knew. But in the ten years since her mother had passed this shop down to her—plus the five she'd worked as a delivery girl—not once had she seen a grown man so helpless. This man really loved this woman, she realized. It took a good ten minutes for her to get him to pull his head from between his legs and look her in the eyes. When he finally did, she poured him a cup of coffee from the back room and then sat across from him at the counter while he began to talk about a woman named London.

3

Living on the East Coast, where she'd been born and raised, Harper had never experienced an earthquake. But, as she began to read the words her sister had written—at least more than a year ago—she imagined an earthquake would feel to the ground much like the sharp pains that were ripping apart her heart. She covered her mouth with one hand and moved her eyes from left to right, slowly, attempting to absorb every word.

Dear Harper,

If you are reading this letter, then you already know cancer has taken my life. I asked Dr. Thorpe to mail you this package one year later. Don't think that I was cheated, though. I wasn't. This disease was part of my purpose in life. God knew that through me other's lives would be touched . . . this is not the end; it is merely the beginning. My memoir, "Mitch & Me", will carry on my purpose in life.

I spent the last eight months of my life writing about my life, focusing the story on the time I spent with Mitch Quinn. You never got a chance to meet Mitch, and I know I didn't talk much about him, but when you read our story you will know why God placed this man in our lives.

I know your life is busy these days, with work, James, and trying to get pregnant—I'm sorry I will not be around to be an aunt. I know you will raise a wonderful daughter or son. Make sure to spoil her or him like I would have.

James . . .

Harper stopped reading soon after the mention of the devil. The letter reminded her that London never knew about James cheating on her. She didn't know that he'd left her for another woman and that they hadn't gotten pregnant like they had hoped to for so long. And although she was glad that he hadn't gotten her pregnant and then left, for a moment she felt as though she had let her sister down.

With that thought eating at her mind, she read on.

To add to your busy life, I am entrusting you with my final two wishes.

First, please check on Mitch for me . . . make sure he knows it is okay to fall in love again.

Secondly, if you and Mitch think my memoir is good enough for a traditional publishing house, please pull some strings for me. With the contacts the two of you have, I know you can make it happen. I only printed this one copy through an online self-publishing company. They have no rights to my work. My wish is that all of the proceeds somehow benefit children who are affected by cancer.

Mitch knows nothing about the memoir; I want it to be a surprise for him, something through which he can remember me. I barely finished it, but God gave me just enough time. After you've read it, please let Mitch be the second person to read the story.

I love you with all of my heart, Harper, and I will always be there for you . . . in yours.

~ Love, London

Cautiously, Harper folded the letter exactly the way it had been when she'd taken it from the book. London's book. It was still hard to fathom that she was holding a book written by her very own sister. Not that she didn't expect London could write a book; London was very intelligent and had always been amazing when it came to telling stories. London was the one in girl scouts whom all the other girls asked to tell a story when they would sit around a campfire out in the woods. But they were never scary like the stories she'd heard about boy scouts telling. London's were about hope and love and magical moments that made little girls realize that dreams were as real as the imagination. London's and Harper's dream of growing up and attending the University of Maryland together had come true. While in college, their dorm room was the one where all the girls gathered late at night. After the girls slipped into their PJ's, London would share memories about yearly summer family vacations in Emerald Isle, where the two of them had played at the water park, fished on the pier with their dad, and experienced puppy love with boys they'd never see again.

Harper couldn't help but notice the worn creases and tear stains, some fresh and some aged, as she'd tucked the letter away. She couldn't imagine the thoughts and the fears that must have been going through London's mind when she'd slipped the paper into the book and sealed the envelope.

As Harper once again studied the package the book had arrived in, she wondered why London had wanted Dr. Thorpe to wait an entire year before sending the memoir to her. Whatever the reason, it had probably been better that she got it in the mail than to have found it in London's apartment when she and her mother cleaned out the place. That day, she remembered, had been more painful than the funeral or even the moment her mother called with the bad news. As the two of them pulled London's clothes from dusty hangers, folded them, and placed them into cardboard boxes, reality hit hard. London was gone. Flipping through picture albums wouldn't bring her back and neither would the gallons of tears she and her mother had poured while wishing the memories would somehow make her real again.

Reading the letter reminded Harper that today was the one-year anniversary of her younger sister's death. Which hadn't crossed her mind since . . . two minutes before the mailman arrived when she was staring aimlessly into the mirror. An empty feeling suddenly swept across her body—the same feeling she'd felt in London's apartment. What would she find as she began to read the cream colored pages of the book that she hadn't been able to set down? Getting through the letter had been painful enough; the thought of swallowing the words that would bring London's story to life frightened her.

I will start reading later, Harper convinced herself. She just didn't think she could take anymore right now. As much as she wanted to read the first word, the first paragraph . . . every word, every paragraph . . . right now . . . all at once . . . she knew she needed some time to clear her mind. She also needed to get rid of this pounding sinus headache. Maybe the medicine would also help settle this overwhelming surprise.

4

Wanting to forget how stupid he'd felt that day at the florist shop, Mitch reared back and let the swing fly, wishing his troubles would fly away with it. But as soon as he looked toward his Jeep in the driveway, he found himself feeling exactly like the plant he had buckled into the backseat after leaving the florist. Somehow, water constantly dripped from the leaves of that darn thing, giving it the appearance that the plant was actually shedding tears. The florist had suggested it, but until this day Mitch still wasn't sure why he had spent twenty minutes weeping profusely while telling her how much he loved London Adams. Maybe it had been because she was the first person he'd tried to talk to since London died. Pastor Kenny had attempted to reach out to him, but Mitch had ignored the knocks on the door and the phone calls. Or maybe it was the look on the florist's face that said I'm here to help you. Although he was pretty sure that look meant with the flowers, and not as a psychiatrist. He'd opened up like a can of soda and poured himself all over her carpet. He could still hear the clicking sound that her old cash register made as she pecked at the buttons before he left. It sounded exactly like London's typewriter, and he remembered thinking of London sitting at her desk as the lady rang him up. On a small card with a picture of a flower at the top, he had accidentally scratched *"Dear London,"* as the heading. But London, he soon realized, wouldn't be the one reading the card. That is when he'd hid his face in his hands and cried a little more. Her family would read the card . . . a family he had never even met. And now, as he thought about all the times she had talked about them, he wondered if he would ever meet them. He hoped to one day, but her funeral just hadn't seemed the opportune time for making their acquaintance.

Mitch continued to push the swing, kicking his feet harder on the porch until the chains sounded like they might snap. He should write the lady from the florist shop a thank you note. Maybe that would get his mind off London for a few minutes. He'd been meaning to do that for the last three hundred and sixty-five days, but he had never gotten around to it. Not because he didn't have the time, obviously. If for nothing else, though, she deserved a "thank you" for canceling the sale on her register and especially for not charging him for the dozen or so used cards he'd left scattered on the counter for her to collect.

The screen door slammed hard behind Mitch as he entered the house. He found a sheet of paper in his desk drawer. Then, he grabbed a book to write on and headed back out to the porch. As he began to scribble a note on the blank sheet of paper, he thought of the words he'd attached to the plant.

My thoughts and prayers are with you during this trying time. Take comfort in knowing that London is in a better place.

— Mitch Quinn.

Now, he wished he'd said more. But what more was there to say? he wondered, as he once again found his head buried in his hands.

Instead of finishing the thank you note, he fussed at God below his breath, which was weird. If he didn't believe in God anymore, why did he keep complaining to him? Why didn't he just forget about him? Mitch knew the answer to that question. God was his only chance at ever seeing London again. He was certain that London's faith, if a person's faith could get her to Heaven, had gotten her there. But like the world around him, God, in his mind's eye, seemed to have taken a leave of absence from his life. If his parents were still alive, he was sure they would tell him to pray about it. "Read your Bible, go to church," they would say. But they weren't around; God had taken them from him, too.

Mitch barely heard the sound that the sheet of paper and the pen in his hand made when they fell to the porch. Every time he tried to pray it made him think of London even more, and after a year of asking God "*Why?*" no reasonable answer had been given. His Bible was covered with dust in the corner of his sock drawer, where London had wedged it after reading a passage in the book of Psalms while leaning against the headboard—the same one that he now often found himself sitting at throughout all hours of the night. He wondered if he would ever open the cover of that Bible again. "You'll always have this to remember me by," London had said. He could still remember the smile on her face when she handed him the world's best-selling book, his name inscribed in silver lettering in the bottom right corner.

5

arper popped a pill in her mouth that would help soothe her sinus headache. A cold glass of water washed it down just right. She couldn't let everything that was going on in her head right now push back her work schedule any further. She was already stretching to meet her deadline. *It was a privilege to be able to work from home, not an excuse to do other things.* Those were the words that Tara, her boss, had used last week when Harper had mentioned the word *extension*. Harper had used that word one—or maybe *ten* was the number Tara had used—too many times in the past year.

Harper's job, for one of the most popular educational television channels on the planet, was to field stories: visit places, interview people, check facts, get the scoop. Then, if the powers-that-be thought the story was worthwhile, they'd send a camera crew with a director and staff to film. Sometimes that meant the story would turn into a documentary; other times it might turn into a reality television show. She'd been in this position long enough now to have a pretty good hunch on which stories would work for television and which ones wouldn't. Recently she'd spent time aboard a popular cruise ship, mainly focusing on the behind-the-scenes life of the crew. She'd spent a good amount of time with the ship's captain, a Puerto Rican-born man with the coolest accent in the world. He was clever and funny, and not at all what she expected a man responsible for thousands of people on any given day to be like. He knew weather inside and out, from storms and currents to the stars and the sun. He reminded her of someone who might have lived in the 1700's and survived off the land. She'd also spent time with the Maitre'D, the room service staff, and some of the ship's guests. When all was said and done, she knew the story had a good chance. It encompassed all of the elements necessary for television: excitement, danger, love, and scandal, which is why she wanted to make sure her reporting back to Tara was accurate and included every possible angle.

Tara must have known that Harper was thinking about her, or maybe even that she'd just now finally opened her laptop and begun to put puzzle pieces together. The caller ID on Harper's cell phone displayed Tara's number. Part of her wanted to ignore the call, but she knew that wouldn't be in her best interest. Instead, she decided that she'd just fudge a little on her progress.

"Hey, Tara," Harper answered, faking excitement.

"Harper, how's the report coming along?"

"It's . . . coming," she replied, honestly.

"Well, put it on hold. I have another assignment for you."

Harper instantly breathed a huge sigh of relief, just not into the receiver; she made sure of that, holding the phone in mid-air, pumping her fist.

Tara's voice continued to flow through the speaker. "This one is time sensitive, and you're either going to love it or hate it." She paused for a moment. "But before I tell you what it is, I'm just going to let you know that I'm not taking no for an answer."

Harper furrowed her brow. It was like a Christmas miracle, but in the summertime. However, it sounded like there might be a catch. "O . . . k." This was Tara, her boss and best friend. One moment one particular thing or person was the most important in the world, then the next moment that all changed to something new. Something shiny.

"Bill is in Hawaii studying hula dancing." Tara's mind shifted to hula skirts and mixed drinks. "Oh, brother, that's going to be a disaster." She paused, collecting her thoughts. "But enough about that. Where was I? Oh, right. Haley is on vacation in California . . . which leaves you." Harper waited for the punch line. Then, it came. "I need you to go to North Carolina."

North Carolina? Had Harper heard right? "You want me to scout a story in North Carolina?"

"Yes, and I know you are familiar with the area, which makes you the perfect candidate for this story." Tara hesitated, but not long enough for Harper to get a word in. "I need you to go to the coast," she insisted, but at the same time realizing a trip to the coast of North Carolina might be somewhat difficult for Harper, since the last time she'd driven down had been for her sister's funeral.

"What?" she questioned. "Why?" Before today, Harper doubted if she would ever even visit the area again.

"Sharks," she said simply.

"Sharks? There are sharks . . ." Harper paused in mid-sentence, but only because Tara cut her off.

"Shark attacks. There have been several on the coast of North Carolina and it's becoming a buzz. The latest was in Emerald Isle." Tara expected Harper to put up more of a challenge if she asked her to go there, which is why she'd decided to give her options. "But you don't have to go to Emerald Isle. There have also been shark attacks reported in Ocracoke and Surf City. I need you in one of these places, Harper. You're the most talented person on this team."

Harper chuckled out loud. "That's not what you said last week."

"Last week is history, Harper. This week is a new week. You can finish the report on the cruise ship when you return from North Carolina."

"So when do you want me to go and for how long?"

"A rental car will be at your place in an hour . . ." Less time for Harper to back out, Tara figured.

Harper raised an eyebrow. "An hour?" she questioned. "Really?"

"You're single. You have no kids. You don't even have a cat. This is the nature of your job, Harper. And I'm your boss . . . and your best friend." She threw in the best friend part, knowing that Harper knew she owed her. If she wasn't her best friend she would have fired her by now. The truth was, Harper had been off her game for a long time, but Tara knew she would make a comeback. "So, I think that formula equals . . . as soon as you can pack your bags."

"What?"

"If you leave in the next hour, you can make it there late this evening."

"Today? You really want me to leave today?"

"Yes, breaking story. Remember? Important. Make a vacation out of it. Have some fun. Meet some guys. Have some drinks. Dance naked on the beach at night." She paused for a moment. "Just don't go skinny dipping?"

"What? Why would I go skinny dipping?"

"Why not?"

"Why would I dance naked on the beach?"

"That part you are cleared to do, just not the skinny dipping?"

"You're making no sense, Tara."

"Sharks, Harper. Remember? The story you're going to check out is sharks! Stay out of the water."

This conversation had turned crazy as soon as it had started, Harper thought to herself. But most conversations with Tara either started or ended up in left field. There was one time Tara had ended up in left field. Literally. At the Baltimore Orioles game, streaking with two sorority sisters. Now that was a funny story. Tara told it all the time at corporate meetings, which was weird because having a record almost kept her from getting hired in the first place. But people always laughed when she told the story, especially the men in the room. So Harper guessed it didn't matter too much. It was just embarrassing to Harper.

"What about accommodations?"

"Once you let me know which location you choose, I'll take care of it and call you on your way."

Dressed in the same pink pajamas her morning had started in, Harper reached for London's memoir—*Mitch & Me*—and then sat Indian style on the comforter that stretched across her lonely bed. There was no way she could leave for North Carolina without starting this book, which added a bright spot to this very odd set of coincides that had happened in the past hour. Going out on assignment would give her plenty of time to read. Sure, she'd have to work each day, but she'd have plenty of free time, too. No one from work expecting the lonely divorcee to go out for dinner after a long day. No yoga classes at the gym. No evening out for drinks with Tara, which reminded her that she'd been meaning to ask Tara why they never went to each other's homes anymore. She'd invited Tara over a handful of times, but Tara always wanted to go out. For the longest time Harper had just brushed it off, but the more she thought about it, the more it seemed odd, like Tara, which was probably the answer.

Harper closed her eyes and flipped open to the first page. Tears began to stream down her face as she read the words her sister had written.

I will never forget the day Mitch Quinn walked into my life. The lanes were filled with strangers, all bowling for a cause—Cancer. I had bowled at the event last year and recognized most of the faces, except for the man bowling on lane fourteen. He was new and smiling from ear to ear . . . had been ever since he walked in. Everyone, except for me, seemed to know him. The younger children were climbing on his limbs and hugging his knees. I noticed that he treated each one like they were his own.

Harper glanced away from the page. Even though London had told her how she and Mitch met, reading the words on paper brought life to their story. After taking a moment to digest the first paragraph, she realized reading the book would be more challenging than she had initially imagined; nonetheless, she went on.

Harold was the one who introduced me to Mitch, the man with a camera that looked more expensive than my car. I could tell Mitch took an interest in me from the moment we shook hands. There was something in his eyes, his baby blue eyes, saying: "I want to get to know you, London Adams." That look brought a smile to my face, and I'd be lying if I said I didn't feel the same way about him; I'd been thinking it since I rolled a gutter ball on my first try.

Mitch invited me to bowl alongside him. At first I declined his offer because I hated the thought of leaving Hannah, who liked for me to call her Hannah the Banana, but after my four-year-old friend called me out in front of Mitch, saying that she wouldn't be jealous of my new boyfriend—the instant title she awarded Mitch—he invited her, too. I'll always remember the instant spark between Hannah and Mitch. I expected his face to turn red, but it didn't. Instead, he laughed and said, "I like you," to Hannah. When he said she was invited, too, she didn't waste any time showing Mitch which ball belonged to her.

After a short conversation with the manager, he was kind enough to add mine and Hannah's names to the screen on lane fourteen. Mitch easily lugged our two eight-pound orange balls—Hannah had insisted we have the same color—to his lane and dropped them in the rack next to his. Of course, his was special with drilled holes filled with white plugs, which he said helped him spin the ball.

"Why don't you just throw it straight down the lane?" is one of the first questions I ever asked Mitch Quinn. I didn't quite understand why he wanted it to hang over the gutter before cutting back toward the middle pin. It didn't make much sense to me, especially since it nearly fell overboard each time he threw it.

Mitch laughed at me, though, and said it scattered the pins better. He even tried to teach me the technique, but in the end I stuck with the tried-and-true method—the quickest way from my hand to the middle pin, which my ball rarely found—a straight line.

After our first of five games of bowling that day, Mitch and I ate pizza that tasted like spaghetti sauce and cheap cheese slapped on a piece of soggy dough. Even though the food was bad, we talked like we had known each other our entire lives. To my surprise, Mitch let Hannah take pictures with his camera. When Hannah didn't have the camera in her hand, she found her way into every photograph that Mitch snapped. The kids smiled because they were happy; Mitch and I smiled because the money being raised would go to help them live another day.

The blanket on Harper's lap doubled as a tear catcher, and as she let the pages close, she continued to sniffle. That was all she could read for now, she decided, even if she hadn't needed to stop to take a quick shower. Even though she had taken precautionary measures by placing a box of Kleenex on the bed, she had neglected to reach for them. She'd been too engrossed in the story. For some reason it felt better to let the tears make trails of their own.

From beneath the blankets, she tugged at the ear of a teddy bear and nestled the face of the shabby animal close to her own. Snuggles had been London's bear when she was a little girl and he had been the first item Harper claimed when her sister passed.

Lying there in her bed, Harper wondered what London had left for Mitch? If he had stared at something of hers for hours, crying as he thought about the way it made her smile? How was he doing? she wondered. Did he think about London every night as he stared at the inside of his eyelids? And why hadn't Mitch come to

London's funeral? Harper had never been able to understand that. She wondered if now, since an entire year had passed, Mitch had moved on with his life, like London wanted him to. She wished she knew more about London's mystery man. In the dozen or so phone calls she and her sister exchanged every month London hadn't revealed much about Mitch Quinn, other than his name. How tall was he? she wondered. Was he an accountant? A policeman? Did he like horseback riding, like London? What was he doing right now? Had *he* replaced the familiar feeling of a warm body with a stuffed animal?

6

For the last hour Mitch had been tossing and turning and he couldn't seem to keep his eyes shut.

Something was missing . . .

He rolled over once and reached the edge of his twin-sized bed. There it was, on the floor, the body pillow he liked to keep wedged between his legs, like London had always done with Snuggles. He wondered if he had thrown it there in his sleep. Sometimes in the middle of these daytime naps he would think he saw someone standing in his room, and he would throw whatever he could get his hands on at the ghost-like image. Of course, there was never really anyone there and he didn't know if it was a dreamlike state or something else, but whatever it was it was weird. He would often wake up, having forgotten all about throwing an object across the room, and find something broken or knocked out of place. Eventually it would all come back to him.

This had been happening regularly since London died, and in the beginning Mitch had allowed his mind to convince him that the image was of her watching over him while he slept. He even talked himself into believing that she'd had Snuggles in her arms, which he later realized was absurd. Before London had died he'd never taken naps in the middle of the day, but now he did after nights when it had taken him forever to fall asleep.

He often wondered about Snuggles. He hoped that the bear was protecting her in some way. If he could have chosen one thing of London's to keep, it would have been Snuggles, but for some reason it just didn't seem right. Still, he knew that holding something in his arms that London had slept with every night would help him sleep better. He often wondered if he should have contacted her family and asked if he could go through her things, maybe keep a few items that he and London had left behind at her apartment. Maybe he would still do that, he considered. There were items other than Snuggles, too, that had meant a lot to London. Like her collection of Snoopy figurines. He wondered if they were in a box in someone's basement now.

A few months back Mitch had purchased a set of black-out curtains to help him sleep during the day. He flipped on the lamp, and he didn't see any shattered glass on the floor that might stick in his feet on his way to the refrigerator. He bypassed the beer shelf and poured a glass of milk. When he was a kid, his mother had always given him milk when he woke up in the middle of the night and couldn't go back to sleep. He figured that should work just as well during the day. He wasn't sure if it had really ever helped, but she had always insisted that it would. One thing he realized quickly today is that it didn't mix well with the taste of beer that lingered on his tongue, and he doubted it would settle in his stomach all that well either. If nothing else, in his younger days the milk had helped him grow strong bones and teeth. At least that is what the doctor said when he was eight and his foot got run over by an old woman behind the wheel of a Cadillac in the church parking lot. He'd walked away without even a fracture, and in thirty-one years he'd never once broken a bone, had stitches for a cut or even chipped a tooth.

Mitch relished the fact that he'd never been in the hospital as a patient, except for when he was born. He'd been there way too many times, though, to visit people he loved; so many times that his outlook on hospitals had become much the same as his thoughts on funerals. He hoped that Hannah would never have to spend another night at Duke or any hospital for that matter. If tomorrow were any other Friday, he would be planning to see Hannah first thing in the morning. Sometimes that meant he would travel to Durham, and other times that meant he'd visit Hannah at Dr. Thorpe's house on the island. Most days lately she had been able to get out of the house and live like a normal little girl: Eat ice cream. Play in the sand at the beach. Climb trees in his backyard. Tomorrow, however, he knew he would end up spending the better part of his day with Myrtle at the adoption agency. She'd said it would probably take a while to finish up the final adoption papers. Myrtle had been very sweet and helpful to him; she was the typical grandmother type. She had frosted gray hair and talked loud enough for the people two offices down to hear every word she spoke. Mitch figured everyone in her office knew his life story by now; he had to talk at twice his normal tone or she would ask him to repeat himself three or four times before she got the information correct. The first time they met in her small office she thought she heard him say his name was Pig Pen. Later that day, after reeling off the names Pig Pen and Mitch Quinn a dozen times out loud to himself, Mitch kind of discovered the similarity, but still, the mix-up hadn't seemed quite as funny as she'd made it out to be at the time. It was funnier to him now than it had been three months after London passed away, but Mitch had never held it against her. She was a kind old woman who smelled like a mixture of moth balls and cigarettes. He knew Myrtle didn't mean any harm by it; he even brought it up himself every now and then to lighten the mood when the process felt like it was dragging along as slow as syrup on a Saturday morning. He'd never anticipated the adoption process being so tedious. But this adoption, in Myrtle's words, was more complex than usual. He'd often wondered if she said that to everyone, and then sometimes he wondered if it had taken so long because she worked about as slow as he had to talk for her to understand him.

For Hannah, this transition from living with her grandfather, Dr. Thorpe, to living full-time with him would be difficult. Mitch knew that. He also knew she understood about as well as a child her age could. She'd even said she did when he talked to her on the phone earlier today, but she wasn't one of those kids that always blurted out the first thing on her mind. Hannah actually thought things through and told people what she thought they wanted to hear, especially if she knew there might be a chance that her response would hurt their feelings. Mitch had always assumed she picked up her ability to genuinely care about other people's feelings from London. She also possessed London's optimistic point-of-view, which was a plus considering that Hannah had been battling leukemia most of her life.

Leaving an empty glass in the sink, Mitch fell back into bed and hoped his mother's home remedy would come through for him once again. He was thankful now that he hadn't started taking those depression pills that the local physician had encouraged. He'd seen all the ads on television and thought he fit the bill. "They'll help you sleep at night," the commercials and the doctor had said. Dr. Thorpe, however, had talked him out of it. He said he'd seen more people go downhill than uphill while taking depression medication. That reminded Mitch he needed to call Dr. Thorpe to get his opinion on a question on one of the forms he needed to turn in tomorrow. He figured he might even take the opportunity to ask if he had been in contact with London's family since she passed away.

Dr. Thorpe was Mitch's only link to London's family, other than Pastor Kenny, and there was no way he was calling him right now. Not because he didn't like the man, but because he didn't want to elicit another visit. He had way too many other things on his plate at the moment to fit in a counseling session. The pastor had run across him in the grocery store a few months back with a case of beer in his cart and told him that he should consider AA. When Mitch had seen him coming, he'd tried his best to cover up the evidence with the three loaves of bread in his cart, but the guy wasn't stupid. He'd spent years at seminary studying theories on human behavior. It was obvious that Mitch was hiding something, and when he tucked himself into bed that night he'd thought about London's famous words: *In bed at night is when guilt often catches up with you. That's God's way of saying you did something you shouldn't have done today.* Most church folk would have stopped there, but London always added: *You know how to know if it's God talking?* She never waited for an answer. *He won't beat you up about your mistakes. That's the guy on the other side of your shoulder.*

Mitch had known he would eventually have to give up his drinking habit, but at that particular point in his recovery—from London's death, not alcohol—he hadn't been quite ready to search for a better way to erase the hurt that accompanied memories of a better life. Although over time, the bitter taste of beer brought on more suffering. In the time it would take the last empty bottle to hit the bottom of the recycling bin, the hurt absorbed by its contents seemed to resurface. Mitch found himself spending warm summer nights on the bathroom floor, hugging the toilet and begging the God he no longer believed existed to take away the pain that was melting his heart. He remembered thinking that if hell was any worse than that feeling he definitely didn't want any part of it.

Instead of seeking help, he passed the days by in solitary, lights shut off and curtains closed. He could vividly remember the night when he'd nearly hit rock bottom. Before he could squeeze the trigger, he'd reached to the shelf above his bed for a small spiral bound journal he'd opened so many times the edge of each page had become worn. The book, filled with London's favorite quotes, saved his life that night. There was one sentence in particular, which he had since committed to memory: "Suicide is a permanent solution to a temporary problem." Below most of the quotes she had jotted down the author's name, but that one she'd left blank. He didn't know if it was one of her own or if she had gotten it from somewhere else, but he would like to find whoever had written it and hug their neck for as long as they would let him. Mitch knew that London had known cancer might eventually take her life, and he often wondered if she had included that quote knowing that one day he might consider ending his own because she was gone.

He knew now that suicide was not the answer, not for anyone. It was as selfish of an act as one could consider committing. There was always a light at the end of the tunnel, no matter how far away it might seem. If you dig long enough and hard enough, he had decided that a man would always come out better than he had been when he first fell in. At least that is what he hoped for now, as the light in his tunnel was starting to shine a little brighter.

Giving up the bottle cold turkey was going to be difficult, but as soon as he'd started the adoption process, he'd decided that there would not be any alcohol in his house once Hannah moved in. She deserved better . . . the best. The home he had planned for her to be raised in didn't consist of anything damaging to a person's mind or body. Along with no drinking, there would be no smoking. No cursing. No cheating. No lying. No stealing. No anything that wouldn't help him in his pursuit to create a better life for a little girl who had been battling a disease she hadn't brought on herself. For that reason, he had absolutely no pity on himself when he sometimes wondered how hard it would be not to have a beer while watching Monday Night Football. If a little girl could beat cancer, and he was determined that she had beat cancer for good, he could give up alcohol.

He wondered constantly about how he would raise Hannah. Would he let her have a TV in her room? Would he let her play video games? Would he let her date before she turned twenty-one? He'd never been a parent before; he didn't even have friends who were parents.

As he stared into the darkness surrounding his bed, Mitch began to see the outline of the picture frames on the nightstand. He knew each pose by memory. London had not only taken over his room, but also his life. When he'd met her, he abandoned all of his friends, and even though they understood why, he wondered now if it had been the right move. London had become his entire universe, and at the same time his friends, like grass in the winter, had withered away. She had also become his only source for comfort . . . the only person he went to for advice. He wasn't too proud to admit that he knew he would need help raising a daughter. There were some things men just weren't equipped to handle on their own. Most of those things, though, would happen years down the road. Training bras. Puberty. Boys. There would be others in the near future. For instance, crying. When he used to help London keep the nursery at the church he'd always handed off the crying babies to her. He liked playing with the ones with dry diapers and smiles on their faces. Of course, Hannah's diaper wearing days were long gone and he shouldn't have to worry about her crying into the wee hours of the morning, but there would come a time when she would cry and she would need a motherly touch. He would do his best; he would tell her that he loved her and that everything was going to be okay, but he couldn't help but wonder if that would be enough.

Thoughts. All these thoughts were keeping Mitch awake, which meant he might as well get out of bed and make the most out of the rest of this day. Instead of sulking, he needed to do something positive.

7

arper was almost finished packing for her trip to North Carolina when a knock came at the door, which meant her rental car had arrived.

The last item she needed to wedge into her suitcase was London's memoir. Earlier she'd flipped through the pages to discover that there were twenty-seven chapters. One for each year of London's life. She wasn't sure if that number was intentional on London's part, but she had a hunch that it wasn't a mere coincidence. She read the handwritten note from London one more time before tucking it away with the book in her suitcase. She slid it gently back into the package and made sure to stuff it between a few pair of shorts and a pair of summer jeans with holes in them.

An hour after her conversation with Tara, Harper placed two bags into the trunk of a Toyota Camry and left Silver Spring in her rearview mirror. Headed down I-95 toward Emerald Isle, she realized she'd probably packed way more than what she'd need. These kind of assignments could take on a life of their own sometimes, she'd learned from experience. She'd prepared to be out of town for at least a week, and the main reason she'd made the unlikely decision to go to Emerald Isle instead of one of the other places—which would have been far less stressful—was because of London's letter. It was as if this trip was meant to be. At some point, after she finished reading London's memoir, she figured she'd fulfill her sister's request. She'd look up Mitch Quinn and check in on him.

She had to admit it was kind of nice to be able to jump in a car and leave on a whim. No animals to board. No man to notify. No attachments. Well, except for her mom, which reminded her that she probably did need to call her mother, as traffic picked up around the D.C. area.

"You're already on your way?" her mom asked.

Harper got tickled just a little, realizing the surprise in her mother's voice. They'd talked earlier this morning, when Harper had absolutely no clue that a trip like this would pop up out of the blue. For some reason her mother seemed to find that hard to believe.

"Yep, I'm literally passing through our nation's capital as we speak."

"I wish you had let me know, I would have gone with you."

Harper knew her mom was just saying that to be nice. There was no way she would leave her dad at home by himself. The two of them were inseparable, always had been. It was kind of sweet. Plus they lived about an hour north of her house, so the timing just wouldn't have been feasible.

"Thanks for the offer, Mom, but I'm going to be working the entire time anyway."

"Well, dear, you make sure to have some fun while you're there. Your sister would want you to have a good time. Make sure to remember all the good times you two girls had in Emerald Isle."

Harper talked with her mom for forty-five more minutes, her cruise set on 70mph. On the interstate there were always crazy drivers, like the one that had just whizzed by her at about 90mph, and then there were the slow pokes. She felt safe somewhere in the middle.

She knew what her mom said about having a good time was true. Even today as she'd read London's letter over and over, she couldn't help but notice the positive tone. London had always remained optimistic, even when cancer was eating at her like battery acid. She was the one who fought the hardest. She was the one who smiled. She was the one who said there wasn't a disease strong enough to keep her from enjoying life. And, the truth was she was right, every time. She never let cancer get her down. Until the day she died, she lived with a joy that Harper had never witnessed in any other human being. If there was one thing she was certain of, it was that her sister had lived life to the fullest. Although London's life had been cut way too short, no one could ever say that it hadn't been a happy and successful one.

It would be bittersweet to spend some time in Emerald Isle. Harper's memory of the place was a blur. The week of the funeral had seemed out of focus for her and the rest of the family who'd driven down in a caravan. Everyone had gone: Aunts, uncles, first cousins, second cousins, childhood friends, even Tara, but none of them had time to notice the towering pines or enjoy the roar of the ocean rolling in as the night sky settled. Before that visit, she hadn't been there since she was a teenager.

When Harper reached the halfway point, according to her GPS, she decided that she better stop to fill up with gas. As she stood at the pump, she realized that she still hadn't heard from Tara. Her mind had been occupied by so many other things that she'd totally forgotten that Tara had promised to call her with the address of her hotel. She tried calling Tara but the call went straight to voicemail. It would have been nice to have an actual physical address to punch in to her GPS, Harper thought. Nonetheless, she would still get there and she knew Tara would come through sometime in the next one hundred miles, which would put her in Emerald Isle in time to grab a late dinner. The soda and snack she'd grabbed inside the convenience store would hold her over until then. While she nibbled on crackers in the gas station parking lot, Harper read the second chapter of *Mitch & Me*. But this chapter wasn't about Mitch at all. It was a glance back at London's childhood, their childhood. London mentioned their first trip to Emerald Isle. She talked about riding horses at their uncle's farm in Montana one summer when she was ten.

Harper found herself crying as she read story after story, especially the ones that reflected on London's battle with cancer as a child. She thought of Hannah . . . knew that must have been why London was drawn to her.

Back on the road, Harper wished she hadn't turned her head and took notice of the grungy looking fellow in the car riding in the next lane. She quickly realized, when he winked and shot her a salute, that he had taken her glance as a compliment. Funny thing was neither of them were wearing camouflage or dress blues. What a weirdo, she thought as she let up on the gas pedal so he would move on by. On another note, since she'd decided this trip was going to be all about a positive perspective, it was nice to know that a man found her attractive enough to flirt with, even if it was *that* guy.

Later in the evening Harper spotted the green sign that announced the North Carolina state line. She sighed. Partially because she was getting closer to her destination but also because she still hadn't heard from Tara, which turned the sigh into more of a huff. She'd left two voicemails and even sent a text when she'd had to stop for a quick restroom break in Virginia. Thankfully, other than one minor traffic accident she'd come across an hour or so ago, the trip had gone very smoothly. She'd been able to keep her mind occupied and even humored herself as she'd wondered how her initial encounter with Mitch Quinn would turn out. She wasn't sure if she'd try to find his number to call him or just show up at his front door one day. She had neither seen a picture of this man nor heard his voice. He could be 6'4" and built like a body builder or 5'6" and built like Screech from *Saved By The Bell*. How would he react if she appeared on his doorstep out of the blue? she wondered. She imagined knocking, smiling as he opened the door: "Hey, I'm London's sister and I am here to make sure you find someone to fall in love with." Sure, that would go over well. He would probably slam the door in her face . . . anyway that's what she would do if she were on the other side of the door.

But that wasn't anything she needed to be concerned with now. She had plenty of time to think about how to approach her sister's request in the days ahead. What she didn't have time for, as she crossed over the high-rise bridge that led into Emerald Isle, was to wait any longer on Tara to find her a hotel room. As she took in as much of the view as possible from the bridge, she worried about Tara. In the dark she could barely make out the beautiful blue water, full of marsh mazes sprinkled with tiny waterways where only small boats and kayaks could explore. She remembered this bridge being as tall as a mountain when she was a kid and she'd always imagined wandering out to one of the sandy beach areas in the middle of the sound. Once she reached the other side of the bridge, she thought again how it just wasn't like Tara not to call with all of the details. The name of the hotel. The room number. The attendant who would be at the front desk when Harper would check in. Instead, she found herself sitting in front of some little rinky-dink hotel. No need in waiting on the bellboy, he wouldn't be coming out to the car like the well-dressed man at the first hotel she'd stopped at. But that guy had only bad news. "I'm sorry ma'am, we are completely booked," he had informed Harper.

Very bad news. The only good news was that the headache she'd had earlier in the day seemed to have subsided.

"I'll be honest with you," he added, "you'll be extremely lucky if you can find a room anywhere on the island. There is a huge fishing tournament starting this weekend. Fishermen and their families are here from up and down the East Coast and beyond."

Maybe that was why Tara hadn't called. She hadn't been able to find a room. And she knew if she had called Harper with this bit of information at any point before she'd stopped for gas, she might have turned around and gone home.

Harper peered out of the car window. *This is the place* that the bellhop had told her to check? *This* was the hotel with the last available room in Emerald Isle? Made sense, though, Harper quickly realized. It looked like a joint where unruly teenagers would sneak into to drink alcohol and fool around.

Once inside, she felt dirty.

"We're full," the lady at the front desk spouted, before Harper even had a chance to glance around. She quickly discovered that the lobby smelled of smoke and was decorated with old, dingy leather sofas and plastic plants that looked as though they hadn't been replaced in years.

On any other night, Harper would have been glad to hear those words from the desk clerk. She wore bags around her eyes and her voice was weak, but somehow intimidating.

"Do you know of any other place that might have a room? I've driven all the way from Maryland and I need a place to stay."

She laughed out loud. "You picked the wrong time to come to Emerald Isle. The big tournament is this weekend." She studied Harper from head to toe. "I'm guessing you're not here to fish, though?"

"I'm here to . . . ," Harper shut off her sentence. There wasn't any need to tell this woman why she was here. She just needed a room. And if she couldn't find one then she'd just sleep in the car tonight. As much as she would hate that option, that's what she'd do if she had to . . . and Tara would never hear the end of this.

"I tell you what, honey," the lady uttered. "Why don't you walk across the street, get you a beer and come back in an hour or two. I might have a room then."

"What do you mean you *might* have a room then?" Harper said with a little impatience in her voice. "One that you don't have now?" she challenged.

"Or you can drive around to every other hotel on the island and see what they have to say. The thing is, honey, I know my customers. You see, Jack and Megan are in room twenty. I just saw them drive up a few minutes ago. To make a long story short, Jack's married . . . but not to Megan. So what I'm gettin' at is that I'll probably have a vacancy before ten o'clock."

Harper wasn't sure how to respond. *Really?* might be a good word. Instead she said, "Okay."

"Don't worry, I'll change the sheets," the lady cackled.

Gross. "Does the place across the street have food? I'm starving," she said, yet realizing she might have just lost her appetite.

"Best mahi-mahi in town. Best shrimp in town. But stick with seafood," she suggested.

8

Earlier, Mitch had removed every beer from the fridge, poured the contents down the drain and threw each bottle, one by one, into the trashcan. He loaded it, along with the recycling bin, into his Jeep and took it off to the dump. No more beer in the house. He knew he would still drink a few from time to time when he went out with friends, but he just wasn't having it in his home.

When he returned from the dump, he straightened the house and cleaned everything from top to bottom. He wanted Hannah's new home to be in tiptop shape. Wanted it to be germ free. Smell good. Look good.

Hannah's bedroom was already set up. She'd helped him pick out a bed, a small dresser, and curtains that matched the sheets she'd wanted. He wished London had been here for that trip to the furniture store. She would have loved picking out items with Hannah, and Hannah would have loved having her there. Mitch remembered imagining the two of them lying on the mattresses in the showroom, testing them out one by one. He figured it probably would have somehow turned into a pillow fight, and then he and London would have remembered just in time that they were adults, and they'd figure out a way to keep from being kicked out of the place. They'd always had fun together. In so many ways they'd been a family already. An odd family, but one filled with love and laughter and hope.

As Mitch's imagination wandered, the house phone on the kitchen counter began to ring. London had always teased that he was the last person on Earth without a cell phone. All the dishes were stacked neatly in the drainer, and he figured he'd put those away later when they dried.

"Hey, Doc," he said a moment after answering. The first time he'd met Dr. Thorpe—the man with more credentials and accreditations than any medical doctor he'd ever known—he'd asked Mitch to call him Doc. Simply Doc.

"Hey, Mitch, my main man. You've been on my mind all day."

Mitch smiled at his shaky voice. Doc hadn't been feeling so well himself as of late.

"I appreciate your thoughts."

"All the time, son."

Mitch wasn't his son, but Doc had always called people young enough to be his son, son.

"How are you feeling today?" Mitch wanted to know.

"The sun's shining, the birds are chirping, and there are plenty of people to love."

He'd always used the quirkiest little sayings. Things that if Mitch said, people would laugh at him, but when such words streamed from Doc's mouth, they just sounded right.

"How is Hannah?"

"She's as delightful as always." He paused. "I can tell she's a little anxious, similar to a kid on Christmas Eve. But she has her bags packed for you to pick her up tomorrow afternoon."

"I guess we're all a little anxious."

This all would have been easier if London were still around, Mitch couldn't help but think.

"Yes. The timing is right, though. Hannah needs you. You need Hannah." Doc paused. "And for me, well, I'm not a spring chicken anymore."

Doc had been able to take care of Hannah when she didn't absolutely have to be at Duke. Mitch had always thought it was bittersweet that the kid who had a cancer doctor for a grandfather would be one of the ones to end up with leukemia. It had saved her a lot of time in the hospital, and it had always helped keep Mitch and London at ease when there were things to worry about. Doc always seemed to have the right answers. That's what scared Mitch the most about Doc's health condition.

"Things will all workout, I'm sure," Mitch said, hesitantly. "Is Hannah around to talk now?"

"Of course."

Mitch could hear Doc shuffling around, like he was getting out of his old rocking chair that overlooked the windows that opened up to the ocean. He could also hear that his breathing was a little heavier than normal today. In a few moments Hannah came to the phone.

"Hello," she said.

"Hey, Hannah," Mitch responded, his smile traveling through the phone.

"It's you," Hannah said, animation lining her voice.

"Who else did you think it might be?"

"I didn't know. Grandpa told me it was a surprise."

"Grandpa's silly," Mitch said.

"I know, that's why I love him." She paused, and Mitch assumed she was thinking about what she'd just said. "You're silly, too, Mr. Mitch."

"No, I'm not."

"Yes, you are."

It wasn't the first time the two of them had this debate. Usually, Hannah won. Actually, Hannah always won.

"Okay, I might be, but you are, too."

"That's what Grandpa just said."

Mitch had heard him in the background.

"Grandpa's always right."

"I know," Hannah admitted. "Are you still coming to get me tomorrow?"

"Definitely. I'll be there tomorrow afternoon after my meeting." Mitch chose his words carefully. A long time back they'd all decided that it would be best to share as little as possible with Hannah about the technical side of the adoption. He was also afraid that if he'd said *appointment*, she would have thought he had a doctor's appointment and it would have scared her. Having spent so much time in the doctor's office and hospital, that's where her mind often traveled when certain words were said.

"Are we still going to the grocery store after you pick me up?"

"You bet, and I'm going to let you pick out whatever you want so that we can have plenty of food that you like at our house."

Our house. It had a nice ring to it.

"So you mean I can put Danish Wedding Cookies and Cheetos in the cart?"

"You better."

Hannah reeled off a dozen more items that she wanted. Mitch could tell she'd actually been working on the grocery list he'd told her to start making last week. He could remember being a kid, and having something to look forward to always made life more exciting for kids. Heck, for adults as well. Knowing that Hannah would be coming to live with him had given him new hope for life. He couldn't wait to make dinner with her tomorrow night. Maybe build a fire in the pit in the backyard and have s'mores.

While talking to Doc and Hannah, Mitch had watched the sun sink below the top of the ocean. Day had turned to dusk and eventually darkness began to fill the house. Mitch flipped on a couple of lights and played some jazz music as he settled in for the evening. He figured he would take it easy tonight. Just as he assumed it would, this day had brought about its share of ups and downs, but somewhere in the midst of the conversation with Hannah, he had gone from being down and out about this being the one-year anniversary of London's death to being thankful for the time that he had shared with London. Grateful for the fact that London had brought Hannah into his life. In an odd way, today was a new beginning, and he had to admit that he was excited about what tomorrow would bring.

9

Harper locked the car and walked across the street. The parking lot was packed; she assumed that was a good sign. The blue and red neon light on the front of the building flashed the words *Bar & Grill*. Inside the front door, she was met by a young girl, probably in her early twenties.

"Welcome to New Name Night!" she greeted loudly and excitedly, obviously trying to talk over the background noise.

A live band was performing in the far corner, their backdrop a live view of the Atlantic Ocean. There were a handful of people dancing near the stage. Others were mingling at the bar and high-top tables. Off to the left there was a row of booths along a hallway that probably led to the restrooms.

"Thank you," Harper said. "What is New Name Night?" she inquired. She'd seen the name of the place on the sign out front, and it definitely wasn't *New Name Night*.

"Oh, every year on the first weekend of the annual fishing tournament we host New Name Night. We give everyone a blank name tag and you have to come up with a new name for yourself."

Harper furrowed her brow.

"It's kind of our version of '*What Happens In Vegas Stays in Vegas*'," the girl with the nametag that read *Bambi* explained.

"Oh, I see," Harper said, catching on.

Bambi pulled out a sharpie and asked, "So, who do you want to be tonight?"

Harper chuckled. The way Bambi had asked the question made it sound like a fairy might come flying in, pull out a magical wand and transform her into someone completely different. "I'll just be me," Harper decided.

"*Me* isn't a name."

"What I meant is that I'll just be . . ."

Bambi quickly cut her off and spoke with a sense of urgency. "Don't say it, don't say your real name. That's one of the rules," Bambi said, pointing to a sign on the wall with a thumb tack poked through it that actually listed the rules for New Name Night. "It's actually a lot of fun," she added. "And this way none of these drunk fishermen know your real name," she teased.

Harper got the point, but in her case it didn't matter. She wasn't planning on sharing her name with any of these drunk fisherman anyway, but since Bambi was so adamant about her making up a name to write on the blank name tag, then she might as well put something other than her real name. This only made sense since she'd rather these people not know her real name anyway. "Addison," she decided, shrugging her shoulders as she spoke.

Loosen up, Addison, she told herself. *Have some fun. Forget that you're Harper and just be Addison.* She could hear Tara's voice in the back of her mind saying the same. With her mind shifting to Tara, Addison couldn't help but think of how much it would help if Tara would call and say she had her a hotel room booked. Then she could get her dinner to-go and head back to a quiet room instead of a noisy bar. Settle into her pajamas and wind down for the night. Here, it looked like some of these folks were just getting started.

Bambi wrote the name *Addison* on a paper nametag, peeled off the backing, and handed it to Addison for her to wear. "Will anyone else be joining you?" Bambi asked.

Addison was accustomed to hearing this question at restaurants when she traveled alone and it didn't bother her anymore to say *no*. When she had first started traveling for work she felt lonely eating at a table with no one sitting across from her. But in time she'd learned how to make the best of it. Mainly, she would just sit back and watch people, which she'd already decided could be a lot of fun in this place tonight. A man near the bar had just spilled a beer all over some lady. Hilarious. Some of the people dancing looked like they'd never seen a dance floor. She was pretty sure the entertainment value at this joint would be well worth whatever the food might cost.

"Just me," Addison said with a smile.

"Okay. We're pretty packed right now, as you can see. So it will probably be a little while before a table becomes available, but you're welcome to try to find a seat at the bar. You can order a drink there or even food if you'd like."

Addison didn't particularly want to eat at the bar, but at this point she figured it didn't really matter. She was starving. Her stomach had been rumbling for the last hour of the drive.

She eased her way through the crowd and found the last open bar stool. It was wooden and nestled between two men.

"Is anyone sitting here?" she inquired. Two sets of eyes immediately turned at the sound of a female voice. The man to her right shook his head no.

"It's your seat now . . . Addison," the guy to the left suggested, after glancing at her nametag.

For some reason she felt the need to look down at it as well, even though she knew what it said and that it wasn't the name she went by. Of course, he knew that, too, which is why he'd kind of smirked when he reeled it off.

It would be interesting to see how this turned out, she thought. Thankfully the only item she'd brought with her was her wallet, so she didn't have to worry about her purse being in the way on the bar or the fear of it being snatched if she sat it on the floor. That had happened once in New Orleans a few years ago. Not a good night.

There was a few feet of space between her stool and the man to her right. He smelled of alcohol and cigarette smoke, so space was definitely appreciated. The man to her left was a bit closer, quite a bit older than her, and she predicted that he would be the less aggressive of the two.

"Hi, my name is Ted," he said.

He had the nametag to prove it, she noticed, smirking on the inside.

Addison exchanged pleasantries with Ted for a few moments and continued to take in the fast-paced atmosphere. Surprisingly, it didn't take long for the bartender to make her way over. Addison placed an order for a Blue Moon and asked for a menu. Everything on the three-panel menu protected by plastic sounded delicious right now, but Addison knew that was because she was hungry enough to eat anything that resembled food at this point. She decided to take the motel clerk's advice and stick with seafood.

"I'll have the flounder," she ordered, five minutes after she'd sat down. The band was on their second song, a Kenny Chesney hit, and they were actually relatively talented, she had to admit.

"The flounder is delicious," Ted offered. "Just so you know, I'm married. So you don't have to worry about me," he added.

He said it with a grin on his face, and Addison didn't quite understand the point he was trying to make.

"How long have you been married, Ted?" She assumed a conversation with him would be harmless.

"Three times," he said.

He obviously hadn't heard the question correctly. All of the noise probably had something to do with that. "No, how long?" she clarified.

"Oh." He paused for a moment and seemed to be working some type of mathematical equation in his mind. "Three years."

Addison just nodded her head. She pulled out her cell phone and for the next five minutes pretended to be listening to voice-mails that she'd saved for one reason or another. Not long after she put her phone to her ear, Ted had diverted his attention to a woman closer to his age that seemed to know him. When Addison set her phone on the bar, she began reading over the rules of New Name Night. The bartender had handed her a copy along with the menu. New Name Night was more than just a name change, she found out. One of the rules was that you couldn't reveal your real occupation. Another was that you didn't have to be truthful about your current relationship status. *Interesting*, she thought.

As Addison waited for her meal, she watched the bar tender jump between customers and listened as the band continued to impress. More and more people were pouring into the bar and everyone except her seemed to love the New Name Night game. When Ted's friend walked away, Addison figured it wouldn't be long before he would start a fresh conversation with her. She'd already figured out that he was the type of guy who liked to hear himself talk.

"What's a pretty lady like you doing with an empty ring finger?" Ted asked.

"It's a long story."

"So you're really single, or you just took your ring off for New Name Night?" he inquired with a wink.

"I'm not married."

"Well, I'd marry you," Ted insisted, taking a swig of his twelfth beer of the night.

Maybe she should have scooted closer to the guy that she *thought* would be trouble. He hadn't said a single word to her. He'd just been minding his own business, watching some sports game on one of the televisions above the wide variety of alcohol bottles that lined the shelves along the back wall behind the bar.

Everything that happened next seemed to happen quickly and slowly all at the same time. It was almost like a traffic accident that you could see coming at the intersection ahead of you, but somehow, even though life seemed to turn to slow motion, you couldn't avoid it. Addison shifted her stool to the right just as a man was wedging his way between her bar stool and the quiet guy. She bumped him and he was the one that said, "Excuse me." Her eyes were level with his nametag, closer than normal comfort level with a stranger: *Ty* is what it read, in big blue letters . . . Bambi's bubbly handwriting.

Ty wasn't the one that caused the incident; he was actually being polite and she could tell he'd purposefully edged further toward the next stool so that he wouldn't rub up against her. A gentleman, she presumed, unlike Ted who'd just made the comment, "Let's you and I get out of here and really get to know each other," he urged, squeezing her thigh and coming way too close to places a woman doesn't want to be touched by a stranger. As his hand traveled closer she jerked in the opposite direction, toward Ty, who'd just ordered a beer from the bar tender who'd just set Addison's food in front of her. Ty was standing, facing in her direction, and he had taken notice of what was happening to Addison.

In one swift motion Ty's right hand reached across Addison— just as she spilled her Blue Moon all over his jeans—snatching Ted's hand. She felt a rough thump on her thigh and then the uneasy feeling of her stool coming out from under her as Ty twisted Ted's wrist, causing Ted's entire body to slam into the bar. Addison was headed backward, toward the floor, and she couldn't believe this was happening. Somehow she had time to imagine that this night was going to end with her in the ER with a concussion. There was no way she was going to be able to catch herself before her head would hit the floor. At the moment that thought entered her mind, she felt Ty's free arm firmly connect with the low of her back, allowing her to fling her arms around him to help steady her balance.

The entire bar grew quiet. Except for the band and the televisions, they both continued to play. The stool below Addison was gone, it had crashed to the floor with a bang louder than all of the other noise in the bar combined.

Addison wasn't sure what to do or say. At the moment she didn't really feel like she could let go of the man whom she was clinging onto. The man who was holding her and somehow still had Ted's face pinned to the bar, while only holding onto his wrist, now awkwardly placed behind Ted's back.

Her eyes were inches from Ty's nametag. He was the first to speak. "I think you owe the lady an apology," he demanded from Ted, twisting his wrist back to make him face her.

Ted's face was as red as the ketchup it had landed in.

"I'm terribly sorry," he uttered, in a cowardly voice, as if all of his testosterone had vanished instantly.

At least fifty sets of eyes were glued on the scene, and when Ty let go of his hand, Ted went squirming out of the bar. Ty pulled Addison back to her feet, and for some reason she kept her right arm around his shoulder. When she noticed that his hand was still on her back, she looked down.

"Oh, I'm sorry. Let me move that," Ty suggested, holding his hands in the air like he was about to be arrested. "A man's hand in the wrong place is what started all of this," he articulated.

Addison somehow summed up the energy to laugh, even though her body was trembling and she had yet to speak a word. She liked the sound of Ty's voice—raspy and intimidating when raised, but somewhat sensual when calm. It surprised her how quickly he'd been able to relax.

"It's okay," she clarified. "I'm so sorry about your jeans."

Ty glanced down, realizing for the first time that there was a huge wet spot that made it look like he hadn't made it to the restroom in time.

"It's fine. I have a washing machine," he said, nonchalantly.

Addison noticed how he smiled easily when he spoke.

"Is this your plate?" he asked.

Addison looked at the bar. Somehow her flounder plate had remained unscathed in the midst of the skirmish.

"Yes."

"Do you still have an appetite?"

Addison laughed again. "Surprisingly, yes."

"I have a table out on the pier," Ty informed her, motioning down the hallway that she had figured led to the bathrooms. "I'm here by myself," he finished.

Addison appreciated the offer. She appreciated what he'd done for her. It was very heroic. But . . . "Thanks for the offer but I really just wanted to eat alone, enjoy some peace and quiet, you know."

"I think you might have come to the wrong place for that. Well, at least in here, anyway," he suggested, mentally comparing it to the relaxed, breezy evening he'd been soaking in on the pier.

She smiled, realizing he was right.

"You'll like it out on the pier. The weather is perfect and the crashing waves are the background music." Ty grabbed her plate. "Come on, you can have my table. I will trade you spots," he added, motioning to the bar stool that was laying on the floor in a puddle of beer.

Addison followed him to the double doors that led out to the pier. As soon as they stepped outside, it was like a new world. The wind was blowing gently and the air smelled of salt water. At the end of the pier, which had to be at least 1,000 feet long, there were lots of people fishing. Between where they were standing and the fishermen, there were about twenty tables lining one side of the pier. Of course only one was empty and Addison assumed it must be the one at which Ty had been sitting. When they got closer, she realized there was a plate of untouched food.

Ty set her meal down across from his plate. "Here you are ma'am," he said as if he were her server. "By the way," he said, "I'm Ty."

Addison just now realized that they hadn't been formally introduced. She assumed he'd probably read her nametag, though, just like she'd read his. "I'm . . ." She almost said *Harper*, but then decided that the way this night had gone she should probably just stick with ". . . Addison."

Ty grinned, realizing how confusing it was to introduce yourself as someone else.

"Nice to meet you, Addison," he said. "I hope you enjoy your meal."

She watched him pick up his plate.

"Hey," she said before he could walk away. "Thank you for what you did in there."

He tipped his baseball cap to her. "It was the only option," he replied and then began to walk back in the direction they'd just come from.

Addison really did want to be alone. She didn't need anything else to complicate this trip. She already didn't have a hotel room. Or she might have a hotel room . . . if Jack and Jill, or whatever their names were, decided to make it quick. She had a story to start working on, too. Plus she wanted to read London's memoir and at some point she had to track down Mitch Quinn.

"Ty," Addison called out, anyway.

Ty was about fifteen steps down the pier when he heard his name. He knew the voice was Addison's. Ironically, he thought about pretending he didn't hear her, walking back into the bar, eating his meal alone like he'd come here to do, and forgetting about everything that had happened tonight: seeing that jerk touch her and making use of years of martial arts training for the first time in a decade. Then, in the midst of it all, meeting the most beautiful woman in the bar, the one with the hazel eyes and light brown hair that he'd just given his table to.

He turned around anyway.

Addison stood and watched the most attractive man in the bar make his way toward her. She hadn't been able to help but notice how his jeans fit just right. His quirky jokes made her smile, and he'd been a gentleman twice. Not only had he put Ted in his place, but he'd given up a table he'd probably waited an hour for to someone he didn't even know. He obviously wasn't trying to hook up with her because he hadn't even remotely tried to take advantage of the whole hero thing. The muscular frame lurking beneath his shirt seemed to fit just right.

"Will you eat dinner with me?" Addison asked.

"Sure," Ty complied, sitting his plate in the exact spot he'd plucked it from just moments ago. "But let me go get the beer that I ordered," he said.

"Try not to start any more fights while you're in there," Addison said, chuckling at her own joke.

Ty grinned and walked away for the second time. Addison was pleased to know that this time he'd be coming back. She figured he would make for good company while she enjoyed her flounder and her beer. *Her beer . . .* By the time she remembered that her beer was soaking into Ty's jeans, he'd disappeared into the bar. When he made it back she would just have to run in and grab another one.

A few moments later Ty emerged from the noisy bar, and when he reached the table, Addison spotted a Yuengling in one of his hands, and with the other he handed her a Blue Moon.

"Thank you," she said. "That's very sweet of you." She suddenly realized he'd noticed more than just her name. Well, actually, she didn't know for a fact that he'd noticed her nametag earlier.

"It's my privilege."

Ty noticed that Addison hadn't even touched her food yet. "Is your food cold? If it is, I can take it back in and ask them to make you another plate."

"I'm not sure," Addison responded.

"Why haven't you started eating? I thought you were hungry."

"I just didn't want to be rude and start eating without you."

"I wouldn't have minded," he insisted.

Now that he was at the table, Addison picked up her fork and took the first bite, trying not to look like a pig but chewing faster than normal. Ty began to eat as well. They didn't say much for the next few minutes. He asked her how the flounder tasted. *Delicious.* And she asked him how he liked the mahi-mahi. He said the same. The moon was bright, the ocean continued to roar, and Addison felt more relaxed than she had in some time.

"So, what would you have done if I had fallen and busted my head on the floor?" she asked.

Ty pressed his lips together, raised his eyebrows, and shrugged slightly. "I guess I would have been apologizing just like the other guy," he said with a snicker.

"Would you have run out of the bar just like he did?"

Ty smiled. "Well, I would have made sure you were okay," he ensured. "Then me and my wet pants would have run out like a puppy with his tail between his legs."

That image in her mind made Addison giggle.

Ty continued talking. "But that wasn't going to happen," he said.

"Oh, yeah," she quizzed. "How can you be so sure?"

"Because your safety was more important than his or mine," he clarified. "I would have done whatever necessary to make sure you didn't get injured, even if that meant letting go of the screaming pervert."

"He did kind of sound like a little school girl on the playground."

Ty and Addison shared a few more laughs about a story that neither of them would most likely ever forget. They cleaned their plates and finished off their second beer. A waitress had come outside to check on everyone, and when Addison asked, "How come you didn't just order your drink from her earlier instead of coming in the bar?" Ty explained that she was the only waitress for all of the tables outside tonight. "When I first sat down, she said that her help had called in sick tonight. So that's when I decided I'd just go inside to get my own beer. Plus that's where all the action is," he teased.

After their third beer together, Addison could tell that she was beginning to feel the effect. She'd loosened up a little more, and she had to admit that she was having a really good time getting to know more about this Ty fellow. But it had been close to two hours since she'd walked across the street from the motel, and she knew she needed to check back in to see if her room was available.

"It's been an adventurous evening, Mr. Ty." Addison giggled at the sound of the words *Mr. Ty*. "But I probably better call it a night."

Ty wanted to spend more time with her, but he knew it was probably best if he didn't. He hadn't come here looking for someone to flirt with. But it had been fun to let his guard down a little. Plus he could tell that Addison was harmless. He was pretty sure she'd had a good time as well, but she'd been careful with her wit, he'd noticed, which probably meant she had a boyfriend. Not that it really mattered. Nothing had happened and nothing would.

"Can I call you a cab?" he offered.

"Actually my car is parked right across the street."

He furrowed his brow. "I'm not sure if either of us should be driving," Ty admitted.

"Driving, oh I'm definitely not driving," she clarified. "I'm waiting for a room at the motel."

"Waiting for a room?" he inquired, his brow furrowed.

"Yeah, it's a long story." This night was full of long stories, she thought to herself.

"Well, let me walk you over, then. Just in case Ted's waiting out in the parking lot for you," Ty teased.

Back at the bar, Ty tried to talk Addison into letting him cover the bill, but she wouldn't let him and she even demanded to pay first.

"Ladies first, then," he finally conceded.

He felt a little guilty when she paid for both of their meals and their drinks, without telling him that was her plan.

"Now we're even," she said. "You saved me from Ted. I paid for your dinner." She paused. "Actually work paid for your dinner."

"Thank you, work," he said as they headed across the street.

The front desk attendant smiled when Addison walked in the door with Ty. "Oh, you found a keeper, huh?" She read his name tag. "Ty, that sounds kinky."

Addison felt a little, make that a lot, embarrassed.

Ty laughed it off. "It's not like that," he assured.

She winked. "It never is," she chuckled, then her eyes moved to Addison's nametag. "Listen, Addison. I have bad news. The room is still occupied. Jack and Megan must be going a few extra rounds tonight."

Ty's eyes widened, wondering what in the world was going on here.

"You two love birds go have a few more beers and come back in an hour or so, and I'm pretty sure your room will be ready."

This was getting old, Addison thought to herself. "We're not . . . ," she started to explain the situation, but then stopped. Why waste her time? It was obvious that this woman was extremely intrigued with her customer's affairs . . . one-night stands, and who knows what else went on in this motel. She knew she didn't need to explain anything to her or to anyone else. "You're sure there will be a room tonight?"

"They've never spent a whole night here," she ensured.

10

The soft sand felt cool beneath Addison's toes as she walked beside the Atlantic Ocean with a man she barely knew. Ty, a few feet to her left, had suggested that they walk on the beach to pass time. At first she'd considered declining, but the alternatives didn't seem very intriguing: sit alone in her car waiting for Jack and Jill to emerge from one of the outside doors of the one-story motel or go back across the street and sit at the bar where she'd been groped earlier this evening.

She and Ty had actually gone back to the bar, but only to order a beer to carry on their walk. Now they were dodging the surf and sipping on what her friend Tara liked to call liquid courage. Addison glanced at her phone again, beyond aggravated that she still hadn't heard from Tara. In fact, she was afraid that something might be wrong, but the alcohol seemed to keep her from worrying too much. Along with the bottle top, she'd pulled off her shoes as soon as she and Ty reached the sand.

"Have you ever seen a shark out here?" she asked Ty. Over dinner he'd told her that he lived here in Emerald Isle, which she wasn't sure she should believe based on the rules of the game in which they were involved. He seemed more like someone that sailed around the world looking for adventure than a man who would settle down in a small town.

"I've seen a few," he revealed. "They like to hang out around the pier, especially when people are fishing."

"Like tonight?" Addison suggested. She figured she might as well start getting some leads on her story now.

"I'm sure there are some in the area," he said. "All the bait and blood attract them. People catch small sharks all the time up on the pier."

"Wow, that's pretty neat," she admitted. The few times she could remember pier fishing with her family when she was younger, she never recalled seeing one.

"It's fun to catch them; they actually put up a tough fight for someone who doesn't have much experience fishing."

"Do you fish a lot?"

"Compared to most of those guys in the bar tonight, the ones in town for the fishing tournament, I'm an amateur. To me, fishing has always been less of a sport and more about enjoying nature."

"What kind of bait does a fisherman use to attract sharks?"

Ty talked in detail about the different kinds of bait used to catch sharks. He explained that there were different schools of thought on catching sharks, as with any other fish. His fishing knowledge impressed Addison, which made her wonder even more if Ty actually had come from out-of-town somewhere for the fishing tournament. She wondered why he hadn't asked her where she was from or really any personal questions at all. Then she realized that maybe he figured she might not tell him the truth either, so it really didn't matter. They weren't at the bar anymore, so technically the rules didn't apply, even though the last rule on the list was that the rules applied for the rest of the night with anyone you met at the bar.

"I understand there have been a number of shark attacks in this area lately," she mentioned, shrugging off her other thoughts.

Ty shook his head. "Three on the coast of North Carolina, I believe, and a recent one here in Emerald Isle."

The pier where they'd shared dinner stood a few hundred yards behind them now, but it remained fairly noticeable. The temperature might have dropped a few degrees, but the air felt relatively warm. They'd only passed a few other people since they'd begun walking. The first, a lady walking her dog. Then, Ty and Addison watched in amusement as a young couple chased one another through the surf and ended up on top of each other making out.

"You think they met at New Name Night?" Ty wondered aloud, as they wandered into the distance.

Addison shrugged. "It's possible, but kicking water on one another seems pretty immature," she suggested, just as she stepped into a couple inches of water and used her foot to fling a string of water toward Ty.

He jumped away quickly, but the spray caught him on the arm. "Don't make me tackle you like that girl did that guy back there."

"You're too much of a gentleman to do such a thing," Addison responded, teasing him but being serious at the same time.

In an attempt to prove her wrong, Ty jolted in her direction.

Ankle deep in water, Addison quickly back peddled to escape his reach. She still didn't think he would tackle her, but it was fun to play the game. At least until she stumbled over her own feet and landed face down in the edge of the ocean.

Ty fought the urge to laugh. "Are you okay?" he asked first, wanting to be certain Addison hadn't injured herself.

Lying in the water, Addison playfully splashed him with more salt water. Ty didn't seem to mind. He continued to walk in her direction, laughing, while extending his arm to pick her up. Addison couldn't help but notice his bicep flex beneath his shirt as he easily pulled her to her feet.

"That was your fault," Addison teased. She wasn't really aggravated with Ty, but she was aggravated. Now her entire body, covered with sand and water and tiny shells, felt icky.

"My fault?" Ty countered. "I didn't even touch you," he pleaded with a smile.

"Yeah, but you ran at me . . . and you bought me one too many drinks," she claimed, raising her eyebrows. "So it's double your fault."

"Let's just say we're even then, since you spilled beer on my jeans."

At the same time, Addison and Ty both glanced at his crotch. The stain that had been there earlier had pretty much settled in.

"Ha, ha." She asserted her best fake laugh as she felt a shiver run across her wet skin. "The water is actually cold," she admitted. "And I feel like I have sand crawling all over me."

"Sand doesn't actually crawl, but if you want to shower off, we passed by my house about . . ." he paused, calculating. "Maybe two hundred steps back."

Addison ignored the sand comment, but thought it to be pretty funny, at least it would have been if she wasn't covered in it. "Really?"

"Yeah, you remember that really big house with three balconies and all the windows that you pointed out?"

"That's your house?" she exclaimed.

Ty smirked. "Nope. After the big house there is a patch of woods and then my house. You probably didn't notice it."

It surprised Addison that he hadn't mentioned his house when they'd walked right past it. She figured most guys would have probably invited her in then. Another check mark for Ty, she noted, while thinking it might not have been so bad if the two of them had ended up rolling around in the surf together.

"It's probably not a good idea for me to take a shower in some strange, good-looking man's house," she said as a joke, yet seriously.

"Oh, you actually thought I was going to let you in my house, wet and covered with sand?" he laughed. "And what kind of man do you think I am? You think I'd let some strange, attractive woman take a shower in my house?" he teased back.

"Well, you are the one that asked, genius."

"Yeah, you're right. But I asked if you wanted to shower off *at* my house, not *in* my house," he clarified.

"What's the difference?"

"I have an outdoor shower."

"Then I'll be freezing even more."

"You're in luck. The outside shower is also hooked up to the hot water heater."

Addison raised her brow. "That's pretty neat. I might go for that."

Ty led Addison through a dozen or so water oaks in his backyard. The shower area was surrounded by a wooden fence about shoulder level high. Inside the enclosure, Ty opened a small plastic trunk and pulled out a towel and wash cloth. A porch light faintly illuminated the area, and the moonlight was seeping in through the tree branches. Addison could make out Ty's silhouette, but not much more. He showed her the nozzles, explaining which one controlled hot and cold.

"It takes just a minute for the water to warm up," he acknowledged.

What Addison did next surprised her just as much as it did Ty. "So if I twist this knob," she said, twisting it as she posed the question, "water will start spraying all over you?"

The spray from the showerhead immediately drenched Ty's shirt, and in the heat of the moment he wrapped his arms around Addison, pulling her into the stream of cold water with him. At first, Addison tensed up, but somehow the warm body she felt pressed against her own caused her to forget about the cold water beginning to trickle down her shirt and into her jeans. Her eyes met Ty's gaze. She could feel his belt buckle against her stomach, his chest against hers. Don't let this happen, Addison's mind warned.

Ty tilted his head, and as their wet lips met, their eyelids collapsed, each of them letting the moment take over. Addison cringed, but in a good way, mainly. This was the first time a man had touched her this way in a very long time.

Before her brain could catch up with her body, she could taste the beer on Ty's tongue. For a split second her eyes opened but then closed again. She wrapped her arms around his waist. Several seconds later their lips parted . . . just long enough for the light from the moon to allow the both of them to see exactly what they were getting themselves into. Before their lips met again, Ty adjusted the nozzles. Then Addison let him slowly lead her backward until her soaked jeans were pressed against the wooden fence panels. Her hands traveled up and down Ty's back, beneath his shirt. Ty lifted his arms, allowing her to pull it above his head, knocking his hat to the wet, concreted pad beneath their bare feet. The water had already begun to puddle there, but neither of them cared to notice.

A few minutes later Addison's shirt fell off the tip of Ty's fingers. She could feel his abs and chest firmly pressed against her body. She'd never been with a man this well built, but it sure felt good as her hands gripped his muscles and explored the areas around them. She could feel Ty's heart pattering. Her own, she realized, was beating twice as fast. He had a tattoo wrapped around each bicep, one a silhouette of a guitar, the other the outline of a snazzy camera. She couldn't help but wonder what story they told.

Ty felt Addison's hands drop to his belt as he gently kissed her neck and shoulder. With her thumb, she unsnapped his jeans and then guided his pants below his boxers. Ty finished what she started, stepping on his pant legs and using his toes to toss them aside.

Addison wasn't sure when the water had turned warm, but it felt good traveling over their half-naked bodies. The cool fence against her bare back felt nice, too. And if steam wasn't already rising from the shower enclosure that overlooked the Atlantic Ocean, she wasn't sure why. They were breathing in unison and her whole world seemed to be spinning. She nearly exploded when Ty lifted her feet off the ground, bracing her between his midsection and the fence. When he let her down, he slid her pants off her legs.

Addison peeked downward. If she would have known this was going to happen, she would have worn sexier panties. These, sky blue and silk, her favorite, were thinning near the top. But an activity such as this had been nowhere in her schedule when she'd showered earlier today and dressed comfortably for a long distance car ride. Making out with a man on a first date had never even been her thing, let alone rounding second base and heading for who knows where. Any other time she would have stopped it; never started it, actually. But something about Ty seemed different. Even though she didn't know him, she trusted him. Oddly enough, being in this moment felt . . . natural.

Ty noticed that his eyes had begun to adjust to the dark, and he took note of Addison's color coordinated bra and panties, following the strap to the point of release. His fingers, trembling and picking, couldn't quite find the spot. He hoped that Addison didn't think of him like most single men who a woman might meet in a bar, who from the very beginning had only had one thing on his mind. He would be fine if she pulled away right now, and in a way he hoped she would. But he wanted her, all of her. Something about her hazel eyes and the way he felt every time he looked into them made him feel helpless, yet in a good way. The sensation reminded him of love, but he didn't know if he even believed in love at first sight. It had never happened to him before, and he honestly didn't even know what it would feel like.

Addison leaned her head against the top of the fence, taking comfort in knowing the man on the other side of the equation seemed as nervous as she felt.

To buy time, Ty continued kissing her neck and shoulders and she thoroughly enjoyed the pleasure of his tongue against her skin.

Beneath a Carolina moon and only a hundred yards from the sounds of the Atlantic Ocean, Addison and Ty gave into vulnerabilities that neither of them had given into in quite some time. Somehow, though, it seemed like riding a bike, but this time a brand new bike with names written on them that didn't belong to either of them.

11

ddison woke up in an unfamiliar bed with soft sheets and Ty's arms wrapped around her. She slept better than she had a single night since James left, maybe even better than she had when he'd been the man with his arms wrapped around her.

"Good morning," Ty said. "By the way, my real name is Mitch."

At the sound of the name that had just fallen from his lips, Addison's body froze, but her mind immediately began to race. Her eyes wandered as she wrestled with the idea of what she might be wrapped up in.

Mitch? The Mitch? London's Mitch? Mitch Quinn?

Addison wanted to ask all these questions, but she found herself absolutely speechless, as the scene from the outdoor shower last night played over in her mind.

"It is?" were the words that she eventually summoned up.

"Yes, my name is Mitch." He noticed that Addison seemed to be caught up in some sort of a daze. Maybe she wasn't a morning person. Or maybe everything that had happened last night was catching up to her all at once. He'd had a similar feeling when he'd woken up, about fifteen minutes ago, and discovered his body flush with her body. What had seemed like a dream had actually been reality, he recognized, and in a way that he couldn't explain he knew that his life would never be the same again. "Did you like me better when you thought I was Ty?" he asked with a smirk, hoping to lighten the mood.

Yes, I most definitely did, she wanted to say. She wanted to press rewind and start all over at the bar last night. Ignore that stupid New Name Game. Tell Mitch her real name the moment they met and ask for his. Then, none of this would have happened. At least not if his last name was Quinn.

Buy some time, Addison found herself thinking. Think of something clever. He's going to want to know your name. "Ty is a nice name . . . ," she uttered, keeping the focus on him.

"Mitch, Ty . . . they're just names. I'm still the same guy you met last night."

Not really.

Addison wanted so badly to ask him his last name, verify what she already had a gut feeling to be true. Seriously, how many Mitch's in his age range could there actually be on the island? It made sense now. She and London had always fallen for the same guys in high school and even in college, but they'd always stepped away when the other staked a real claim.

"So, what's your name?" Mitch had been dying to ask. He almost asked last night. He thought the New Name Game was kind of silly, but he didn't know how Addison, or whatever her real name was, felt about it. So he'd just followed the rules. "You know, your real name," he added, as she continued to appear lost.

"I have a confession to make," Addison admitted, as she spotted a photograph on his nightstand. The dark curtains shielded most of the early morning sunrays, but she could make out London's facial features just fine. At least now she didn't need to ask for his last name.

"Okay." Mitch waited. He really hoped that this amazing, attractive woman wasn't about to tell him that she was married. That would ruin everything. It would make him feel terrible for all of the decisions he'd made last night. He hadn't even planned to go out and definitely hadn't planned to meet Addison and bring her back to his house.

"My name is . . ." How was this possible, Addison contemplated, as she began to put a string of words together, ever so slowly. *How could this happen to me?* Last night she felt like she could be falling in love with Ty. But now . . . Not Mitch. She couldn't fall for Mitch. "My name is Addison," she finished. She said it with a frown, but not for the reason that she knew Ty . . . Mitch would assume.

"Oh, so you cheated?"

In more ways than you can imagine, she wanted to say. *Tell him now, tell him you cheated because you went to bed with the man your sister loved. Tell him you had no idea that Ty and Mitch were the same person. That you wished you could take it all back. The initial innocent flirting. The romantic walk on the beach. The intimate moments beneath the shower and the night sky.*

"Sorry, I thought the game was kind of college-ish."

Mitch laughed. "I'm pretty sure college-ish isn't a word."

Addison, all of a sudden, didn't like him correcting her. Last night the crawling sand comment seemed kind of comical, but now things had changed. She needed not to like this guy, at least not in a romantic way, which meant she needed to expose his faults. There was number two. Number one, a giant number one, was that he slept with her last night while a picture of another woman—her baby sister—had watched over them.

A lull filled the room.

Even though the lights had been dim when they'd come into the bedroom last night, she couldn't believe she'd been so caught up in his web that she hadn't noticed the picture. Stupid her and stupid recessed lighting. This house was too old for recessed lighting anyway. Why in the world had someone installed it? Did they not imagine that something like this might happen? She knew the answer: Things like this didn't happen. What were the odds? Her randomly meeting Mitch? Out of all the people in Emerald Isle—even though the island was fairly small—the chances had to be slim. Thousands of tourists were here for vacation and the fishing tournament. Why couldn't she have met one of them? Why couldn't Ty have been one of those guys?

Mitch spoke again. "Honestly, I thought the same thing about the game." He paused, a little concerned about Addison's current demeanor. "That's why I used my middle name."

Really? You used your middle name, too? How ironic. An image of her driver's license randomly popped into her mind, the name Harper Addison Adams in bold letters. Her mother had wanted to name her Harper and her father had wanted to name her Addison. Both sounded more like first names to her parents, but in the end neither gave in, except for her father in a way since Addison ended up being her middle name. Her mom had won that battle because she said everyone would end up calling her Addie, which she didn't like for some reason.

It didn't surprise Addison that both she and Mitch had a middle name that the other had never heard, but she found it interesting that they each had it written—by Bambi—on paper nametags that had been ruined by the shower. That shower had probably also ruined any friendship that could have ever been possible between the two of them, Addison recognized.

"That's clever," Addison admitted, her mind continuing to run a hundred miles a minute.

Mitch reached out for her hand and leaned in to kiss her.

Addison pulled away, covering her mouth, hoping he would just write it off as fear of morning breath. "I need to use your bathroom?" she said.

Beneath the covers, only a bra and underwear—that Mitch had been thoughtful enough to toss in the dryer last night—covered her body. He'd also been sweet enough to put her jeans and shirt in the washing machine. He'd promised to dry them this morning, while he made breakfast, and suggested that she could wrap up in the covers until her clothes were clean again.

Mitch couldn't help but peek as he watched her walk quickly toward the bathroom door. She had an amazing body for a thirty-year-old, but the entire time he watched her hips shake all he wanted to do was gaze into her beautiful eyes again.

— ~

Standing at the bathroom sink, the first thought that entered Addison's mind brought tears to her eyes. She wondered how many times London had stood at this very mirror. How many times had her sister walked back to Mitch's bed and fallen into his arms? She wanted to cut her own arm with the razor laying on the counter, run out the back door to the ocean and become shark bait, which was dumb and inconsiderate. But thoughts like that only proved she was human. Humans think stupid things. Things they would never actually do. They also do stupid things, she reminded herself, like sleep with Mitch Quinn.

— ~

Mitch's feet found the solid wooden floor and he headed for the kitchen with breakfast on his mind. Scrambled eggs. Bacon. Biscuits. Grits. He'd promised Addison last night that he'd mix up a variety of southern favorites. When she'd asked if he liked to cook, he'd told her he loved to cook . . . because he loved to eat. She'd laughed and he had, too. He started pulling out pots and pans and ingredients, then he remembered he needed to move Addison's clothes into the dryer.

———

Addison continued to think of all the things that had gone wrong last night. The scenarios that had led to this perfect storm. It started with every hotel room in this town being full. Then Ted—dumb, perverted Ted—putting his hands where they didn't belong. Mitch just happening to be there with his *Ty* nametag covering his true identity, then going kung-fu on Ted. Ty offering her his table. Her not letting him walk away. An otherwise harmless dinner and drinks. Then, Jack and Jill going the second mile in her hotel room. Of course, she just had to take Mitch up on his offer to walk on the beach. Like that wouldn't lead to anything. The guy was handsome, sweet, and one of the finest southern gentlemen she'd ever met. His house being a football field from where she fell into the water. The shower . . . oh, the shower. The image still gave her goosebumps. His abs, his . . . *You're getting off track,* she told herself. *He's not attractive. He's not thoughtful. He's not for you.*

———

The sound of the dryer tossing Addison and Mitch's clothes around reminded him of why they were there in the first place. How they'd come flying off their bodies and landed at their feet. Somehow, he had no regrets from last night. He should. He knew he should. But . . . he didn't.

He had to move forward with his life. Today, he would officially become a dad. At some point he would have had to start dating. Start looking for someone to build a family with him and Hannah. He cracked open an egg and watched it slide into the mixing bowl.

He was thinking too much. He and Addison had only known each other one night. He hadn't even known that he knew her real name until this morning, but that wasn't the point. The point was he had to move forward, and last night had been a great start. Not the start he would have ever imagined. Instead of wading out into the shallow end, he and Addison had just dived right into the deep end.

The first slices of bacon began to sizzle, filling the quaint home with the unique aroma only known to fried bacon. Mitch had always loved that smell. It reminded him of his childhood, of good times.

As breakfast cooked, he found himself wondering if Hannah would approve of Addison.

Addison thought about climbing out of the bathroom window. Marching down the beach in her bra and underwear. It's not like she'd look much different than the other women that would be out there in their bikinis. But then what? Then where would she go? That was the second half of this perfect storm. After getting to know each other extremely well in the shower, Mitch had built a small fire in the homemade pit in the backyard. They'd sat around and talked about stars and sharks and the sounds the ocean made at night whether or not anyone was there to listen. An hour later Addison pulled her clothes off the branch Mitch had used to make a clothes line and slid her still nearly soaking wet clothes back on. He gave her a towel to wrap around her and walked her back to the motel. She still couldn't believe what had happened there. The initial part, when the front desk clerk grinned from ear to ear and said, "Somebody's been skinny dipping," hadn't been a shock at all. Mitch had played right along and said, "It was amazing. We made love in the ocean with sharks swimming around us. You should try it; it's a high like you'd never imagine." Addison still couldn't believe he'd made the lady blush. Her eyes had widened, and then she'd shared the news that Jack and Jill had decided to stay the night. "Jack's wife must be out of town," she'd suggested. When Addison and Mitch had walked outside it got worse. That's when she noticed that her car wasn't between the two white lines where she'd parked it. "I'm so sorry, I didn't know it was your car," the clerk said when they went back inside. "It didn't have a parking pass on the dashboard and we had a guest waiting for a space, so I had no other option but to have it towed." When Addison asked where it was, she found out that she could pick it up . . . in the morning, at the impound lot. That's how she ended up back at Mitch's house. Go figure. What were the odds? she thought again. All of that happening in one night. Tara would love this story if she ever decided to tell it to her.

12

Mitch smiled when Addison stepped around the corner and into the kitchen with a bath towel wrapped around her body. He'd slipped into a pair of gym shorts and an old t-shirt. His feet were bare, like Addison's.

"Nice toes," he said. They were painted pink. He'd noticed the polish by the fire last night but the conversation had been so steady that he hadn't even gotten around to bringing it up.

Mitch watched Addison glance down as if she needed a reminder of what color nail polish she'd used.

She smiled. "Thanks, and good morning," she offered. "I never said good morning earlier."

Before she'd come out of the bathroom, she'd decided that this wasn't his fault. He didn't deserve for her to start treating him badly. She just had to be an adult and figure out how to handle this extraordinarily unique set of circumstances they'd stumbled into. She thought about just coming right out and telling him the truth, but doubted she had the guts. Why couldn't he have been the one to find out first, she thought? So he would have to deal with this burden. She wished she had said her first name before he said his.

"Thanks." He paused, feeling kind of awkward for not saying *good morning* back to her, but he'd already said it and thought it would also be kind of weird if he said it again. "So, you're an artist," he asked, pointing at her toes with the spatula.

"I'm a reporter." So it wasn't the whole truth, but it was close enough. She didn't want to lie to Mitch, but at the same time she had to be careful how much she revealed about herself. She had absolutely no idea what all London had told Mitch about her.

"You said you're here for work, what's your assignment?"

"Sharks."

Mitch wrinkled his brow and nodded his head. "So that's why you were asking so many questions about sharks last night?"

"Exactly. I didn't expect to meet an expert on my first night here," she said with a smile.

Mitch laughed, "I'm far from it."

"What about you? What do you do for work?"

"Well, I've been a photographer my whole life, but I pretty much gave that up about a year ago. Now I'm embarking on some new adventures," he said, leaving it at that for the time being.

That explained the camera tattoo wrapped around his bicep. Maybe she'd find out more about the guitar later. Addison wondered why he'd given up photography. Based on the timeframe, it sounded like the decision had something to do with London's passing. But she didn't want to pry, especially into anything that might bring up her sister.

"Breakfast looks good," she admired. "I could smell the bacon all the way in the bathroom."

"I figured that might draw you out."

"Is there anything I can do to help?" Addison offered.

"It's pretty much all wrapped up. I just need your help making a decision."

Oh, no, she thought to herself.

"Should we eat inside or outside?" he asked.

"Outside, definitely outside," she chose. Right now she couldn't stomach coming across any other pictures of London that might be in the house. She already felt like London was now watching over her every move.

Each of them made a plate and then found their way to a table made from pallets on the back deck, overlooking the blue ocean.

"What does your day look like?" Mitch wondered aloud as they began to eat their second meal together.

"I guess my workday will start at the police station, since I'll have to go there to bail my car out of jail anyway." Mitch laughed and Addison continued. "Law enforcement officials are usually fairly helpful with my stories. I may go back to the pier and interview some fishermen."

"How long will you be in town?" He'd wanted to ask that question several times, but he was kind of afraid of the answer. No matter how long she said, he was afraid it wouldn't be long enough.

"About a week, I suppose."

Mitch hoped to be able to spend as much time as he could with her. He didn't want this to be a one night fling. In fact, if he'd had even an inkling of intuition that such might be the outcome, he wouldn't have let one thing lead to another last night.

Addison took another bite of her eggs. They were actually delicious and so was everything else on her plate.

"I appreciate you letting me stay at your house last night," she said. "I'll find a hotel for the rest of the week, though," she mentioned, wanting to go ahead and get that out of the way.

"I'm afraid you're going to have a hard time finding a room," he said.

Addison had figured he'd most likely try to talk her into staying at his house. Last night when she'd considered the thought, the answer would have been *yes*, but after what she'd found out this morning it would have to be *no*.

"I searched on my phone before I came into the kitchen," she confirmed, wanting him to know that she'd already been looking.

"Any luck?"

She shook her head. "But I'm sure something will open up, even if it's at you-know-where."

Mitch laughed. "I would hate for you to have to stay there. That place is nasty. I wanted to offer for you to stay at my house as soon as we walked across the street after the exciting bar fight and dinner last night, but I didn't want you to get the idea that I was the type of guy that meets a girl at a bar and asks her to come home with him."

"Too late for that," she reeled off with a snicker, temporarily forgetting that she needed to guard her words a little more carefully now. "Just kidding," she said. "I can tell that you are a gentleman." She paused, taking in the smell of the morning air, a mixture of salt water and dew-filled grass. "I'll be fine, I've stayed at all types of places," she finished.

"I wish I could offer for you to stay here again, but I have other plans tonight."

Mitch's comment threw her off. Other plans? Like another woman? Not that it mattered. She had no stake to Mitch. She didn't need to have one, anyway. So why should it matter? Maybe because London had at one point? She wasn't sure. Her emotions were all over the place right now.

"Oh, okay," she said simply.

"I guess I picked a bad time to come to Emerald Isle." The comment had a double meaning, at least for Addison.

Bad times . . . Mitch had encountered plenty of those lately. Maybe Addison had picked the wrong time, but maybe she'd also picked the right time to stumble into his life, he thought.

"Depends on how you look at it," Mitch suggested.

Addison frowned. "If you could see it through my eyes, you'd know what I mean," she said, wishing he could. "Don't take that the wrong way. I'm glad we met. I've had a lot of fun with you, Mitch," she said honestly. "I'm just in a tough spot in my life right now. Things are not quite what they seem." She wanted to at least prepare him for the inevitable.

"I have an idea," Mitch offered. "Did you happen to notice the house next to mine?"

"The huge one with all the windows on the ocean side?"

Mitch laughed, remembering their conversation about his house last night, sensing deja vu. "Not that one, the one on the other side."

From their viewpoint in the backyard, patches of woods kept them from being able to see either of the neighboring homes. "I might have, but I'm not sure," she said, looking in that direction anyway.

"I don't know if you would be interested, but it's vacant," he acknowledged.

What was he suggesting?

"Do you know the owner?" she asked.

"I do."

"It's not five stars, but I promise it doesn't have roaches either, or a lady at the front desk who will be all up in your business. Plus the rent is reasonable."

Money wasn't the object, Addison knew. Work would pay for it. She'd stayed at places that cost more per night than her townhouse cost to rent for a month. The bigger question was did she want to be staying in the house next to the one owned by Mitch Quinn.

"If I were to decide to go that route," she began to quiz, wanting to make sure she left her options open. "How would I go about getting up with the owner to ask him if I could stay there for a week or so?"

"You wouldn't have to ask him," Mitch said.

Addison furrowed her brow. "What are you suggesting? That I break in and just stay there, hoping the owner doesn't show up and kick me out? Or call the police? I need the police on my side for this shark story, and I'll already have to do a little digging to get out of the hole I've dug by letting my car get towed," she said with an easy laugh.

"I wouldn't kick you out or call the police on you. And you don't have to ask me if you can stay there. It's your house for as long as you need it. I haven't rented the place out in three years."

"Oh, so you own the house?"

Mitch nodded. "I've been looking for a good reason to tidy it up a little, maybe make some minor repairs. I wouldn't mind putting it up for rent at some point." He paused, trying to think this scenario out. He'd somewhat put the buggy before the horse. "The floors need sweeping and the place could use a good dusting; the furniture is kind of old, well, ancient maybe, but it's in good shape."

Addison hesitated, "I don't know . . ."

"How about this, I'll start working on it some this morning after I take you to pick up your car."

"You don't have to do that. I can call a cab. You don't have to do any of this, Mitch."

"That's nonsense; there's no need to call a cab. I have a perfectly fine Jeep sitting in the driveway."

Addison racked her brain for a way to get out of staying at Mitch's house next door, which seemed to be the only vacant place on the island. "I'm not sure how much help I would be with cleaning. I might not have much free time. And as far as repairs are concerned," Addison admitted. "I once smashed my . . ." She barely caught herself, nearly blurting out that she'd smashed London's hand with a hammer. ". . . friend's hand with a hammer," she finished.

Nearly every story Mitch heard these days reminded him of one London had told him. He remembered London telling him about a time when she had found her hand wedged between a piece of particle board and a hammer swung by one of her friends, or maybe it was her sister that had smashed her finger. Honestly, he couldn't remember the details, and it kind of frustrated him. He didn't want to forget a single thing about London, but time seemed to have a way of stealing memories, which was one of the reasons why he used to love taking photographs.

Addison noticed the expression on Mitch's face and feared London had told him that story. "My father was a contractor," she quickly offered—a bold faced lie. "And one day when I was a kid, my friend and I were helping him build a house and I missed the target and hit her thumb."

It was really London's knuckles, and they were putting together an entertainment center.

"Ouch, that had to hurt."

"She cried for a really long time."

She hated to lie to Mitch, but like the hammer, the story had just slipped out. She would have to be more careful, she knew, if she wanted to complete her assignment and read London's memoir before she told Mitch that she was London's sister. Being next door definitely wouldn't help with her new plan, which consisted of staying away from Mitch until it was time to leave Emerald Isle.

13

Addison cranked her car and seriously thought about crossing the bridge out of Emerald Isle and heading back home. In fact, she'd spent the entire ride to the police station with Mitch thinking about the best way to wiggle out of the stickiest situation she'd ever been a part of. The two of them had barely talked, and she knew that he had to have been wondering what happened to the woman he met last night. She hated doing this to him, but she had no other choice. She'd taken down his phone number—although she still found it hard to believe that he had never owned a cell phone—but she hadn't offered her phone number in return. She figured the area code would probably raise a red flag, plus she didn't want him to have it anyway. This way she didn't have to worry about him calling her while she was in town. It would be up to her whether or not they saw each other again before she had to drop off London's memoir. No matter what happened, she knew she had to do that.

"Would you like to get together on Saturday?" was the last question Mitch had asked.

"I'll call you later," Addison had replied. *Later* meant anytime, so she felt good that she hadn't lied to him again. She *would* call him later. Later . . . She knew he would be expecting her to call about staying in the house next door. That conversation had kind of been left open ended. The way she preferred.

The officer at the police station—a gentleman in his mid-fifties with salt and pepper colored hair and a gold bar across his left chest that read *DUNLAP*—had been a huge help in jumpstarting the investigative part of Addison's assignment. She'd meant to introduce herself as Addison; she'd decided she would just stick with that name as long as she remained on the island. Keep confusion to a minimum. But when the officer asked for her driver's license, she responded to Harper as he glanced it over.

He'd been generous enough to provide her the police reports for all three shark attacks, which she was somewhat surprised to find in his possession, with each taking place in a different location. The reports included solid details. Pinpoint locations. Victim's names. Witness's names. Time of day. Officer Dunlap informed her that he'd been a first responder to the Emerald Isle attack. She felt chills when he told her how it looked worse than any crime scene he'd ever witnessed. It had basically happened on the shore, in knee deep water. He also gave her the name and a cell phone number for the head lifeguard, who'd been the first on the scene. She knew she would need to talk with him at some point.

Work would have paid the fee for her car being towed, but when Addison pulled out her credit card the officer—Pete, he'd said she could call him Pete—told her the bill had already been taken care of.

"By whom?" Addison inquired.

"The individual requested confidentiality," Pete Dunlap responded. "Said to tell you they felt bad for what happened."

Addison smirked, knowing it had to have been the clerk from the motel. The person who'd basically told her to leave her car there and walk across the street to the bar to eat dinner. Maybe she wasn't so bad of a person after all, Addison contemplated.

Instead of being a coward and heading out of town, Addison parked her car under a shade tree in a public beach access parking lot not too far from the police station. She slammed the trunk shut and opened the book. She realized after what had happened between her and Mitch Quinn last night, the memoir, for her, would never come across as London had imagined it would. Nonetheless, she'd been dying to read the next page.

When Mitch arrived at the park I wasn't quite sure who was happier to see him, me or the multitude of ducks, heads arched and beaks stretching for Heaven. He'd brought with him three loaves of bread that he'd picked up from the local bakery on his way over, and as we ate lunch at a picnic table close by the water, the furry little creatures begged for food. When we finished our meal, we fed the swans and mallards; the seagulls quickly became jealous because we weren't including them, and eventually Mitch fell trap to their squalls and began tossing clumps of bread into the air.

"You better watch out," I advised, "seagulls are greedy; once you feed one, they all come."

Minutes after I finished my sentence, a swarm of them soared in the air above, and it wasn't long before Mitch's hair color suddenly gained a splotchy white tint. I have no idea how I escaped the bombing.

I tried to hold back my laughter as he ran for the car and then held his head perfectly straight on the drive to his house. He looked so helpless, as my amusement seeped out from time to time as we passed an onslaught of beach traffic.

Once we made it inside, I couldn't help but notice the muscles on his back as he slowly and carefully maneuvered his shirt over his head. It was the first time I saw Mitch with his shirt off and as he knelt beside the tub I felt my body tingle. When he leaned over the low wall and began rinsing his hair beneath the faucet, I reached for a bottle of shampoo. I noticed tattoos on his biceps as I massaged his scalp until it turned as red as a fire engine and just as I was finishing, a stream of water trickled down his spine. Before I knew it, a water fight broke out; Mitch and I were on the floor, his body hovering closely

above mine. It wasn't the first time we had kissed, but my body felt urges it had never felt
before, and we forgot that we both needed to get back to work . . .

It hurt Addison to read those words. Not because she was jealous in any way but because she'd crossed a line without even knowing one existed. Just as London had, she'd studied Mitch's physique as his shirt came off, and she understood firsthand the same urges that her sister had felt. Mitch was a handsome man. Tanned from lying out on the beach behind his house, she assumed. But she felt guilty for thinking those thoughts, for having a picture of London and Mitch in her mind one moment and then the next moment she couldn't escape the image of her and Mitch beneath the shower last night.

She wanted to puke out of the opened window. How had she let this happen? That was the thought on her mind when her phone began to ring. She considered letting the call go to voicemail, avoiding the caller. Then she considered throwing her cell phone out the window and starting a new life. But she didn't.

"Hello?" she said, her voice raised.

"Harper, I'm so sorry. Do you forgive me?" Tara begged.

"Not a chance," Harper blurted out.

For a moment the only sound came from the wind nudging the branches on the tree dangling above the car.

"I have a good reason," Tara promised.

"Oh, yeah, let's hear it."

Harper sometimes talked to Tara like her boss and other times like her friend. This time she was a friend and Harper wasn't giving any ground. Tara had left her hanging. Come to think of it, this whole situation that she was now in with Mitch was Tara's fault. If she'd had a hotel room reserved, none of this would have happened.

"I was at the hospital."

The parking lot was beginning to fill up with beach goers, but up until Tara's last comment Harper hadn't even cared that the couple in the next parking spot—plucking chairs and towels and bags from their trunk—could hear every word of her conversation.

Harper's tone changed immediately. "Are you okay?" was all of a sudden all she wanted to know. She thought about rolling up her window now, but it was already too hot outside to be cooped up in a car.

"Yes," is all Tara offered.

"What happened?"

"Well, I was trying to book you a hotel room. I called a dozen places in Emerald Isle. There is some stupid fishing tournament . . ."

Harper interrupted. "Not with the hotel room, Tara, with you?"

"I'm okay," Tara said.

"You're okay? That's it? Did you spend the whole evening in the hospital? The night? I tried to call you over and over. I was worried about you. Mad at you . . ."

"It's nothing, just a little scare and I'd rather not talk about it over the phone," she insisted.

"Tara, it's me. What's going on?"

"I'll tell you all about it when you get back."

That wasn't the answer Harper wanted to hear, but Tara seemed adamant about not talking about it for now.

"You promise?"

"Yes."

"But you're okay?" Harper paused. "At least tell me that much."

"Yes," she hesitated. "I'm okay." Then she changed the subject. "Like I started to mention, the fishing tournament . . ."

Harper cut her off again. "The fishing tournament . . . I know all about the fishing tournament, believe me. This place is nuts about this fishing tournament. There are no hotel rooms available anywhere on the island or any of the towns within thirty minutes of here," Harper informed her. She'd checked.

"Yeah, that's what everyone was telling me, too. So where did you stay last night? Please don't tell me that you slept in your car."

Harper shook her head. "No, my car was locked in the impound lot at the police station all night."

"How in the world did that happen?"

"It's a long story," she admitted. "Basically, though, everything comes back to the fishing tournament."

"Oh, brother. So, then, where did you stay?"

"That's an even longer story," Harper offered.

"Well, I want to hear it," Tara insisted.

Tara had chosen to keep quiet about her hospital visit, and for now Harper's lips were sealed shut about what had happened between her and Mitch Quinn last night. Sure, she wanted to tell her best friend all about one of the most amazing nights of her life, one that Tara would have definitely been proud about. She'd been urging her to move on ever since James left, even told her that a one night fling was the cure all. But Harper wasn't sure she would ever tell anyone about what had happened. And she now knew that a one night fling wasn't a cure-all. It was the worst decision of her life.

14

Mitch's morning had been filled with emotional highs and lows. He'd woken up to a different woman than he'd gone to bed with, that he knew for sure. In fact, he wondered if he would ever hear from Addison again. He kind of hoped she'd take him up on his offer to stay at his house next door, but with the way she'd acted earlier he just didn't know if he had the time to deal with this. He couldn't help but wonder if Addison was bipolar. For now, though, he had more important things on his mind. He'd been sitting in Myrtle's office for the past hour.

"Sign right here, Mitch Quinn," she pointed out. "Just make sure not to sign Pig Pen," she said, laughing out loud.

Her comment tickled Mitch. Dr. Thorpe laughed, too; Mitch had told him the back story behind the name. Maybe that was the name he should have had Bambi write on his nametag last night, he thought to himself as he glanced at the lawyer sitting across from him. Mitch decided that Myrtle's inside joke would be too confusing to explain to the man in the suit at the moment.

All of these legal documents had been in the works for what seemed like forever, Mitch thought, as he literally crossed the final 't' and dotted the final 'i'.

"If any questions arise about any of these documents, do not hesitate to contact me, Mr. Quinn," the lawyer reassured him.

Mitch shook his head. The reality of the moment seemed overwhelming. He was now officially a dad. The biological part didn't matter. He was a real dad. He'd just sworn to make Hannah his responsibility. He would. Every day. He would love her and care for her and make sure she enjoyed the life she deserved. The life London had always wanted her to have. The life London would have given her if she had been able to become her official mom. In so many ways London had been Hannah's mom already. She'd loved her like her own child. Been there for her through the good times as well as the bad. Physically, there had been more bad times than good ones, but London had always known how to turn the bad times into good times. Mitch wished she were here as he watched the lawyer lift his briefcase, shake each person's hand, and head out of the room. Mitch, Doc, and Myrtle remained behind.

"You're going to be a great father, Mitch," Myrtle assured him.

Mitch just smiled. Myrtle hadn't stopped smiling.

"You definitely will be," she added. "Just like your lawyer said, if you have any questions, I'll be here for you, too. You have my contact information and you know where to find me."

Mitch hugged Myrtle and walked Doc to his car. Outside, the conversation shifted gears, somewhat.

"If he ever comes around," Dr. Thorpe said, "you call the police and call me, too."

He was Doc's son, Donald, Hannah's biological father. Doc had been through the history with Mitch a dozen times. Mitch knew the story, knew what to expect. Doc had been the one to break the bad news to Donald years ago. The moment he found out Hannah had cancer he'd disappeared for months. He couldn't handle it, he'd said. He'd already lost his wife in a fatal shooting only months before. Doc had told Mitch that the shooting might have been ruled a random act of violence, but he never thought that to be the case. Donald had gotten mixed up with the wrong crowd in college. He'd dabbled with drugs in high school, but when he went off to college the freedom got the best of him. He met a girl, got her pregnant, and made all the wrong choices. Her family didn't want anything to do with Donald or Hannah, especially after their little girl was killed. They blamed Donald for hooking her on drugs and alcohol. Doc had never once heard a word from them since his son had agreed to give him full custody of Hannah. He'd told Mitch that he doubted they would ever want to see her or have anything to do with her. But Donald would show up every once in a while wanting to see Hannah. Sometimes he would be drunk, other times high, and sometimes sober. Doc had never let him in the house. He'd always told him that they needed to talk first, make sure it was in Hannah's best interest to spend time with her dad. Donald had never been up for that. He always wanted to see her right then. One night he'd thrown a beer bottle through one of the windows at Doc's house. Another night he'd pushed his father down and kicked his car on the way out.

Mitch shook his head and gave Doc a big hug. "I will," he promised.

What hurt Mitch the most was that Doc took the blame for how Donald turned out. He said he'd waited too late in life to have a child; that he was too old to play ball with him and do all the things a dad should do with his son which, along with his health, added another reason that Doc had liked the idea of Mitch adopting Hannah. He couldn't do the things for her that a dad needed to do. Doc said after he lost his own wife to a horrible case of pneumonia he'd become a workaholic, which had only further harmed his relationship with his son.

Mitch and Doc got into their vehicles and headed in the same direction. A babysitter had been watching Hannah at Doc's house ever since he'd headed out to meet Mitch.

Hannah had been waiting near the front window, playing with her baby dolls all morning. As soon as Mitch pulled into the driveway, she ran out the front door of the enormous house—the only real home she'd ever known—and jumped into his arms.

"I missed you," she exclaimed.

"I missed you, too," he declared.

"Will you play dolls with me later?"

"Of course I will."

A minute later Doc pulled in next to Mitch's car, and as soon as he stepped out, Hannah attached herself to his leg. Mitch smiled. Doc had always been good to her. Mitch knew that in a way Doc had tried to make up for all the lost time with Donald. He hadn't spoiled Hannah with materialistic things, although she had her fair share of belongings, but he'd given her his time and his love.

"Mitch is going to play dolls with me later," Hannah informed her grandpa.

"He is," he responded with excitement.

"Grandpa can't get down on the floor and play dolls," Hannah, acting like a grown up, told Mitch. "He says he's too old, so we just play at the kitchen table. Sometimes they have tea with us," she shared.

Mitch already knew these things, but he smiled anyway. Hannah was too cute. They would have so much fun together; he knew that without a doubt.

"Let's go get some lunch," Doc suggested. He and Mitch had planned to take Hannah out for lunch, and from there she would go with Mitch. That way she wouldn't watch them pack all of her bags in the car and then wave goodbye as she and Mitch backed away from her home while her grandfather waved from the front door. It seemed too sad. She'd already had enough sadness for one lifetime. They wanted this moment to be happy.

"Can I ride with Mitch?" Hannah asked.

"Of course."

After Hannah put her dolls in their bag, Mitch strapped her into the booster seat that had become a permanent fixture in the back row of his Jeep. It was a little more rugged than what she was used to, but she never complained and Mitch knew it was safe.

"Let's put the top down," Hannah suggested, as usual, even in the winter months.

They rode in style, as Hannah liked to call it, to a restaurant a few miles down the road. Mitch ordered a burger, Hannah had chicken strips, and Doc ate a wrap. The food tasted good, but the company proved to be even better. Mitch knew they would do this often, which made it easier to take on this new role. He'd have full support from Doc, and Hannah would still be able to spend plenty of time with her grandpa.

After filling their bellies, Doc hugged and kissed Hannah and headed home. Mitch knew it had to be difficult for him to walk away, and in a way Mitch felt like he was taking someone that belonged to another person. But he loved Hannah dearly; he knew that for sure.

The two of them ended up at one of her favorite places, the grocery store. They found a parking spot and Hannah climbed into the basket part of the grocery cart.

"Grandpa always lets me do this," she declared.

Mitch figured that statement would become reoccurring in the days and months to come. Hopefully, he and Grandpa would be on the same page with many of the ways that each of them would raise Hannah. As for riding in the cart, it was fine by him. As long as it made her happy, it made him happy.

Inside the medium-sized brick building—the only real grocery store on the island—Mitch pointed the cart down the first aisle.

"Let me know if you see anything that you want," he declared.

"We might need to get another cart, then," Hannah insisted, her blue eyes growing with her statement.

They laughed then and a handful of other times as they weaved in and out of aisles and around people in the crowded store. The fishing tournament caused every public place to be busy. In fact, Mitch hadn't had to park as far out in the parking lot as he did today since two years ago when the tournament had been in town. Last year he hadn't ventured out. Another reminder of London. The tournament, he remembered, had started the weekend after her funeral. He hadn't really felt like eating, so he made by on what little he had in the house until he ran out of food altogether.

"You're silly," Mitch revealed, choosing London's optimism on the outside, even though he felt a little different on the inside.

"I know," she testified.

Hannah made the sound of wheels squealing as they rounded turn number nine. Mitch had called out each aisle number as they left it in the dust, and Hannah had made the sound of screeching tires each time. This time, though, Mitch had to slam on the brakes, causing Hannah and the twenty items surrounding her to slide toward the front of the cart. Hannah, facing Mitch, had a look of surprise on her face. She immediately silenced her sound effects and stared at Mitch with those bulging eyes again. Mitch wore a similar look on his face but for a different reason. Having to stop so he didn't run into someone hadn't surprised him at all. There were people everywhere, conversations all around, random announcements on the intercom, a lot going on in a little space. What threw Mitch for a loop was the person that Hannah hadn't seen yet—a person he had never even imagined running into on his first trip to the grocery store with Hannah.

15

itch stood speechless for a moment. Hannah continued to stare at him, still unaware that someone was standing in the way of their cart. The set of eyes that Mitch had locked in on stared back at him then looked down at Hannah. Mitch watched closely. He didn't know what to say. What to do. He could tell that Hannah being in the middle of them presented a question.

"I'm sorry," Mitch offered, referring to the screeching halt.

Mitch wondered what would happen next. What would be said? If this would be as awkward as he thought it might.

Suddenly, he felt himself tense up as Hannah turned to see the person on the other side of the apology.

"You're fine," Addison responded, motioning with her hand. "Who is this?" she asked with a grin.

Mitch smiled. *This is my daughter*, he thought proudly. He wanted to speak those words, not just to Addison but to the whole world.

"I'm Hannah," Hannah offered before Mitch could introduce his daughter for the first time.

She'd never been shy, Mitch relished.

"Hi, Hannah," she responded, "I'm . . ." She paused for a split second. ". . . Addison." She'd almost done it again. Almost said *Harper*.

Hannah giggled, then looked at Mitch. Then back at Addison. "Are you his girlfriend?" Hannah asked, referring to Mitch.

Mitch wasn't sure what to say. He couldn't believe Hannah had said that. Well, actually, it wasn't the first time she'd said something like this. She'd called him London's boyfriend the first time they'd met.

Addison glanced up at Mitch, then back down into Hannah's blue eyes. They were even more beautiful than she'd imaged when she'd read about little Hannah in London's memoir.

"I'm a girl," Addison stated, "and I'm his friend."

"So you are his girlfriend."

"Why do you think that?" Mitch asked.

Hannah swiveled her head from Addison to Mitch and then back again. "Because that's how you looked at London . . ."

Mitch didn't know how to respond.

Addison found herself speechless, afraid the expression on her face might offer a clue to her real identity.

Hannah, on the other hand, seemed to be doing just fine with words. "And I never seen you look at any other girl that way."

Addison wanted to cry. She even thought she might have felt tears trying to form in the corners of her eyelids.

Mitch glanced away, his body working overtime to hold in his own emotions.

"You look at him the same way London did, too," Hannah mentioned to Addison, before pausing for a second. "London was kind of my mommy." She paused again. "Mitch is my daddy . . . my real daddy now," she said, proudly.

Mitch smiled as best he could. He knew he had some explaining to do. Well, maybe. He had some explaining to do if Addison decided again that she liked him like she had last night. If she liked him as little as she seemed to earlier this morning, then none of this probably mattered at all. If the latter was the case, she was probably already searching for a way out of this predicament, just like she had been when he'd given her his phone number. Mitch had a good idea that she wouldn't call. At least that is what his gut feeling had been.

Hannah continued to dominate the conversation, or more precisely, to fill the lull that presented itself between Mitch and Addison. "You should have dinner with us," she suggested.

Addison felt the pressure to respond. She wondered if the red had worn off of her face yet. "That's mighty sweet of you to offer," she replied. Buying time seemed to be the theme of her day.

"You're more than welcome to," Mitch added, not knowing what else to say but glad the conversation had moved away from London. "But I know you have a lot going on with work," he finished, leaving her a way out of the invitation. He didn't like the idea of twisting her arm, especially after the way she'd acted this morning.

"Please," Hannah begged. Then she turned to Mitch. "Oh, and she can even pick out her own meat since we're at the grocery store."

Addison furrowed her brow.

Mitch decided he'd better clue her in on the plan. "We're having a cookout this evening. Those are the plans I mentioned to you earlier today." He paused for a moment, kind of happy that Hannah had invited Addison. He probably wouldn't have in fear of being turned down. He didn't need that right now. "I told Hannah that we could come to the grocery store and pick out our meat for the grill."

Hannah chimed in. "I'm having hot dogs," she exclaimed. "And Mitch's having hamburgers. He makes really tasty hamburgers."

Addison couldn't help but smile at the way Hannah pronounced hamburgers. It almost sounded like ham-buggers.

Mitch shrugged his shoulders. "They're okay," he said with a grin.

Addison wanted to say *yes*. She also wanted to say *no*, but something in the way Hannah looked at her made her feel like she should take the opportunity to get to know this little girl that her sister loved so much.

"Sure," Addison finally answered. "I'll come."

"We're having ice cream, too," Hannah blurted out.

"Wow," Addison replied. "It must be a special night."

"It is," Hannah said simply.

"We're celebrating," Mitch mentioned, pointing to a cart filled with junk food.

Addison had noticed the candy and cookies already; she'd also seen apples and oranges and toiletries and cleaning supplies.

"Which flavor ice cream is your favorite?"

Addison grinned again, loving how Hannah's v's made the sound of b's.

"I like mint cookies and cream."

Hannah shrugged her nose. "Yuck," she responded honestly. "But we'll get you some."

"Hannah has an unlimited budget today," Mitch said with a chuckle, pointing at the list in Hannah's hand, as if the cart didn't offer adequate proof. "I made the mistake of telling her she could get anything she wants today. So if there's anything else you want just let her know and she'll add it to the list."

Addison could tell that Mitch's offer was honest, whereas most people in his spot would have probably said the same thing but with a hint of sarcasm.

"I think the ice cream will do." Addison, for the first time since they'd begun talking, took in her surroundings. A new set of people wandered by. A new song played on the circular speakers sticking out from the faded square ceiling tiles. She hadn't realized how engrossed she'd become in the conversation with Hannah and Mitch. "And the hamburger, of course," Addison added.

"Sounds great," Mitch affirmed.

"Where's your cart?" Hannah questioned out of the blue.

Mitch hadn't even thought about her not having a cart or hand basket or even any items in her hands.

Addison touched the cart that Hannah was sitting in. "I'm actually not grocery shopping," she said. "I'm working."

"You work here?" Hannah asked, not allowing Addison an opportunity for a response. "I've never seen you here before. What time do you get off?" She continued. "Dinner is at . . ." Hannah turned to Mitch. "What time is dinner?" she asked him.

"Addison doesn't work at the grocery store," he explained to Hannah.

Totally confused, Hannah furrowed her little brow.

Addison, noticing her expression, chimed in. "I interview people, which basically means I talk to them. I'm at the grocery store to talk to a man who works here," she explained.

Mitch wondered what the grocery store had to do with shark attacks, but he didn't want to ask any further questions on the subject since Hannah was already confused. Not that it mattered anyway.

Hannah took it at face value. "Oh, okay."

16

After parting ways with Mitch and Hannah, Addison spent the next thirty minutes talking to the meat manager at the grocery store. His daughter had been the victim of the shark attack in Emerald Isle. Addison hadn't expected to chat with him this long; she'd even initially asked if stopping by the family home later might be more convenient, but he'd said now would work perfectly. He was just about to go on break, and he didn't mind eating his turkey sandwich while they talked, as long as she didn't mind sitting out behind the store while he ate lunch and smoked a cigarette.

The scene out back reminded her of a few other locations where she'd interviewed people over the years. This job had led her to all kinds of places, like restaurants and bars with alleyways out back. Some dark and scary. At least this time it was daylight. She spotted a couple of large dumpsters nearby that smelled of outdated meat. Even a couple of scraggly, skittish cats meandered around. On the other side of a makeshift table made of old plastic bread crates where she and the meat manager were currently sitting, Addison could see a cluster of hand carts, a forklift, and a few wooden crates.

"I'm going to record our conversation for my own personal notes, if that's okay with you?" she asked. "None of what you say will be shared with anyone," she promised the man. When she'd first introduced herself—making sure to refer to herself as Addison—and told him the name of the company she worked with, she could tell he thought it was impressive that she was here to talk to him. She knew from experience that he'd pretty much agree to whatever information she requested.

"Sure, that's fine," he confirmed.

Thankfully, this man's daughter hadn't been injured badly. She did suffer a few gouges that, to the naked eye, looked pretty intense. A slew of photos were in the police report that Addison had studied after her conversation with Tara this morning. Given the presumption that a six-foot shark had taken a hold of the girl's leg, everyone involved knew it could have been much worse. All-in-all twenty stitches had fixed her, and now she would have a scar to prove a story that she would probably tell for the rest of her life.

While the man ate his sandwich and puffed small rings of smoke into the warm air, Addison could feel herself beginning to perspire. She fired a few rounds of questions to get some background on the family, things that weren't in the police report. Why they went to the beach that day? Whether they'd ever seen a shark in the past? If they'd ever go back to the beach? If the girl had nightmares? If the family blamed anyone in particular?

The dad answered every single question, some taking more thought than others. One of the interesting thoughts that Addison had about shark attacks at this point in her investigation is that sharks didn't have preferences. It didn't matter if the victim was poor or rich. Lived in town or came to the beach for a vacation, which made the story more interesting. One note Addison made in her cell phone was not to allow this story to become entertainment. The shark attacks were real. The people were real. This man's little girl had made it out with minor injuries, but the others had been more life altering. A middle-aged man in Ocracoke had a chunk taken out of his hip, and a teenager in Surf City lost part of his leg. This story would be about how a single encounter with a creature in its natural habitat could alter the life of an individual. A family. A community. A region. Even a nation.

Three cigarettes and thirty minutes full of conversation later, Addison had what she needed. More than what she needed, since the second-hand smoke felt like it was burning her lungs. She thanked the man for taking the time to talk to her and handed him her business card.

"If you think of anything else that might be helpful, feel free to send me an email."

Tara had always given Addison a hard time about choosing not to include her name and phone number on her business card, but unlike Addison, Tara liked the attention, especially from the male interviewees. When Tara had trained her, Addison had noticed how she'd practically enticed men anywhere near her age to call her about anything. Email just made things easier, Addison thought. The communication channel offered her a record of conversations, just like she had when she recorded her live interviews. As for her current name situation, it brought a smile to her face when she remembered that even her email address was generic. It would be better if no one in Emerald Isle knew her real name.

— ~

Mitch and Hannah finished putting away two-weeks-worth of groceries before bringing Hannah's suitcase into the house. Mitch let her go into her room to play with her Barbies while he brought them in. Throughout the last few weeks, he and Doc had been slowly migrating Hannah's belongings to Mitch's house. They thought the transition would be easier this way. Doc had been bringing Hannah over more frequently as well, to play in her room and become more acquainted with the house. She'd been here off and on throughout the past year, more so in the past six months, but when London was around they'd spent most of their time together at London's house. Hannah had asked about Doc a couple of times today, but the thought of him not being around hadn't seemed to bother her as much as Mitch thought it might. He was afraid, though, that the reality of the situation might catch up with her tonight.

Mitch had smiled when Hannah placed apple juice and yogurt in the spot where he'd always kept his beer.

For the next hour, Mitch jumped back and forth between the kitchen, Hannah's room, and his bedroom. He wanted to give her some space, but at the same time let her know that he was here if she needed anything. A couple of times when he peeked in she asked him to sit on the floor and play with her. He laughed and let himself be drawn into her stories. The last time he was in her room he told her about a special project he needed her help with. "I've never even been over there," she said, when he mentioned cleaning the house next door.

"It will be fun," he said, leaving out the reason for cleaning it. He'd almost decided that it was a waste of time before he and Hannah had run into Addison at the grocery store. Now he figured the chances of her deciding to stay there might be a little greater.

— —

Mitch and Hannah were walking out the front door with buckets and brooms in their hands when a car neither of them had ever seen before pulled into the driveway. Mitch wondered who it might be, as the sun poured onto the windshield.

"Addison," Hannah called out when she stepped out of the car.

Mitch was surprised to see her here two hours early. He'd told her that dinner would be around six o'clock. He found himself wondering if she'd come to say she wasn't coming.

"Hey," Mitch sounded, as he watched Hannah run toward Addison.

Addison smiled and returned the hug that Hannah shared with her.

"Hi, Mitch," Addison said as he walked toward her.

"Want to come help us clean," Hannah asked. "We're going next door to Mitch's other house to clean it," she shared, pointing to the house.

"Sure," Addison replied, looking at Mitch for approval. "I hope it's okay that I came early. Honestly, I need a . . ." She searched for a word other than *shower*, knowing that the word *shower* would only bring back memories. For her, it had already. "Well, what I was going to say, is that if your offer still stands, I think I'll take you up on it," she confirmed. The more she had thought about it the more it made sense. Seeing Hannah had opened her eyes, and once she'd agreed to dinner, she'd decided that she'd just go ahead and tell Mitch tonight why she'd acted the way she had this morning. The real reason—not some excuse like she wished she could conjure up just so that she could let him hold her in his arms one more time. Softly kiss her lips again. Let the moment lead to wherever it wanted with no sense of guilt or shame.

"I'm a man of my word," Mitch said.

"Then I guess we better start cleaning," Addison suggested, reaching for the broom and washcloths that Hannah had dropped on the ground when she'd come running her way. "You may have to put some of that soap on me, Hannah. I smell bad from working outside in the heat today."

Addison really did wish she could jump in the shower. It was the reason she'd arrived early. Now she felt inclined to help clean, since

Mitch was tidying the house just for her anyway, and it wouldn't matter that she was already a little icky. Cleaning the house would most likely bring on more of the same.

Mitch carried Addison's suitcase into his bedroom and shut the door behind him when he walked back out, so that she could change clothes.

"Once we clean a spot for your luggage next door, I'll carry it over for you," he mentioned.

Addison changed into a pair of yoga pants and a tank top and then met Mitch and Hannah on the front porch of the house next door. Once inside, Mitch, Addison and Hannah developed a game plan for tidying up the place. Mitch suggested that today they only needed to focus on cleaning the living room, kitchen, bedroom, and bathroom since those were probably the rooms that Addison would use the most. Then the three of them scattered across dusty wooden floors into all of the rooms, opening every window in the house, inviting in the smell of the ocean. Some of the old windows were a bit stiff, so Hannah ended up supervising for the most part on that project. She seemed to enjoy calling for Mitch when Addison came across one too difficult to pry open. Opening the windows reminded Mitch of growing up on the island. At night, his parents had always allowed him to keep his windows open, and he'd loved falling asleep to the sounds of the ocean: the roar of the waves, the ships passing by, and all of the birds that migrated through the region. He hadn't realized how special it was until he'd moved away, and it had been one of his favorite things to come back to.

Hannah did her best to help Mitch and Addison remove the dusty plastic coverings from antique furniture that filled the house Mitch had grown up in. This had been his parent's home until they died in the car crash three years ago. Since then, he'd only stepped through the front door several times. After what happened to London, though, he knew it was time for him to face the fear that neither she nor his parents would ever be coming back. They would both want him to move on with his life. Letting Addison stay here would be a good transition for him. It wasn't like renting or selling the place; Addison wouldn't be making any changes or even redecorating. For the most part, it would still be the home he remembered growing up in and coming back to when he would visit his parents once a year.

As dust floated loosely through the stale air, Addison began to sneeze.

"Bless you," Mitch and Hannah said simultaneously.

"Thank you," Addison responded.

Hannah swept the living room floor with her little broom that she'd asked for at the grocery store. Addison followed behind her, collecting all the loose particles. They both worked together to put the sand, dirt and dust into the dustpan. Hannah wanted to dump it outside, so Addison let her. Mitch had been in the kitchen filling a bucket of mop water and putting trash bags in the trash cans. When the girls finished sweeping the living room, he started mopping. They danced from room to room just the same.

Mitch was amazed at how nice the floors looked after a simple mopping. Addison started dusting, but then suddenly began sneezing frantically.

"Are you okay?" Mitch asked, concerned.

"Allergies," she answered, sneezing again and again.

"I'll get you some tissues," he uttered before darting out the door. He'd already noticed that there weren't any in this house.

When Mitch made it back, Addison and Hannah were sitting side by side on the concrete steps outside the front door. He handed Addison a roll of toilet paper and propped his leg up on the porch. "Sorry, I don't have any Kleenex," he said.

She smiled, red nose and all, and she looked beautiful in a way he had yet to notice. A simple elegance, a feature many professional women had lost sight of, he realized.

"This is fine," she said, looking kind of funny with a roll of toilet paper in hand.

"Do you need some medicine? There is a drug store just down the road."

"Fresh air," she responded. Mitch furrowed his brow. "That's all I need," she clarified.

"How about a walk on the beach?" he offered. "Salt water and ocean air are the best medicines known to man. In addition to salt water being a natural treatment for cuts and scrapes, the ocean air can work wonders for your sinus cavities."

"It's worth a shot," Addison admitted, feeling a tad bit embarrassed by her sudden sneeze attack.

A mile down the beach, Mitch, Addison and Hannah decided to make a U-turn and head back to the house. They had stepped out of their shoes and onto the sand nearly thirty minutes ago and walked slowly as the sun pounded at their backs. Mitch had lathered Hannah's shoulders and face with sunscreen, and Addison had done the same for herself. Even though the only things she felt comfortable talking about were things that had happened during the last year of her life, she and Mitch had kept the conversation flowing. Hannah helped in that area, too, but she had spent much of the walk playing with sea shells, chasing seagulls and dancing in the edge of the water. Addison realized she'd been keeping a close eye on Hannah, nervous after talking with the guy at the grocery store this morning. Before today, she'd never known a shark could attack in only a couple feet of water. She'd always thought it would go after a surfer or someone swimming fifty yards from the shore.

When Mitch nonchalantly asked Addison if she had ever been married, she found that she felt safe talking about her divorce. She just had to make sure not to mention James by name, or maybe she should just use his middle name, she thought, laughing inside.

Ultimately, she decided he didn't need to be named, and she doubted Mitch would ask.

"Has anyone ever cheated on you?" she asked Mitch.

"Not that I know of."

"I didn't know either until after the fact."

"How did you find out that your ex-husband had cheated on you?" Curiosity had been eating at him ever since she'd mentioned that the reason she'd divorced was infidelity.

"The day he left me he decided to tell me that he had been seeing someone else."

"That had to be difficult."

Addison only shook her head.

"Did you know the woman?" Mitch asked.

"To this day, I have no idea who it was. I didn't want to know so I didn't ask, and of course he didn't offer."

As they continued walking, Addison could feel the sun slowly trying to paint her face just like it had tried to draw on her neck when they were walking in the other direction. She was so glad Mitch had offered sunscreen; otherwise, she'd probably already be burnt.

"Have you ever been married?" she asked Mitch. London had never said much about Mitch's past, and before taking the chance of finding out in the memoir, she figured she might as well ask him herself.

London immediately entered Mitch's mind. "I once wanted to get married, but it didn't work out."

"How come?" Addison asked, instinctively, but as soon as the words escaped her mouth, she wished she'd have kept it shut, knowing he was probably referring to London, and vividly remembering the way her sister's cold ring finger looked and felt the last time she'd touched it.

Mitch stared at his feet as he spoke. "God," he said.

"What do you mean?" *Crud*, she'd done it again.

"After years of searching, I finally found my soulmate, but God had other plans for us . . ." Addison noticed that he seemed to clam up after spilling that bit of information. "Needless to say, God and I haven't seen eye to eye for some time."

"I'm sorry," was all Addison knew to say, and she wondered who had been there to console Mitch Quinn after the loss of his soulmate . . . her one and only sister.

Just in time to break up a conversation that had begun to penetrate the gray area, Hannah came running back toward them with an orange shell; she handed it to Addison with a cute little grin crossing her face. Addison sighed, then smiled back.

"This one's for you," Hannah announced.

"Thank you, Hannah."

Mitch winked at Hannah.

"I'm going to find one for you, Mitch," she said as she ran ahead of them again. Mitch had granted her permission earlier to wander around on the beach as long as she remained in front of them where he could see her as they walked.

"Do you think you will be okay in that house? Your allergies, I mean?"

"I'll be fine. As long as it's okay to leave the windows open and let it air out the rest of the evening."

"Of course," Mitch confirmed.

⌐ ⌐

Addison felt like a new person when she stepped out of the shower. She toweled off quickly in the small, steamy space and then wrapped the towel around her to walk out into the bedroom. A nice breeze blowing in off the ocean traced her skin. She doubted that Mitch and Hannah were in the house, but earlier Mitch had asked if it would be okay if he and Hannah brought over a few things he'd picked up for the house while she showered.

After slipping on a fresh set of clothes, Addison found a handwritten note and three paper grocery bags on the kitchen table. She smiled as she began reading the words Mitch had written.

Addison,

> *Hannah and I thought you might need a few things to make you feel at home. Also, I hooked up the refrigerator. We put a few cold items inside: milk, eggs, butter, etc. I checked the washer and dryer, too, and you're all set to wash clothes if you'd like. We're looking forward to having dinner together this evening. See you shortly.*

> *–Mitch Quinn*

Addison began sorting out the contents from the bags onto the kitchen table. She grinned when she pulled out a box of Kleenex and a bottle of Tylenol Sinus. She doubted she would ever tell Mitch that the medicine probably wouldn't help, but his thoughtfulness was much appreciated. Allergy medicine had become useless in her case; she had tried every pill on the market. None of them seemed to work, and neither did the various nasal sprays her doctor had prescribed over the years. The last preventative measure she had taken was allergy shots, and after four months of needle holes in her upper arm, she found out she was allergic to the shots themselves. After all of that, she gave up on allergy medicine altogether and hadn't really felt any worse or any better ever since. Her allergies acted up the most on days like today when dust got stirred up in an enclosed environment or if there was a lot of pollen in the air.

Out of the corner of her eye, she caught a glimpse of her purse. She'd tucked London's memoir in there earlier, and for a moment she worried that Mitch might have seen it. But upon further inspection, the snap was still closed and the zipper was tight, just like she'd left it. Inside, nothing seemed disturbed. She doubted very seriously if Mitch had taken a peek in her purse, and it was nice to know that there were still men out there who respected a woman's privacy. James never had. For some reason he never had trusted her; he'd always snooped through her purse and the files on her laptop computer. She'd even suspected he'd figured out her email password and read every email word for word. He had always seemed to know a little more than he should, even if it was about something petty like her having a bad day at work and telling her mom instead of him. He would make a big deal of it like he wasn't her priority if he didn't know every single thing about her life before anyone else. It seemed that the times that she did choose to confide in him, he would only fuss at her and tell her to stop complaining or give her some fix-all advice when what she really needed was him to just listen and tell her that everything was going to be okay.

She'd once heard that a husband who didn't trust his wife is likely that way because he has unfaithful tendencies and figures his spouse must, too. In the end, James had been the one with the infidelity issue, not her. She had never even considered being with another man while they were together. When she'd said *I do*, it had meant *I do* and that was that. Neither leaving nor cheating had ever been an option in her mind. Of course he'd always said the same, but the day he left there was no stopping him; he had another woman waiting, and as far as he was concerned the marriage had ended long before that day.

Like so many other people on the short end of the cheating stick, Addison had since experienced many lonely nights. On more than one occasion, usually on the weekend, she'd considered walking into a bar, picking out one of the many men who'd go home with the first woman who would agree, and have a wild night of meaningless sex. In theory, it seemed like a great way to get back at James for what he'd done to her. She'd even stretched a skin tight dress over her curves several times, slipped into her high heels, and lined her lips with bright red lipstick. She had never shared these thoughts with anyone else, and she doubted she ever would, especially after last night. In a way, she couldn't help but think that she had ended up living out her fantasy. But last night was different. Even after what she'd found out this morning; last night had meant something. It was special, magical even. But now the memory seemed tainted.

All of these thoughts were surfing through her mind as she plucked more things from the bags: cereal, bagels, coffee, and some other items had been in the second bag. The third bag contained paper towels, toilet paper, shampoo, and soap. She'd had her own bathing items, but she realized Mitch hadn't known that when he'd bought these items at the grocery store earlier today. The Q-tips, dental floss, and tweezers might come in handy, though, she thought.

Once she finished putting away the groceries, she went back to her purse and pulled out the memoir. Before sitting on the couch, she made sure all of the doors were locked, just in case Mitch and Hannah decided to come over for any reason. She knew she had a little time before dinner, and she'd decided to spend that time in the story.

On our third date, Mitch & Me went out to see a movie. He picked me up around six o'clock and we headed straight for the theater. We'd each eaten dinner at our own homes. He'd actually asked me if I wanted to go out for dinner but I hadn't really felt like it. Not because I didn't want to be with him but because I'd been slightly nauseous all day. I thought a movie would be easier. We did eat some popcorn, which didn't seem to bother me. Mitch threw a piece at me before the movie started and I threw a handful back at him. I absolutely adored his playful personality, and what girl doesn't like to be flirted with? Especially when the man flirting is as handsome as Mitch Quinn. He had kiss-me eyes and a body to match.

When the room turned dark and the previews began to play, we made out in the back row of the movie theater like two high schoolers hiding from adults. As the screen flickered I caught glimpses of Mitch's face, tanned and scruffy. He probably hadn't shaved since we'd first met. I kind of liked that. I knew I shouldn't be opening my eyes as we kissed, but I couldn't resist looking at him. What I liked most was that he was twice as fun as he was good looking. When the movie started, we were sharing a bottle of water that he'd dumped two straws into because, in his words, it was romantic. "Whatever you think," I replied to that comment with a grin. It was romantic—not because on several occasions our lips were inches from each other's but because he was just being himself. We weren't sharing a milkshake in a diner in the fifties, we were drinking water . . . out of a bottle. Plain but perfect.

I honestly didn't pay much attention to the movie that night. It was a decent roman-tic comedy, but Mitch & Me had our own romantic comedy playing out. We continued to toss popcorn at each other, and I think it even annoyed the teenagers sitting in front of us. They turned around several times, and we just snickered when they turned back to face the screen.

When Mitch took me back home, we sat on my front porch and talked for almost an hour. That was the night that I told him about my battles with cancer since childhood. I could tell that he felt bad for me, but he didn't look at me the way other people did when I told them I'd had cancer. He just listened to my stories and held my hand as we watched the stars from an Adirondack chair made for two. He didn't act like I was fragile or talk like he was frightened by my disease. In fact, he left me with a goodnight kiss that made me wish I had invited him inside.

17

When evening began to settle in, Mitch started the grill. Earlier, he'd formed the hamburger meat into patties and seasoned it after a second round of cleaning at the house next door. He and Hannah had dusted the furniture, curtains, and lampshades while Addison put fresh sheets on the bed, cleaned the kitchen counter, and erased any lingering germs in the bathroom. After he'd retrieved Addison's suitcase from his house, Mitch and Hannah had dropped off the groceries while Addison was taking a shower. Hannah seemed super excited that Addison would be living next to them for a week.

"I'm glad Addison is moving in," she said.

"Me, too," Mitch replied. "But remember it's only for a little while. She has to go back to her home eventually."

"Where is her home?"

Mitch suddenly realized that he didn't know the answer to that question.

"You'll have to ask her when she comes over."

Addison followed the easy sounds of a strumming guitar around to the backside of Mitch's house. She slowed her pace as his voice sailed through the summer air. She noticed that his back was turned to her as she reached the corner and leaned against it, taking in his voice— a mixture of Johnny Cash and Chris Isaac, singing an Aerosmith classic. The lyrics floated through the air like an eagle in the wind: *". . . I don't want to close my eyes. I don't want to fall asleep cause I'd miss you baby . . ."*

The way Mitch sang it assured Addison that he had attached images of London to the words and she wondered how often he had sung for London. Today he was singing for Hannah as she sat at his feet with her Barbie dolls and not a worry in the world. She hadn't noticed Addison, either.

Whether singing or talking, Mitch's distinctive voice was very recognizable. After meeting him for the first time yesterday, Addison had played it, along with the familiarity of her sister's voice, in her mind while reading their story today. She would describe his voice as deep and crackly. Not crackly like the sound of a teenager reaching puberty, but instead it had a harmonious sizzle to it.

Mitch had yet to notice Addison, but as the final chord floated toward the sky, the sound of her hands clapping together echoed beneath the porch's roof. Mitch twisted his body, pulling his shirt snug against his chest. His biceps flexed as he stood with the guitar in one hand. Shaking away thoughts that had entered her mind, Addison forced herself to glance at the grass below her feet.

"You startled me," Mitch admitted.

Hannah looked up, smiling.

Mitch watched Addison glide toward him in a simple blue summer dress that fell just above her knees. She wore it well, he couldn't help but notice.

"I didn't want to interrupt such a beautiful song," she stated. Mitch's song would have definitely received a standing ovation if he had been singing at the bar last night.

Mitch shrugged off the compliment. "Hannah asked if I'd sing for her while we sat out here waiting for you."

Hannah chimed in. "And he's going to sing me a bedtime song tonight, too."

That is sweet, Addison thought while smiling.

"Did you find everything you needed?" Mitch asked.

Addison tilted her head, crossed her arms, and found a standing point. "Yes, and you didn't have to buy all of those groceries. I could have run out to the store later this evening."

"We were just being neighborly," he said. "Has the dust settled yet?"

"Mostly, but I might have to sweep again," she teased. "I had to get out of there before I suffered another allergy attack," she added with a smile.

"Maybe the medicine will kick in soon." He paused. "You did find it, right?"

Addison shook her head but said nothing.

While Mitch had showered earlier, he'd wondered how tonight would turn out. He was glad that he hadn't planned to take Hannah out for fast food for dinner since she'd taken it upon herself to invite Addison. Even though tonight wasn't exactly a date, the thought of Addison telling people about this guy that took her out to a fast food joint on their first date would have made for an interesting story. On second thought, he decided that might would have been more memorable than a cookout. Not that it mattered.

"Addison, come play Barbies with me."

"*Will you* come play Barbies with me?" Mitch suggested to Hannah.

"Will you?" Hannah added politely.

Addison sat down on the steps near where Hannah had her Barbie dolls spread out. She wasn't sure whether to be happy about the way things were working out or if she should feel guilty for not having been honest with Mitch. She'd learned a lot about him already and dinner with him and Hannah would definitely give her more insight into the life of Mitch Quinn. In a way, she felt like a secret agent. Her mission: get to know Mitch Quinn without revealing her true identity. She hated it, the lying part at least.

Mitch noticed how Addison's knees were clasped together like magnets, freshly shaven legs leading to a pair of flip flops. He'd slipped on a pair of khaki shorts and a lightweight button-down shirt he'd owned for ages. Suddenly, this felt a lot like a date. He wondered if Addison's mind was in the same place.

He wanted to know more about the woman he couldn't stop glancing at out of the corner of his eye as he worked the grill. She was beautiful and intriguing. Out of nowhere, she had wandered into his life and for some reason he felt like he'd known her for years.

"This doll is you," Hannah said handing it to Addison.

"She's pretty," Addison responded.

"Like you," Hannah said without looking up.

Hannah reached for the only male doll on the deck. "This one is Mitch," she said.

"He looks like a fairly nice guy," Addison complimented.

Mitch grinned in the background. If Addison noticed his response in her peripheral vision, she hadn't shown any sign of it.

"This one is me," Hannah said, showing off her little girl doll.

"She's almost as beautiful as you," Addison revealed. She noticed a smile grow on Hannah's face and then watched her play for a few moments. "Who is the other doll?" Addison asked referring to the only one she had yet to introduce.

"That's London."

When Mitch heard the reference, he kept his eyes steady on the two hamburgers he'd just flipped. He should have told Addison about London by now. This was the second time Hannah had brought up her name, and he figured Addison had to be curious. She probably assumed that London was Hannah's mom. He and Addison hadn't had much alone time today, but he could have found time to tell her at the beach earlier while Hannah played with the shells and chased the birds. He now regretted not taking that opportunity.

"She's really pretty, too," Addison said. She didn't want Mitch to see the way she'd wrinkled her lips to help hold in her emotions, so she faced the ocean until her face straightened back out. The wind was blowing her hair slightly in his direction.

"They're all having dinner together," Hannah informed her. "Like us." She paused and picked up London's doll, holding it close. "But London won't be here. She's in Heaven."

Mitch still hadn't looked up, and in a way, he was kind of glad that Hannah had shared the part about London being in Heaven. He admired how kids possessed such a simple, straightforward way of revealing their thoughts. He wished he had a beer right about now, though, as he felt a stream of stress running through his blood.

"Addison, would you like anything to drink?" he asked after a minute of awkward silence. "I just realized I haven't asked you yet." He needed something to do to move around a little bit.

"What do you have?" she asked over her shoulder.

"Sweet tea, apple juice, orange juice, and water."

"A glass of ice water sounds nice," Addison answered.

When Mitch brought the glass back outside, Hannah and Addison were walking the dolls around on the deck, making up stories. It was really cute, he thought.

"I have a confession to make," Addison said when Mitch handed her the cold glass.

Mitch cocked an eyebrow. A confession? They'd only known each other for a little more than twenty-four hours. What in the world could she be confessing? "What is it?" he wondered aloud.

"I should have told you earlier." She paused, knowing she needed to limit the lies if she wanted to increase the chance of Mitch ever trusting her. "I didn't take the medicine you brought me."

"Oh," he said, not expecting the confession to be about something harmless and not sure what else to say. It wasn't a big deal.

Addison spent the next five minutes talking about allergies and all of the medications that went along with her condition. A couple times during the conversation Hannah made Addison's doll sneeze, which caused Addison and Mitch to laugh out loud, especially the first time.

"You were really allergic to the shots?" Mitch quizzed, almost in disbelief that someone could be allergic to allergy shots. It just seemed to be a double negative or something.

Addison smiled. "No one believes it, but it's true. After injecting you, the nurse makes you wait in the office about ten minutes to make sure you don't have a reaction, and for three months I didn't have any issues. Then one day out of the blue about twenty minutes after I'd been given the shot, I started feeling dizzy. I was in the car on my way home, and I turned the car around immediately. When I got back to the doctor's office, they said if I hadn't come back right away the reaction could have been fatal."

"That sounds scary. Did you have to go to the hospital?"

"No, thankfully, I didn't," she gasped. "They gave me another shot to counter the first one and about thirty minutes later I felt fine again."

It felt relieving to tell Mitch something about herself that London wouldn't have known. Only because this had happened earlier this year. Otherwise, London would have most likely been one of the first people she told.

"Are the hot dogs almost ready?" Hannah asked.

"Just about," Mitch promised.

"The food smells really good," Addison commented. "Actually, I could already smell the grill on my walk over here."

"I usually grill the meat really slow."

"So that the neighbors will be jealous?"

Mitch laughed. "Well, for that reason and so that all of the flavor won't cook out."

A few minutes later, Mitch plopped hamburgers and hot dogs onto the plates that Hannah and Addison set around the outdoor table. While Mitch fixed Hannah's hot dog just the way she liked it, Addison scampered indoors to refill her water as well as the glass that Mitch had been sipping on while grilling. She also grabbed a juice box for Hannah.

"This burger is amazing," Addison exclaimed after taking the first bite.

Hannah giggled. "You should try the hot dogs. Mitch makes the best hot dogs on the planet."

Mitch smiled at the compliments. He loved to grill. It had always been one of his favorite things to do in the evenings when the weather was cooperative. Something about grilling out seemed to force the world to slow down just a little.

When Mitch and Addison finished their first hamburger, Addison let him talk her into splitting another one with him. She kind of wanted a whole one, but there was no way she was going to admit that tonight. Hannah ate two hot dogs, and all three of them had chips and baked beans as their sides. Eventually, they left the table and walked out past the outdoor shower and sat in some chairs closer to the beach. Every time Addison had glanced at the shower, she'd had visions of a night she knew she would never forget.

"Can I play in the sand?" Hannah asked.

"Sure. Just stay where I can see you," Mitch instructed. Hannah had always been a well-mannered child, and Mitch knew he could pretty much trust her to do exactly what he asked, which would definitely make his life much easier. What didn't make it easier at the moment was figuring out exactly how to bring up London to Addison.

Once Hannah was out of earshot, he gave it a whirl. "Just in case you were curious, London was my girlfriend. She's actually the person who introduced me to Hannah." Mitch stared straight ahead at Hannah while he talked. "They were the perfect mix, like mother and daughter, and best friends. But London wasn't actually her mother. She just kind of fell into that role."

Addison felt guilty for already knowing all of this, but she let Mitch continue as if she had no idea.

"London passed away from cancer a year ago. It's been tough on both of us," he openly admitted. "Hannah got sick a lot after London passed away. I did, too, but for different reasons. I started drinking too much, hoping it would help me forget about the pain." Mitch felt tears in his eyes, but he didn't shed them.

Addison wanted to cry, and she could sense that Mitch did, too. She also wanted to ask him why he didn't come to the funeral if he loved London so much. But now wasn't the time, and if she was entitled to her secret, then maybe so was he.

"The reason I didn't offer you a beer tonight is because I decided that once I adopted Hannah, I wasn't having that in my house ever again," he shared.

"Mitch, don't feel like you have to tell me about all of this. I know Hannah brought up London, but . . ." she trailed off, not sure what else to add. She thought about saying that it was none of her business, but London wasn't just her business, she was her sister. She wanted to tell Mitch that right now, but how could she? How could she just slap him in the face with the big secret in the moment he had decided to confide in her? She hated this. Hated this so much. She'd wanted to tell him tonight. Make this right. But now it would have to wait. She would have to keep lying to the man that was opening his heart up to her.

"I just want to be up-front with you, because I know you must have a lot of questions circling your mind. I don't have a ring on my finger, but I have a daughter. Hannah kept mentioning London, so I just wanted to shoot straight with you."

"When did you adopt Hannah?" Addison asked, curious to know but also wanting to shift the subject away from London for a moment. She just couldn't take anymore.

"Funny you should ask," Mitch said. "Today."

"Today?"

"This morning, just after I dropped you off at the police station. I had a meeting to sign all of the final paperwork and make the adoption final."

"So that's why you said you had plans this evening," Addison realized, putting the puzzle together. "This is your first day with Hannah?" She paused. "And I'm totally intruding on this special time for you two. I shouldn't be here," Addison revealed, thinking about the two reasons. One now obvious to Mitch, the other not so obvious.

"Please, stay," Mitch pleaded. "Hannah invited you, personally. She wanted you here. She's been talking about you all day," he admitted.

Addison stood with her arms crossed. "It's not fair for me to come between the two of you like this, though. You had plans, and I know your plans didn't include me."

"It's not like that, Addison," Mitch demanded.

For the first time since they'd met, Addison heard frustration in his tone.

Mitch continued. "Our first day together isn't about me," he said referring to Hannah. "It's about her. If having you here makes her happy then that's what I want."

There were two ways Addison could have taken Mitch's comment, but she knew he meant it in the most unselfish of ways. It was obvious that he wanted to make this little girl happy. Addison knew that Mitch had wanted her here, too, but she also realized that what Hannah wanted today trumped what Mitch wanted. She respected that, and she was honored that Hannah had asked her to be here on such a special occasion in her life. Mitch's, too.

"Mitch, I think you are a wonderful man. I think that what you're doing for Hannah is one of the most admirable things I've ever known a person to do. But I don't deserve to be here. I don't deserve to be a part of this."

Mitch interrupted, "That's . . ." One word was all Mitch was able to get out as Addison took over the conversation again.

"Mitch, you don't know me, and if you did . . ." She wanted to cry, wanted to let emotions from the words that had been said by both of them since Hannah walked down to the sand just spew right out.

"If I did, what? I'd love you . . . ?"

Addison's eyebrows rose, and Mitch stepped toward her. She found herself temporarily speechless as she listened to the words that came next.

"I'd love that you are being honest? I'd love that last night we made love and this morning you felt bad about it because you're not that type of woman? And all day long you've probably been worried that I'd think you're someone you're not?"

Addison began to shake her head. He had no idea. She shook it until Mitch grabbed it, gently, one hand covering either side of her face. Then he kissed her. She kissed him back, soft and slow and perfect. For a moment Addison closed her eyes and forgot all about the problems that existed. All the problems that Mitch knew nothing about.

She felt like she loved him, too. That was the biggest problem of all. She loved everything she knew about him, which is why she had to pull back before she gave in.

"Mitch, there is something about me that you don't know. Something I can't tell you right now. Something that will change your mind about me."

"What? What is it? Because unless you're married or an ax murderer I really don't see how anything you can tell me would be that big of a deal."

Mitch had somehow managed to keep one eye on Hannah off and on throughout this entire conversation, and now he noticed her walking toward them with more shells in her little hands.

"You can't trust me, Mitch," Addison said simply. "But you have to trust me on this . . . you don't know me."

With those words, Addison began to walk away. Hannah was getting close, and she didn't want to hurt Hannah's feelings by letting her see her like this. Hannah deserved better. Hannah deserved London.

18

"Why did Addison leave?" Hannah queried.

Mitch didn't know quite how to answer her question. Honestly, he didn't really know why she had left. He didn't understand what she was trying to say without saying. He wished he did, maybe then he could make sense of it, or help her make sense of it. But maybe she didn't want his help, which was fine, and he would have been just fine listening to whatever it was that scared her.

"Her allergies were bothering her again," Mitch fibbed. He hated hiding the truth from Hannah, but he realized in his first day as a parent that sometimes shielding his child from the truth—whatever that might be in this situation—was necessary.

"I thought I heard her crying," Hannah shared.

Mitch fought back tears of his own. "She was sniffling," he said. "I think she hurried away so she could get some tissue."

"Is she coming back?" Hannah then wanted to know.

Mitch had no idea, but he seriously doubted it. The way things had just ended it wouldn't surprise him if he heard the sound of an engine cranking in the next few minutes and rocks crunching as Addison's car backed down the driveway. One thing he knew for sure, he wasn't going over there. She could stay or she could leave, but he didn't want to push her in either direction. His focus now had to remain where it had been all day—on making Hannah happy. At the moment, he was a little upset with Addison for leaving without saying bye to Hannah, regardless of her reason. Why hadn't she just found a better way to leave?

Addison dove face first into the bed in the house that Mitch was letting her borrow. She beat on the pillow she'd covered with a clean pillow case earlier today. Then she cried on it. The words from her sister's letter played over and over in her mind: *Make sure that he knows that it is okay to fall in love again.* She might as well put a green check mark beside that one then add a huge red X over top of it. She'd succeeded and failed all at the same time. On the drive here yesterday she remembered wondering how in the world she was supposed to convince Mitch to fall in love again when even she didn't believe in love at this stage of her life. Yet now, one day later, she did.

This was killing her. She had to do something. Something to ease the haze in her mind so that she could think clearly.

Addison unrolled the purple yoga mat she had packed in her suitcase. Then she glanced up at the television in the living room. "You're kidding me," she uttered, as she stared at what had to be the last tube television in America. She had noticed it earlier, but she hadn't even considered the fact that there was no DVD player next to it. If there was it probably wouldn't even connect. Oh well, she'd just have to use her laptop to play her workout video, she decided, which led her back into the bedroom where she'd left it, and then she set it up on the bed. She pulled the curtains shut and shimmied a pair of running shorts on beneath her dress. Then she pulled the cotton dress over her head and replaced it with a tank top. She'd always liked how this pair of shorts made her butt look. Rarely did she wear them to the gym or out running unless she'd been feeling down and out.

Addison spent the next thirty minutes with her eyes glued on her Italian Stallion yoga instructor. His voice was almost as sexy as Mitch's. She forced that thought to the back of her mind and continued to work up a sweat, allowing her mind to thaw out. Yoga had always been able to relax her mind and body, and she prayed that it would work tonight.

When she finished the video, she had way more trouble getting her clothes off than she had putting them on. After taking a cool shower, she crawled into bed and switched on the lamp. In a way, it didn't feel right to open the book with London's name on it, but she knew she had to. Not knowing what happened between Mitch and London made things worse.

The lamp shined for nearly an hour as she cruised through the pages allowing her mind to take her to the places that London and Mitch had visited. Right now, she felt like a fly on the wall of the local fudge shop. She could hear rolling laughter eroding from London's lungs as Mitch raked the sample spoon across her tongue.

"This is the best," I said to Mitch.

"You said cookies-n-cream was the best . . . and the same thing about orange swirl," he reminded me.

"I know, but they're all soooo good."

That was when I felt his breath tickle the minuscule hairs that covered my ear as he whispered to me, and I imagined this was the way leaves felt when the wind blew them across the yard—weightless, and in the arms of something more powerful than themselves. I would go anywhere he would carry me. If he wanted to stop and enjoy the sun, we could stop. If he wanted to dance across the grass, we could do that, too.

"I can't afford them all," he said. "It's nine fifty per pound and I didn't bring much cash," he laughed.

In the time I'd known Mitch, I'd learned that he bought everything with cash. He didn't even have a single credit card in his wallet, which looked like one he'd kept in his back pocket since he was a kid.

We left the fudge shop with a block of cookies-n-cream. He'd said it was his favorite and I wanted to make him as happy as he was making me. It didn't matter to me that he was broke. I didn't care if we got one flavor of fudge or none at all. I just wanted to be with him.

Addison closed the book but only long enough to reposition herself. She'd been sitting against the headboard with a pillow wedged between it and her back. She suddenly realized how much brighter the room seemed now than it had when she'd first shut off the overhead light and turned on the lamp. With Snuggles nestled beside her, she decided to lay flat on her back and support her head with two pillows. As she held the book up, images of London and Mitch began to bombard her mind again.

On our one-month anniversary, Mitch picked me up and took me out for dinner at my favorite restaurant on the island. We shared the largest plate of crab legs I had ever seen, and by the end of the night our stomachs were bulging and our laps covered with crab shells. I'd been looking forward to this night for some time, not just because it was the first milestone in our relationship but because Mitch had never eaten crab before. How he'd grown up on an island and never eaten crab, I have no idea. But, until that night, he hadn't.

"Tools," he said. "I have to use tools to eat my dinner?"

It took a while for him to master the use of the nutcracker—I guess he had never eaten nuts either. He even shot a crab leg across the restaurant and almost hit a waiter carrying a tray to the family at the table adjacent ours. Afterward, we went back to his place for a walk on the beach. We sat in the sand for hours and talked about the best month of our lives. And when most men would have been trying to take my clothes off,

Mitch wrapped his jacket around my shoulders, and as the ocean breeze blew my hair in all kinds of directions, I was glad we were different than other couples. Mitch was the first man I ever dated who respected my choice to save sex for marriage.

Ten minutes later, Addison read the last word of the chapter about Mitch and London's one-month anniversary. With sand in her shoes, London had heated a pan of milk on Mitch's oven—the way their mother always had—and then stirred two cups of hot chocolate to rid the chill bumps on their arms. Addison wondered if, by the end of the story, London and Mitch would end where she and Mitch had started—making love. She'd always known her little sister had vowed to wait for marriage, but if she knew that cancer was about to rob her of her life, surely London hadn't let cancer also rob her of one of the greatest experiences this life has to offer.

Addison flipped to the next chapter.

Hannah's face gleamed when Mitch entered the room holding my hand. She hadn't seen him in a week, and before we reached the bedside, she jumped out of the sheets and pulled out the plastic container that held her G.I. Joes.

The week after Mitch met Hannah and me, he went to the store to buy her a gift for her birthday party. She had demanded that we send him an invitation. I clinched my teeth as she opened the package, but like most children with cancer, she didn't care what was inside—Army figurines were just as good as Barbie dolls.

"G.I. Joes were my favorite when I was your age," Mitch explained to her with boyish jubilee.

"They're my favorite, too," Hannah replied.

Then Mitch handed her another present, one I hadn't realized he'd picked up. Hannah smiled even bigger when she opened four Barbie dolls.

"This is your real present," he said. "The G.I. Joes are to remind you of me and to protect the Barbies."

You would have thought that what Mitch said was the funniest thing that kid had ever heard. When she stopped laughing, she walked gingerly to her dresser.

"I made you a birthday present, Mitch . . ."

Mitch furrowed his brow and glanced in my direction.

I shrugged my shoulders. "Honey," I said to Hannah, "it's not Mitch's birthday; it's yours."

She handed him a drawing.

I watched his eyes water over but couldn't see what she had drawn.

When he sat the piece of orange construction paper on the bed and kissed her bald scalp, I picked it up and saw Hannah, Mitch, and myself—sleeping in her bed at the Children's Ward at Duke.

She wrapped her arms around Mitch. "This is my birthday wish," she mumbled. "I want you and London to live here with me."

Addison snatched a tissue from the box on the nightstand. This morning at Mitch's, she had seen *that* drawing on his refrigerator framed with magnets. Until now, she hadn't known exactly who the stick figures represented although she'd had a good idea. She read on.

A variety of gunshot sounds echoed off the walls as Hannah and Mitch battled in the jungles of Vietnam. I left them in their own world to visit with Dr. Thorpe.

"She's improved over the last few weeks," he informed me.

"Do you think she will ever be able to leave this place?"

"If it were anyone else asking, I would say no." He paused. "But you did." He smiled. "She has the best role model in the world."

Addison chuckled, remembering the day her father walked into the bathroom and found her with her head half shaven. Other kids at school had been teasing London, and Addison had decided if her hair matched her sister's, then London wouldn't have to take on the teasing alone. She still had photographs from the two years it took to grow their hair out and could vividly remember everyone thinking they were twins with cancer.

When I was Hannah's age, I battled through the same disease she was now fighting, and even though Mitch deserved to know about the chemo treatments and the many sleepless nights I had spent in the hospital he had been visiting with me for weeks, at this point in our relationship I had not yet told him. He thought I volunteered at Duke out of the goodness of my heart, which in fact I did, but he didn't know there was a story behind my charity, a story that changed my life . . . that would ultimately change his.

Addison's body slowly sunk into the sheets, and she pulled her tank top strap to her mouth. *Why didn't you tell him, London?* she gritted, but then she realized that she had to turn her pointer finger back at herself. *And why haven't I told him?*

Mitch didn't know that when I came to see Hannah, I sometimes visited Doc's office for a check-up of my own—in addition to an update on Hannah's condition, of course. When Mitch came with me, I'd make up an excuse to sneak away. He knew that Doc and I were close, so I don't think he ever expected the worst.

At a young age, Hannah's father had left her with Doc, who thank God was her grandfather. Hannah's mother had recently died, and her father decided he could no longer love this blue-eyed angel with cancer. Doc is the reason I'd moved to Emerald Isle. He lived there, and he had treated me when I was younger. In a way, he'd always been like a second father to me.

When I found out Hannah had no one else to visit her, no one else who cared, she became my sweet angel. I read her stories like Good Night Moon, *her favorite, at bedtime. Once was never enough, though, and if I had to guess I would say I read that book more times than every other book on my bookshelf combined. We had ice cream sandwich parties often, and I even taught her how to sew a quilt. The first one we made together was covered with Peanuts characters: Snoopy, Charlie Brown, Lucy, Linus, Peppermint Patty, Pigpen, Woodstock, Sally, Franklin, Rerun, Marcy, and Schroeder. They were all there, and she could recite their names in less than five seconds without missing a single beat. To her, it was pertinent that each character occupy a square on the blanket.*

Doctors say that cancer isn't contagious, but from experience I would have to disagree. Though the disease itself cannot be transferred from one human being to another, cancer has its own way of spreading. When Mitch Quinn followed me into Duke for the first time, I knew his face would be filled with tears as soon as he walked out of the Children's Ward. I was right.

I didn't ask nor expect him to donate time or money, but he did both anyway. In fact, for the longest time, I thought he was a broke beach bum. I later learned that he was a big time photographer, all the while I'd thought he was just a normal photographer trying to make ends meet. Two days after we left the hospital he wrote a check for ten thousand dollars, a thousand less than what he had made at a photo shoot he'd recently shot in Cancun—models on the sandy white beaches. I'd once thought this man that lived life on necessities alone wasn't very well off financially, but now I knew that his perspective on life was even more well off than his bank account.

Another thing I'd learned is that there is nothing worse than watching a child suffer and nothing greater than watching her smile when you want to cry. When Mitch handed me that check, I cried. I held it in my hand and dropped to my knees. I thanked him, for me, for Hannah, for all the children at the hospital. I knew the money—whether spent on research or cleaning supplies—would be well spent.

Addison added one more tissue to the pile next to the bed. When her eyelids became so heavy that they were closing on their own, she reached for the chain that hung from the lamp on the nightstand and fell asleep with Snuggles on one side and London's memoir on the other.

19

Mitch woke up the next morning similar to the way he had the morning prior—a smile on his face, but this time he couldn't feel the curves of Addison's warm body. A different type of joy flooded his heart when Hannah jumped into his bed and snuggled up next to him.

"Good morning, beautiful," he greeted.

Hannah just smiled, resting her head on the soft pillow next to the one he was attached to.

"Did you sleep okay in your new bedroom?" Mitch asked, noticing that she wasn't there to fall back asleep. Her eyes were wide-eyed and beautiful as ever.

"Yes," she assured him. "Can we have cereal for breakfast?"

"Of course," Mitch agreed.

Hannah ate two bowls of cereal. Mitch ate three. Between bites, they talked about what they wanted to do today. The final decision was to spend the day at the beach. For Mitch that used to mean surfing, tanning and relaxing, but he knew that wasn't what Hannah had in mind. For her, a day at the beach meant playing, playing and playing. Sounded fun to him, too, he decided.

"You think Addison will come with us?"

It didn't surprise Mitch that Hannah asked about Addison. "Probably not. I think she has work to do today." He had somewhat prepared himself for the question; the answer, he knew, was honest.

"Let's go ask her anyway," Hannah suggested. "She might need more medicine, too."

Mitch grinned, impressed by how much Hannah cared about the well-being of others. "I doubt it," he replied. "We left her almost a whole bottle yesterday."

A couple of conversations later, Mitch and Hannah headed out the back door as the clock on the microwave flipped to eight o'clock. The sun wasn't scorching quite yet, but it would be soon. Mitch had made sure to apply sunscreen on Hannah from head to toe. During his days as a photographer, he'd learned a lot of tricks on how to avoid many of the skin issues that the sun can cause. The most important rule of thumb was to pick out a quality sunscreen. Applying prior to going out into the sun was also important. Over the years he'd noticed that many parents waited until they were already at the beach to apply sunscreen on themselves and their kids. He'd made sure to cover Hannah just before they began eating cereal so the sunscreen would have ample time to work into her soft skin.

They pulled the beach gear they needed from the 10x10 shed next to the outdoor shower: Chairs. Umbrella. A plastic bucket with a handle, filled with beach toys. Hannah had played with them before and knew exactly where to find them. Mitch was still inside the shed when Hannah stepped out and blurted out, "Addison."

Mitch watched Hannah's little legs run away as he walked out and clasped the lock on the door to the shed. He kept his head down, but he could see Addison from the corner of his eye—and now Hannah clinging to her leg. When he turned to face her, he wondered if the expression of shock that had fallen on his face had vanished yet.

"Good morning," Addison said in a chirpy tone.

Mitch immediately felt his guard go up. He didn't mind that she'd walked out on him, but Hannah was a different story. Hannah had nearly cried last night when she found out that Addison wouldn't be eating ice cream with them. She'd begged Mitch to wait an extra hour because she just knew that Addison would come back for ice cream, but she hadn't. Eventually, Hannah ended up falling asleep without eating even a single bite of her favorite ice cream.

"Hey," Mitch replied.

Mitch could tell that Hannah had already forgiven Addison, but for him it wasn't quite that simple.

"Mitch, can I talk to you for just a second?" Addison asked.

"Sure." One word answers seemed appropriate.

"Hannah, will you go get me one of those pretty shells like you gave me yesterday?" Addison asked.

"Yes," she said, turning quickly to make a dash toward the sand, oblivious to the reality of the request.

"Remember to stay where I can see you," Mitch reminded, his voice following her as she skipped off.

When Addison felt Hannah was far enough away, she began her spill. "First, I owe you an apology."

"Yes," he quickly agreed.

Mitch's blunt reply kind of caught Addison off guard, but she knew she deserved it.

"I'm sorry, Mitch. I'm sorry for what happened two nights ago and for what happened last night."

"Last night—I agree with you on that one, but don't be sorry for what happened the night we met," he insisted. "That was the best night I've had in the past year."

She liked how straightforward Mitch spoke. She knew she had to continue in order to keep her own bearings straight. She'd come here with one thought in mind, her new plan. "Honestly, it was a great night for me, too, but Mitch, the last thing I need right now is a relationship, whether it's for one week, one month or whatever. What I need to say is . . ." She paused, searching for courage. "Can we just be friends?"

Mitch held her gaze for a moment. "Sure." Even though Mitch didn't quite know why he wanted to be around her after the roller coaster they'd been riding the first two days of knowing each other, he just couldn't shut the door on the opportunity to spend more time with her. If that meant being *just friends*—whatever that was about—he was willing to give it a shot.

Addison exhaled. *Back to one-word answers again,* she noticed. "When I leave here to go back home, I'm going to tell you something that is going to shock your mind, and you're going to have a good idea of what I've been dealing with for the past two days."

Mitch furrowed his brow. What in the world was she talking about? He couldn't help but wonder now if maybe she had some type of mental issue. Maybe that is why she thought he wouldn't want to be with her. If so, she might end up being right. He didn't need a psycho in his life. He had a daughter to raise and a life to get on with.

"By the way, where exactly is it that you live?" Mitch asked, somewhat chasing a squirrel. He had also been keeping one eye on his little squirrel. Still searching for a complete shell, he recognized. She never kept the broken ones.

The question surprised Addison, and she knew the look on her face revealed it. "You'll find out the day I leave."

This just got even weirder, Mitch thought to himself. "Okay." If she ended up saying she was an angel or some ridiculous crap like that, he'd be forced to kick her out of the house. He almost wanted to ask her if she was part of a cult or some backwoods religion.

"I know this all sounds crazy. It is, in fact, crazy, but I need you to know that I'm not crazy. Not normally, anyway," she said hoping the sincerity of her comment would encourage him to crack a smile for the first time since she'd set her eyes on him this morning, but his lips didn't even budge in an east or west direction. "I hope you won't hate me after this week is over. I really do want us to be friends. We just can't be anything more. No more holding hands. No more kissing. No more looking at me like you want to rip my clothes off." She couldn't handle all of that, especially the latter. Mostly because of the urges she would have to fight not to give in.

Mitch didn't mean for his eyes to dart up and down her body at that instant, but they did. He'd wanted to rip her clothes off every moment he'd been with her since the intimate shower they'd shared. He couldn't imagine not touching her, but what other choice did he have?

"Pretend I'm your sister," Addison suggested.

"And why is it that you just can't tell me this big secret right now?" he asked.

"Because you would kill me."

"I doubt it."

"Trust me, you would."

Trust you? He didn't know if he could, but in a way he kind of felt like she had been honest with him the whole time. Even though there was something she wasn't telling him at least she was letting him know that there was *something*. Something very strange, indeed.

"As long as you don't hurt Hannah again, I'll let you live," he said, finally cracking a smile but with a somewhat serious tone.

Addison actually appreciated the parental instinct.

"Fair enough," she admitted.

"With that said, the person that you really owe an apology is the little girl down there in the sand searching for a perfectly shaped seashell for you. She waited all night for you to come back over for ice cream even though I told her you weren't coming back." He watched Addison's faint smile turn into a real frown. "I bailed you out, so don't let me regret it," Mitch meant. "I told her that you left because of your allergies."

Addison's lipped curled upward just a little. "Thank you," was all she said. *Why do you have to be so darn sweet?*

"She even wanted to ask you to join us at the beach today, but I told her you probably had to work. Honestly, I doubted we would see you again. I kind of expected to find a note attached to my front door saying you'd left." He figured that he'd leave out the part about actually checking first thing this morning, when he'd spotted her car still collecting salt in the driveway.

"Well, I was actually planning on spending a good part of my day at the beach. I need to interview random beach goers, gather some thoughts on various perspectives about the shark attacks. So, if you will allow me to hang out with the two of you, I'd love to try to make it up to Hannah."

"Sure."

Sure must be Mitch's word of the day, Addison decided.

The wind always blew at the beach, but today the breeze felt as calm as it ever had. Mitch liked days like today. He hoped he would like this day. Hoped Hannah would, too. Hoped he wasn't setting himself and her up for more disappointment.

— —

Thirty minutes later Addison found Mitch and Hannah building a sandcastle near the edge of the Atlantic Ocean. On her walk toward them, she noticed two regular-sized empty chairs and one small one, surrounded by toys and covered by an umbrella. Mitch had mentioned that he'd carry down an extra chair for her, and she was thankful for the nice gesture. In her haste to leave Silver Spring, she'd forgotten to pack her own beach chair.

Mitch spotted Addison walking in his and Hannah's direction. He forced himself not to stare as she drew near. She was wearing a pair of neon green shorts, much shorter than a pair she might wear in any other public setting, he imagined, and a matching top. Of course, this was a judge of character based on knowing her all of two days, but he'd always been a fairly good judge of modesty. In the business he'd been in he'd seen both ends of the spectrum and everything in between. He'd always declined the nude photo shoots that came across his desk, but he'd still seen his share of naked women. About half of the models that he photographed over the years had absolutely no problem changing from one outfit to another right in front of him and anyone else on the set. Most of them were fairly professional about it but others not so much. He vividly remembered one model who had spent more time out of her clothes than in them. She'd also spent a lot of time touching him. It was one of the rare shoots when they were absolutely alone, under a waterfall in Brazil. She'd all but begged him to take off his clothes, too. Mitch was sure most men would have jumped at the opportunity, but those type of women had always turned him off. He could tell that she wasn't accustomed to being rejected, and looking back he was so glad he'd kept his clothes on. Addison, on the other hand, he presumed didn't know how attractive she really was. Even with both pieces covering whatever she was wearing below, there wasn't another woman on the beach that he'd want to photograph more. The features he'd always found most attractive on a woman came from within—her character, her personality—things that mattered at the end of the day.

"Hey, guys," Addison said.

Hannah immediately asked her to help build the sandcastle. The three of them scooped sand, molded it with water, and talked as the sun climbed the sky. Mitch had taken his shirt off earlier, and he could feel the rays beating on his back. Addison kept her focus on Hannah, and when Mitch would talk, she'd make sure to look in his eyes. It wasn't dark today, like the night in the shower, and she'd caught a healthy glimpse of his tight pecs and well-defined abs when walking up earlier. His tattoos had also stood out, and now that she'd heard him play the guitar, she understood the second tattoo.

When Hannah decided it was time to take a break, they grabbed some snacks from the cooler and sat down for a little while. Addison had been keeping an eye out for sharks, and she'd also been people watching. The family next to them had shared pleasantries earlier, and Addison had even been able to ask them a few nonchalant questions about the shark attacks. She'd found out they were from Raleigh and that they weren't at all afraid of encountering a shark while in the water. They'd spent over an hour swimming around already, they said. Mitch and Addison had agreed to keep Hannah away from the conversations with others about the sharks. Mitch didn't want her worrying about being attacked by a shark. They hadn't been in the water yet, but he'd told Addison that he was fine with Hannah being out there as long as he was with her.

"We'll probably stay within twenty yards of the shore," he said. "It's a little safer there."

Addison mentioned the attack near the shore.

"It happens," Mitch acknowledged, "but it's rare."

Hannah had started playing with a little boy who had just walked up with his family. They'd set up camp on the other side of the space Mitch had claimed before the crowds began to gather, and they were well within talking distance. The guy, in his early thirties maybe, had carried a surfboard under his arm.

"Have you been out on your board yet this summer?" Addison queried.

"Yes, several times," he responded.

Addison noticed the letters A.C. scratched into his surfboard.

"I've been a little scared of him going out there, with the shark attacks that have happened," added the lady Addison presumed to be his wife. She was gorgeous in a natural sort of way that most women would die to possess. Neither of them were wearing a ring, but a lot of married couples didn't wear their rings to the beach. The fear of losing such an important symbol of marriage in the sand or water seemed to take precedence.

Addison would rather the people she talked to be the ones to bring up the shark attacks. That way it didn't seem like she was prying or trying to worry them.

"We haven't been letting little man go in the water, though." the gentleman offered. "He's not crazy about it in the first place, so we figured it's not worth talking him into going out there." He paused, glancing out over the ocean. "I definitely keep an eye out while I'm on my board," he said.

"Most surfers tend to feel like they should help look out for sharks," Mitch mentioned. "While you're waiting for the perfect wave, there's not much else to do."

"At least not for those of us who are in a relationship," the other guy teased.

Everyone laughed.

"Where are you all from?" Addison asked.

"New Bern."

"How about y'all?"

Mitch waited to see if Addison would respond.

Addison glanced out of the corner of her eye at Mitch. For a moment a lull took over the conversation.

"Actually," Addison started, turning her body. "Mitch lives right there," she pointed.

The four of them continued to talk while the kids played. They found out the man worked in real estate, but the lady didn't mention what she did for a living. Addison wondered if she was a stay-at-home mom, but she didn't want to pry. Instead, she asked a few more questions about sharks and their viewpoints on the recent attacks. These conversations were strictly for idea gathering purposes, not so she could use these people's words in any report or expose them in any way that might cause them to feel used. That's why she didn't mention her job. Also, she loved meeting new people and learning about how they live their lives.

As they discussed life, none of them had any idea that less than a mile down the beach a teenager on a surfboard had just been bitten by a shark. At least not until two officers on four-wheelers came flying past the crowds, followed by a truck with red flashing lights and a siren sounding. Many of the people nearby began following the path the wheels had left in the sand. Addison whispered to Mitch that she wanted to go check out what was happening. Of course, everyone feared the worst. Another shark attack.

20

Complete strangers began talking up and down the beach. Word of what had happened quickly traveled for miles in either direction of the tragedy. Addison had been gone for less than five minutes when a man with a red hat spread the word to Mitch. Moments later he watched two orange and white Coast Guard boats shoot across the horizon, headed in the same direction Addison had. Mitch talked with both families that they'd met earlier and all of them wanted to believe what they'd heard had been exaggerated. Mitch understood why Addison had been in a hurry to make it to the scene, but now he feared that what she might see would haunt her. Of course, she couldn't call him because he didn't have a cell phone. Circumstances like this were the only reason he'd even thought of caving into the societal norm, but then he looked at Hannah and remembered a better reason not to have a phone in his hand at this very moment. In his mind, a cell phone equaled one more distraction, one more reason not to interact with the people right beside him. The people that, in most cases, mattered most. Eventually, he and the surfer-dad began digging in the sand with the kids. Maybe it would keep their minds off what was going on down the beach, he considered, plus they could make sure the kids didn't overhear the popular adult conversation. A worthwhile distraction, but everyone's mind kept going back to the news they'd just heard.

⁓

When Addison reached the scene, she quickly realized why Mitch had wanted to stay behind with Hannah. Hannah didn't need to see this. No one needed to see this. She was furious at the parents who were allowing their children to stand around as paramedics took over the spots where lifeguards and good Samaritans had knelt beside the body of a teenage girl. Blood and sand didn't make a pretty sight. In fact, it made Addison want to hurl. Others had. The evidence scattered all around in the midst of plastic shovels, broken seashells, and restless sea foam. Addison knew she had to do something more than just stand there. She spotted Pete Dunlap in his police uniform urging people to move back, but on a busy day at the beach, the amount of people flocking to the incident proved overwhelming for just one man.

"Keep your kids away," Addison shouted, working from the opposite side as the man in uniform. She could tell it was all he could do to keep people back on one side at a time. "They don't need to see this."

This was someone's daughter . . . someone's friend . . . someone's girlfriend. From what Addison had heard the instant she arrived, the boyfriend had been a hero out in the choppy water. He and his blonde haired, blue-eyed girlfriend had been straddling their boards when a shark ripped her off of her longboard, an overweight gentleman with obvious sunburn had shared. Instinct had taken over, he'd told Addison and a few others. Apparently, the boyfriend saw the shark just as it surfaced and opened its jaws. The boy had jumped off his board and onto the shark. A few men also took the heroic risk of swimming out to where the girl was floating in the water. They hastily helped the boyfriend—who'd luckily managed to scare off the shark with his bravery—carry her to shore and began yelling for people to bring shirts and towels. Addison had seen the remnants, soaked with blood and laying all around the victim. She'd also seen the horrifying sight of blood-drenched towels wrapped around her leg near the knee. The lower part of her leg completely severed. Addison had taken one look at the girl's right arm hanging by *something*, and that's when she'd began helping clear the area.

Officer Dunlap recognized Addison and, once he realized her intentions, made a quick gesture of thanks with his hand as she helped the only way she knew how. Others began to chime in with her.

More police officers, firefighters, and paramedics began showing up in swarms. In no time they established a clearing around the scene and created a lane for the truck that had sped past Addison and Mitch earlier to drive out. Addison found the communication between the first responders to be absolutely amazing. "A chopper can't land here in the sand," one man said. "Let's hoist her onto the truck," another suggested. "We'll transfer her to the ambulance as soon as we reach asphalt," a paramedic insisted. "The helicopter will meet us at the Coast Guard Station."

Addison knew that Coast Guard Road was at the foot of the bridge she'd crossed over two days ago to reach Emerald Isle, and it led to the edge of the island where the Coast Guard Station was housed. It was also the area known as *The Point*, where vehicles were allowed to gain access to drive on the beach during the winter months. Probably less than five miles from their current location, she assumed.

No longer needed to help direct, Addison sat in a Yoga position that she'd spent hours in throughout the last year of her life. It usually relaxed her muscles. Relieved the tension of life. But today it didn't seem to help much at all. She found her head buried in her hands, tears streaming from her collapsed eyelids. In all the talk about shark attacks—from the moment she'd received the first phone call from Tara to the conversation she left behind when she jogged away from Mitch—Addison had never even imagined she'd see firsthand the damage a single shark could cause. If she had it to do all over again, she wasn't sure she would have followed the crowd down here to find out what had happened.

As she thought about the two teenagers, one hanging on for dear life, thoughts of London began to bombard her mind. She realized that the thought of tragedy always reminded her of her sister. Then, for some reason, she thought about James. She'd also remembered him earlier this morning as she'd eaten a bowl of Frosted Flakes. When she'd finished her cereal, she'd sipped the remaining milk—a bad habit in James's eyes. He'd always hated when she slurped down the milk in the bottom of the bowl and ended up looking like one of the actresses in a *Got Milk?* commercial. She must not have been as pretty as those women, though, or he wouldn't have quit on their marriage. "Why let good milk go to waste?" she would always say to him. "There is stuff floating around in there," he would reply. "Yeah, James, granules of the cereal I just finished putting into my mouth." Just to appease him, she'd stopped drinking the milk from the bowl. Now that they weren't together, she didn't feel obligated to refrain from a habit she'd enjoyed since childhood. She could do whatever she wanted.

Thinking back to how the morning had started reminded Addison of the words she'd read in the memoir. She wished now that she'd just kept reading. Wished she could go back to the first time she'd cried this morning.

"We can fight it," Mitch said. "We can beat it."

It was nice to hear the "we", but I knew the fighting could only go on so long. If I could have figured out a way to get around it, I would have never told Mitch I had brain cancer. But when most of the people I knew took a step back, thinking the disease would spread like a virus, he touched me. He took my hands in his and told me he loved me. It was the first time I heard those words roll off his tongue and I knew without a doubt that he meant them. If he was thinking angry words, the compassion in his voice overshadowed them. Many men would have walked away or at least faded away in the next few weeks but not Mitch. If there is an optimist in this world, his name is Mitch Quinn. If he would have had the time, he would have gone to medical school, studied cancer, and found a cure for me. That is how much he cared.

The next morning he picked me up for breakfast at eight o'clock and when I asked why his eyes were so red, he started crying. I soon found out Mitch had spent eight straight hours researching cancer on the internet. He had been to dozens of websites and read hundreds of articles, and he hadn't shut down his computer until thirty minutes before arriving at my place to drive me to Duke so that I could start a round of chemotherapy.

"Before last night," he admitted. "I didn't even really know what chemotherapy was." He knew it was a treatment for cancer, but that was the extent of his knowledge on the treatment.

"That's okay, Mitch. Most people don't know much about chemotherapy or radiation. The average person doesn't know that surgery is often the first treatment for cancer patients."

Between last night and this morning, he found out. As we talked over coffee and bagels, it seemed he knew as much as I did about the disease that was eating the cells in my body. He discovered that cancer cells can grow anywhere in your body, and that by the time a woman can feel a lump in her breast, it could have been there up to six years. He knew that removing the main tumor mass didn't assure the cancer hadn't spread. We talked about radiation—treating only the area of the body exposed to radiation—and how that hadn't worked for me either, at least not permanently. Temporarily, maybe . . . which was a word that seemed more realistic to me when it came to curing cancer.

The night before, I described how chemotherapy kills rapidly dividing cells and treats the entire body. I told him I had been through chemo before and that it hadn't worked. I explained to him that this round of treatment was probably my last hope.

"I will be here with you the entire way," he said. "I am not going to work another day until this is over." Mitch meant it, every word of it. I knew that.

Someone tapped Addison's shoulder, distracting her from the words she'd read earlier. She looked up to find Officer Dunlap standing over her. "Thanks for your help," he said. "I was going to call you once we finished up here, but then I looked over and saw you directing people." When Addison had been at the station to get her car back and obtain the police reports, he'd promised that he'd call her if he heard about any shark attacks in the area so that she could be a part of the investigation. No need for that call this time.

The two of them chatted for a few more moments, then he hurried off. He asked her to pray for him. He was the one who would have to track down the family and tell them what had happened, he'd said. The boyfriend had been in shock and didn't want to be the bearer of bad news to his girlfriend's parents via a phone conversation. "It's probably a good thing the girl's parents weren't here to see her like that" were the last words Addison spoke to him. He nodded his head, then said "I'll be in touch," and she was pretty sure she'd seen a tear stream down his face.

A few minutes later, she forced herself to stand up. She wondered if Mitch had been worried that she hadn't come back yet. She knew him well enough to know that he wouldn't venture down here with Hannah, so she headed back in their direction. When she came to the spot where they'd been earlier, she didn't see them anywhere. The chairs and umbrella were still there but no sign of Mitch or Hannah. She checked the water. Only a few idiots were in the water. She noticed that the folks who had been on either side of them earlier were gone, too. But those family's belongings were also gone, so she assumed they'd packed up and left the beach for the day. She didn't blame them. Beach goers had left in swarms. She wanted to do the same. Wanted a cold beer and a soft couch.

Maybe that's where Mitch and Hannah were . . . back up at his house.

The hinges on the screen door squeaked as the spring tightened. Addison poked her head in and called out, "Anyone home?" A moment of silence passed. "Mitch?" she said before walking toward the kitchen, letting the door close behind her. She stopped at the refrigerator, taking a moment to study the picture Hannah had drawn. She walked into the hallway that led to the bedrooms and bathroom. "Hello," she said as she peeked into each room. No one answered. Then she noticed the door at the end of the hallway again. It had caught her eye yesterday when she'd noticed that it was shut. She stood in front of it for a moment. Turned to see if anyone had come up behind her, then knocked. "Are y'all in there?" Part of her wondered if Mitch and Hannah were playing hide-n-go-seek from her, but then she realized that wouldn't be the case, not after what had happened down at the beach. After no one answered, she twisted the knob.

When Addison stepped into the room that had been hidden behind the closed door, she felt her knees buckle. Her heart skipped a beat, maybe two beats. *London.* She spoke her sister's name slowly and softly. Then she uttered it once more, just the same. *London.* Her eyes began to travel around the room—a room literally filled with London's smile. The walls were overflowing with photographs of her sister. Some included Mitch, some didn't. Some were of London and Hannah. It reminded her of an art gallery with perfectly placed pieces. Shadow boxes covered the floor. Frames, of every shape and size, covered the walls. There must be at least a hundred photographs, she figured. Some were on canvas, and many of them looked more like paintings than pictures.

Slowly, Addison worked her way around the room, taking in each photograph. London and Mitch pinching one another's nose with crab claws; Mitch and Hannah playing G.I. Joes; London with a hat on backward and a goofy smile; London, Mitch, and Hannah in what appeared to be Hannah's room at Duke; London in a bikini on the beach; London with a drop of ice cream on her chin.

Addison stumbled to the middle of the room and fell to her knees. Since the moment she had walked in, she hadn't stopped sniffling. This time allergies had nothing to do with it. Sitting Indian style, she sunk her hands into her hair and absorbed the moment. Thoughts of her sister flooded her mind. Thoughts about the life London had started with Mitch Quinn. Then this whole situation Addison had gotten herself into with Mitch bombarded her thoughts. She wanted to stay in this room all day. Wanted hours all to herself to take in every photo—photos she'd never seen before—which in some unique way seemed to make London real again. Now wasn't the time, she suddenly realized, as she heard the back door squeal and then slam shut.

Mitch . . .

She couldn't let Mitch find her in here. That thought leapt into her mind as she bounced to her feet and quickly pulled the door shut behind her, hoping he wouldn't be able to tell that she'd been in the room filled with London.

She was standing just outside the closed door when the heavy footsteps came around the corner. If she hadn't been careful enough to put down a photograph of London that she'd picked up just before she'd heard the door, she had no doubt in her mind that in this very moment glass would be shattering on the floor all around her. That's how afraid she was when his voice filled the narrow hallway.

"What are you doing in here?" he demanded to know.

Addison glanced to her left, to her right. He looked at her with such anger that she even thought of opening the door behind her and locking herself in.

"I asked you a question," he yelled walking toward her with his eyes locked on her eyes.

Standing only a few feet from a man she didn't recognize, Addison found herself speechless.

"Who are you?" she finally uttered, her voice soft and trembling.

"You don't ask the questions," the man instructed. "I do."

Addison could feel her lips trembling. Her knees felt wobbly all of a sudden. She wondered if she should run, but there was nowhere to go. The only two doors that led out of the house were at the other end of the hallway, blocked off by this strange man with hate-filled, midnight brown eyes.

"I don't care who you are," he said grabbing her arm.

She always thought she'd run or fight back if she ever found herself in a situation like this. One of those scenarios you see in a horror film where the helpless victim just stands there while everyone in the movie theater is yelling: *Run!*

Addison couldn't move an inch, especially now, with his rough hand squeezing her delicate arm, turning it bright red and hurting it.

"I only need one thing from you," he demanded. Addison could smell much more than a trace of alcohol on his breath, which explained the slur in his voice. *Oh, God,* she thought. Sex. This man wanted sex. This wasn't happening. It was a dream. A nightmare. It wasn't real. It couldn't be. Things like this weren't supposed to happen in real life.

Out of the corner of her eye she could see the bed in Mitch's room. This man was going to rape her. Right there. In the same bed where she'd slept with Mitch Quinn just two nights ago. Suddenly, she felt like she might faint. Then, he spoke again. "You tell Mitch Quinn that I'm looking for him." The stranger's worn out face was inches from her face. What had Mitch done to cause this man to come into his house in search of him? Addison found herself wondering, somehow, in the midst of five hundred other thoughts bombarding her mind.

"Who are you?" she asked again, even quieter this time. Maybe he wouldn't rape her. Maybe he wanted something else. She felt weak when his hand released her pulsating arm and pushed her into the closed door at her back.

"You don't need to know my name," he roared. "But I know your name," he said with a wink. "And I know you live next door," he added, smirking. Then he shifted the conversation back to Mitch. "You just tell your boyfriend Mitch that I'm in town to get my little girl."

21

Addison sat against the closed white door and cried softly until she felt sure the man had left the house. Then she suddenly felt the urge to run out the back door, back to the beach where there were people.

It seemed to take more energy than normal to stand. Her legs were still trembling. Her hands, too.

It only took three strides for Addison to reach the end of the hallway and cut the corner where she knew she'd find a straight shot to the back door. In less than five seconds her feet would hit the hot sand and she would be safe, but when she rounded the corner at the end of the hall, she slammed on the brakes and found the barrel of a black pistol only three inches from her temple. For a moment, she thought this was it—the end. Then Mitch lowered the pistol and pulled her safely into his arms. She knew he could feel her heart beating up against his chest. Neither knew exactly what was going on, but instantly she felt safe.

"Is he in here?" Mitch asked immediately.

Addison could hear the tension in Mitch's voice; she could feel it in his body. He had one arm wrapped around her like a security blanket and with the other he had lifted the pistol back into the air, waiting to see if someone was going to follow her around the corner.

"I don't think so," she slurred out.

"Did Donald hurt you?" Mitch wanted to know, glancing down and meeting her gaze.

"I'll be okay," was all she said.

Mitch tucked the gun into his board shorts and kissed the top of her head.

Addison hoped he would never let her go, at least not until she stopped shaking, which could be years from now.

"I thought you were him," Mitch said. "I had no idea you were in the house."

It took a moment for Addison to find the words she was searching for to respond. "You and Hannah weren't out on the beach when I came back, so I thought you might be in here. I looked around for you." She stopped, suddenly realizing that reliving what had just happened still seemed nearly as terrifying as the experience itself. "I heard the back door, and I thought it was you." She couldn't hold back the tears. Sounds of fear and relief exited her mouth all at once, and she found herself buried in Mitch's chest once again.

Mitch had slowly turned their bodies to put his back against the wall. Addison, lost in the moment, hadn't even noticed. He wanted to make sure he could see the back door and the entrance that led into the kitchen, just in case Donald decided to pop back in. Addison had said that she thought he'd left, but she didn't seem certain enough for him to lower his guard.

The two of them held each other for a few more minutes. The waves in the ocean continued to roll. The clock on the wall continued to tick. Warm air drifted through the screen door and into the house. Everything around them appeared normal, but everything inside of them knew better.

"How did you know he was here?" Addison finally asked, wondering where Mitch had been and how he'd known to come into the house with a gun. And where had the gun come from? Had he had it with him at the beach the whole time? But where? In his shorts? In one of the bags where the kids could get to it? She began to worry about things that didn't really matter at the moment. Questions she could ask later.

"While you were down the beach, I started playing with Hannah. When we were down in the sand, I just happened to look up and see Donald standing in my backyard surveying the beach." Mitch paused, thinking back over the whole thing. "The family sitting next to us had just decided to leave. The parents didn't want the kid to hear about the shark attack. So I grabbed Hannah and we inconspicuously blended in with them as they walked to the public beach access where they'd parked."

Addison suddenly felt the need to interrupt. "Where is Hannah now?"

"She's safe," Mitch replied. "I used the man's cell phone to call Doc, who was actually in his car, headed to my house."

Addison furrowed her brow.

Mitch continued his explanation. "Apparently, Donald must have come to my house this morning just after we went out to the beach. When he realized no one was home, he went to Doc's house. Doc said Donald grabbed him by the shoulders, shook him, and pushed him up against the wall." Mitch could feel fury running through his veins. He'd wanted it to be Donald that had run around the corner when Addison had. His finger had been on the trigger. If it had been Donald, he knew he would have applied a couple more pounds of pressure. One squeeze would have solved this problem for good. Thank God he'd been able to hold his finger steady when he saw Addison, though. He would have never been able to forgive himself if he'd pulled the trigger. He'd lost London, and he couldn't bear the thought of losing someone else that he loved, which reminded him of what Addison had said earlier about being friends. He'd lied to her. He couldn't be just friends. He couldn't keep his promise. If she had a problem with that, he'd just have to deal with the consequences. That's when he decided to let his natural tendencies take over.

Addison hadn't seen this coming, but she had felt it too, just like Mitch. The strong desire to let her feelings lead further than just wrapping their arms around one another. His lips met her lips before she had the time to think about what might happen next. She'd thought she'd be strong enough to hold back the temptation of falling for Mitch Quinn again, but that was before the last few hours had changed their lives, again. With Mitch things had been up and down, but she liked it best when things were up.

This time, Mitch was the one up against the wall. Addison felt herself pushing her hips into him as they made out like two characters at the end of a dramatic movie, which is what life felt like right now. When she felt the pistol pressing up against her thigh, she arched her back and pulled her lips away from his face just long enough for both of them to laugh out loud. Then they stumbled to the couch. Mitch set the pistol on the floor. He'd made sure to click the safety on earlier when he'd tucked it into his shorts.

Addison could feel the soft couch cushions beneath her as Mitch settled in on top of her. She let him kiss her neck, then her stomach quivered as his lips traveled downward and traced the skin below her bikini top. She loved watching his muscles flex as he hovered above her body. Suddenly, a calm came over her and for the first time since she'd found out that Ty was really Mitch, she felt okay with it. London had asked her to make sure Mitch knew it was okay to fall in love again. He had. And she had fallen in love with him. She knew it wasn't what London had in mind, but love was love, and she didn't want to look back five years from now and wish she had made a different choice. Her whole life she'd made safe choices, but all that had changed when she met Mitch. She kind of liked it this way. Maybe things would work out for them, maybe they wouldn't, but there was one thing she knew for sure—she was no longer willing to put a limit on love. This had all happened for a reason. All of it, and as crazy as it seemed, she decided to embrace it.

Mitch kept expecting Addison to stop him, but she didn't. He took his time. Touching her. Kissing her. Caressing her. He wanted more. He wanted to go further. Break all of the boundaries. But the door was still open, and he felt vulnerable in more ways than one. At any moment Donald could come marching back into his house. He'd already been here twice today. In the midst of his thoughts, Mitch heard a loud bang as the front door busted open and slammed against the wall.

Addison watched Mitch jump. Thank God their bathing suits were still on, she thought, as she saw him reach for the gun.

22

"Police!" a voice hollered out. Then another voice shouted, "Police." A third followed, "Police". Mitch could hear feet scampering, tactically, on the wooden floor in the front room. Once he realized that the three voices shouting "Police" couldn't possibly be Donald, he quickly tossed the pistol into a nearby recliner. He assumed the officers would be trained well enough to hold their fire even if he had kept his gun at his side, but he didn't want to take that chance. Neither did he want to risk dropping it on the floor and startling their raid nor tossing it on the couch and putting Addison in danger. It had always amazed Mitch how quickly and calmly a human mind could think in a situation like this. Maybe that was a gift he had, or maybe it had come from his martial arts training.

"Put your hands in the air," the first officer to round the corner into the living room instructed when he locked eyes with Mitch. The second turned his back flush with the first officer and faced the hallway where Addison had been confronted by Donald earlier. The third quickly analyzed the positions of everyone in the room and instinctively pointed his Glock at Addison. "Don't move," he demanded.

Addison hadn't moved since they'd barreled through the front door. Mitch, standing next to the couch, had his empty hands lifted. Addison shifted her eyes toward the officers but made sure to keep her body stiff. Her hands were covering her belly button.

"I live here," Mitch swiftly clarified.

Addison could tell by the look on Officer Pete's face that he was trying to connect the dots. She just hoped he wouldn't pull the trigger. His gun just happened to be the second one pointed in her direction today. It baffled her that in all twenty-nine years of her life, before today she had never had a gun pointed at her.

"You know this man, Harper?" Pete asked quickly and somewhat fuzzily, making sure whatever had been going on here, before he and his officers entered the house, to be consensual.

"Yes," she replied hoping Mitch hadn't caught the name Officer Pete had just called her, and now she found herself wishing she had asked Pete to call her Addison, not just at the station on day one but when she'd talked to him on the beach less than an hour ago. She was aggravated with herself for forgetting that important detail, but thankfully one of the other officers had said something to Mitch about the same time that Pete had called her by her first name.

"Is there anyone else in the house?" the officer with his firearm pointed at Mitch had asked.

"No, sir," Mitch replied. He'd always been taught to show law enforcement the utmost respect regardless of the situation. Although he had to admit, it felt somewhat intruding that they'd busted into his home with guns drawn. Why they'd come, he wasn't quite sure, but he had a good idea. He'd asked Doc not to call the police, but Mitch had noticed that Doc hadn't seemed so sure about that when he dropped him off a block from his house. That's when Mitch had asked him to drive Hannah somewhere off the island and not to stop for anything until he called him. At that point, he figured they'd make a decision about where Hannah needed to spend the night. Mitch knew he didn't want her to be around if Donald decided to come back later.

"Why is that gun on that chair?" Officer Pete asked.

All three men still had their guns drawn. Mitch, shirtless, still had his hands pointed at the flat ceiling. Addison felt like her body was glued to the couch cushions. Everyone's eyes were darting back and forth. Checking out each other. Glancing at Mitch's gun.

Addison began wondering again about where the gun had come from in the first place. After she had found it pointed at her temple, one thing had led to another and other ideas had taken over her mind.

"It's mine," Mitch confirmed. "I'd had it out for protection, and then when I heard you guys coming in, I tossed it out of the way."

Pete sidestepped to the chair where Mitch had tossed the weapon, placing himself between it and everyone else. Once he felt it no longer to be a threat, he picked up a blanket strung over the armrest and tossed it to Addison. "Just in case you want to cover up," he offered.

Mitch didn't feel jealous that the eyes of the other officers had darted in Addison's direction more than his once they figured out that they could lower their weapons on Pete's command. In all honesty, Mitch had been sneaking glances at Addison all day. The weight she'd mentioned gaining after college must have all gone to her butt, he'd assumed. In fact, it filled out her bikini bottoms just fine. Thankfully she was still lying on her backside, so the officers would miss out on her best physical feature. Mitch was fine with that as he watched her drape the blanket around her body as she sat up.

"We received a call that an intruder had entered your residence."

As everyone settled down, Mitch began to explain the story. He wasn't surprised when Officer Dunlap said he knew of Donald Thorpe. "From past encounters" is how he explained it.

"We're sorry to have barged in on you all like this, but we had reason to believe that you were in harm's way, and believe it or not, bad guys don't usually come answer the door when they're up to no good."

Mitch laughed. Addison smiled. Her legs were still shaking.

"I'm going to let Officer Johnson finish up here. He won't take up too much more of your time, but he does need to ask a few more questions and fill out a report," Pete said. Then, he sighed, and his lips grew tight before he spoke again. "When I got the call to come here, I was on my way to find the parents of the teenage girl who was attacked by the shark earlier."

"How is she?" Addison asked.

"I'm waiting for an update on her condition," he said. "She was being airlifted to Vidant Medical Center in Greenville."

Pete excused himself while the other two officers remained behind—one longer than the other—and Mitch and Addison answered questions for the next ten minutes. When Officer Johnson asked for the best way to contact each of them, Mitch could tell that he found it odd that he didn't have a cell phone. Mitch thought it was weird that Addison asked if she could write her number on the report for him. He was surprised that the officer agreed to her request, but Mitch had always known that attractive women could get away with things that most other people couldn't. Part of him wanted to watch the numbers as she wrote, her hands shaky, but he decided to give her the privacy even though he still didn't understand why she didn't want him to know her phone number. Mitch called Doc to let him know that everything at the house had turned out okay. He didn't go into all the details about Addison being confronted by Donald and guns being drawn. Partially because he didn't want to frighten Doc any more than he had already seemed earlier but even more so because he didn't want Hannah to catch on any more than she probably already had.

When the officers left, Mitch locked the doors. Addison scooted close to him on the couch. It felt safe there. "I'm scared," she admitted.

"I understand," Mitch said simply.

She'd expected a more macho answer. *You'll be okay. I'm here to protect you. I have a gun and I know karate.*

"Donald knows that I'm staying in the house next door."

Mitch had taken note of that fact when she'd disclosed that bit of information for the police report.

"We'll move all of your things to my house, and you can stay here tonight."

Mitch was somewhat surprised when Addison agreed with a simple nod.

"Doc is going to take Hannah to a friend's house that lives in Durham. It's a couple of hours away and Donald will never find them there." Mitch paused to think about what move Donald might make next. "He's not that type of criminal. He won't put forth the effort to piece together a puzzle. He comes back to Emerald Isle because he has buddies here and he begs his dad for money, then he decides he wants Hannah and these things happen." Mitch sighed, rubbing his hands across his slick head, finding only a few particles of sand left from playing with Hannah. He prayed that she'd be okay. He'd made sure not to mention anything about Donald as they'd quickly fled the beach. He'd simply told her that they should walk their friends out and see if Doc wanted to meet them so Hannah could spend some time with him today. "If we lived somewhere else we'd probably never see him," Mitch finished.

"Have you ever thought about moving?"

Mitch shrugged. "This is home. Ninety-nine percent of the time life is peaceful in Emerald Isle. Plus Doc lives here, and I can't take Hannah away from him."

Addison could tell Mitch had wrestled with these thoughts a time or two. "I understand, but . . ." Addison halted her thought, not wanting to overstep her boundaries.

"But what?" Mitch tested.

"Well, isn't Hannah's safety more important than comfort?"

Mitch could feel his body temperature rising. "That's one of the reasons Hannah is living with me now."

Addison knew she didn't need to push Mitch's buttons right now, but she also knew how much Hannah had meant to her sister, and she felt like if anything happened to this little girl that London, in some way, would hold her accountable. She couldn't just turn a blind eye to what was going on here. Once she had seen reality, it wasn't like she could just unsee it.

"So you're saying that since you have a gun and know karate, you're going to be able to protect Hannah?" As soon as the comment flew out of her mouth, Addison couldn't believe she'd chosen to use the exact words she'd just given Mitch credit for not using.

"Yes," Mitch declared. "I will protect Hannah. I would give my life for Hannah." He paused for a moment, working to keep his cool, holding in a few choice words. "Heck, I would give my life for you, Addison. When a man loves a woman, or a little girl, that's instinct."

Addison felt honored by his words, and she knew they were more than just words.

"All I'm asking is for you to think about it."

"Fair enough," Mitch agreed.

Addison felt like they needed to raise their voices more. Throw something across the room. That's how arguments with James had always gone. He had a temper. A bad temper. He'd never physically hurt her, but she'd been scared on several occasions, including the day he walked out on her, especially when she'd heard the sound that her hand had made when she slapped him across his fiery red face for the first time ever. With Mitch it seemed different. He was so in control of his emotions. In a way, it made her jealous. Mitch had been as steady as the pier they'd had dinner on the first night they'd met, and she'd ended up being more like the waves below. Calm one moment, crashing against him the next. He probably didn't know if her true spirit was a gentle wind or a turbulent hurricane. In all honesty, it was probably somewhere in between. Hopefully, one day she could show him her true self, but first she knew she would have to tell him her true identity.

23

Addison locked Hannah's bedroom door and walked back to the small cast iron framed bed where Mitch had set her suitcase earlier today. A Peanuts character-themed blanket and dozens of stuffed animals covered the mattress. Barbies and G.I. Joes were hanging out in one of the corners on one side of the room next to an antique white dresser that matched the bed. Beneath the window on the other side of the room, a bookshelf with an assortment of kids' books lined the wall.

When Mitch had walked Addison over to the other house earlier this afternoon to gather her belongings, she made sure to keep a clinched handful of the back of the t-shirt he'd pulled over his head once the police officers left. The two of them went carefully from room to room checking every nook and cranny to make sure Donald wasn't hiding out in there. When they made it to the bedroom Addison had slept in, she exhaled a breath of fresh air. She thought she'd remembered to tuck London's memoir and Snuggles into the bottom of her suitcase before she'd left for the beach this morning, but she had been second guessing herself ever since the idea of moving over to Mitch's came up. It had only taken Addison about ten minutes to pack all of her belongings, make the bed, and tidy up a few things. Mitch placed the items from the refrigerator into a couple of plastic bags and let Addison carry those as he shouldered her luggage.

Addison had made sure to pull the curtains to in Hannah's room before she kissed Mitch goodnight. His lips tasted like salt, and she'd wanted the kiss to linger a little longer. She also wanted to read another chapter in the memoir. With the soft blanket covering the lower half of her body, she began where she'd left off.

Mitch and I had spent every single moment together since the day I told him that I had cancer. I didn't tell him that I might not be around to open Christmas presents, but I think he knew. When my hair began to fall out, Mitch tried to pick it up sneakily so that I wouldn't realize how much I'd been losing. But I had watched my hairbrush rob me of the strands of silky, dark-brown hair that had taken years to grow. When my mouth was dry, Mitch brought me water. When I felt too fatigued to take off my pajamas the entire day, he would lay in bed with me and watch movies. He waited on me hand and foot, just like he'd promised.

I hated for Mitch to see me go through this, but I was glad that he was the only one. Not counting Doc, of course, but he had seen the worst side of cancer thousands of times. In no way had he become numb to it, especially in my case. It wasn't that he was a better doctor than that, he was a better man. He loved me like a daughter. He treated me like the father that I didn't have by my side. I didn't tell Mom and Dad or Harper how bad things had become. I know one day they'll be mad at me for that, but I just didn't want them to see me like this. I didn't want Mitch to see me like this either, but I thanked God for him every day. I wasn't supposed to fall in love with a man whom I couldn't grow old with, but I did.

Addison read two more chapters and sniffled through every word. She was mad at London for not letting her and their parents know how bad things had become. She wished she could have been here to help, to spend the end of her sister's life with her. She still didn't understand why London hadn't wanted them here. She doubted she ever would, but she knew that London always felt like her cancer was a burden on everyone else, although it really hadn't been. When Addison finally set down the book, she wondered if Mitch had fallen to sleep yet. She hadn't heard him moving around in the house. She hadn't heard much of anything, actually. Every time she started reading the memoir, she found herself so entranced in the story that the world around her seemed to disappear. She liked that. She enjoyed being swept away into another world, a world that she kind of knew but kind of didn't. She knew London and she knew Mitch, but she didn't know them together. She'd never spent a single day with the two of them; never even seen a picture of them together. At least not until she walked in the room just down the hallway. Oh, and she had seen the one on Mitch's nightstand the first morning, but Mitch wasn't in that one.

"Mitch," Addison whispered, since the house was dark other than a dim lamp illuminating the area at the end of the couch where she found Mitch resting as soon as she tiptoed out of Hannah's room. Yoga had helped her be light on her feet, but she was pretty sure he'd heard her coming. His eyes had already shifted in her direction by the time she'd spotted him.

"Hey," he said in a hushed voice, matching Addison's tone but not sure why it mattered. They were the only two people in the house. He was sure of that. He hadn't even dozed off once, and the last time he'd looked at the clock it was past midnight.

"Why aren't you in your bed?" Addison inquired.

"Because you're not there." Mitch shuffled in the chair. Addison spotted the black gun sitting on the coffee table beneath the lamp. "I didn't mean that like it sounded," Mitch cleared up. "I know we're supposed to just be friends, and I already overstepped the boundaries earlier." He paused again, and Addison waited for him to go on. She could tell he had more to say. "I just feel more comfortable out here where I can keep an eye on everything."

By everything, he meant her. She knew that.

"Thank you," she said.

Mitch smiled in the dark. He was wearing a pair of black gym shorts, a matching tank top, and the hat he'd been wearing the night they'd met, which meant he hadn't even been trying to fall asleep, Addison gathered. At least no one she'd ever known liked to fall asleep in a hat.

"I can't sleep," Addison admitted. There were several reasons for that, she knew. "Is it okay if I sit out here with you for a little while?"

Mitch lifted the newspaper from the couch cushion next to him. He hadn't read a word of it, but he'd set it there just in case. He watched Addison settle in. She reached for the blanket that had covered her when she'd been wearing her bathing suit earlier, then it surprised Mitch when she rested her head on his shoulder.

"This is much better," she said.

For some reason, he felt butterflies in his stomach and a lack of words in his mouth, so he simply allowed himself to enjoy the moment. Neither of them spoke another word as the hands on the clock began to circle. The next thing Mitch heard was Addison's breathing when he woke up to sunshine cutting through the curtains. She looked so peaceful, her body rising and falling with each breath she took. He didn't want to wake her, so he let her sleep until she woke up on her own.

When Addison's eyes opened, she realized that she didn't even remember that they'd ever closed. The last thing she recalled was nestling up close to the warm body next to her. She could still feel Mitch's arm rested on her left side, his hand settled on her thigh. It felt so fitting that she didn't want to move. She glanced up and saw that Mitch was already awake.

"Good morning, sleepy head," he greeted.

Tilting her head to see his face better, Addison grinned. "What time is it?"

"Morning time," Mitch said with a smirk.

"Ha. Ha."

"I would kiss you but my breath probably smells really bad. Plus I really don't want to move."

"You haven't moved since you fell asleep."

"I know, I can't believe it. I slept so good." She paused, realizing that this was the second time she'd slept all the way through the night with Mitch. "Did you get any sleep?"

"Actually, I did. I've only been awake for about thirty minutes."

"Thirty minutes? Why didn't you wake me?"

"You looked so cute with your eyes shut and your mouth open," he teased.

Instinctively, Addison covered her mouth with her left hand. "I don't sleep with my mouth open," she said between her fingers, although she knew that she had ever since childhood. Allergies and sinuses attributed to that characteristic.

"Yeah, you do," he ensured her, "so maybe all of your bad breath snuck out, which means you could kiss me."

"I like how you just twisted that from joking me to trying to steal a kiss."

Addison climbed up his body and kissed his cheek. "That'll have to do for now," she said falling back into place.

"I'm not picky," Mitch admitted.

Addison furrowed her brow. "Today is Sunday, right?"

"Yes, it is. Why?"

"I love Sunday," Addison offered.

"How come?"

"Because I don't have to work."

"That's always nice."

"Do you ever work?" Addison asked.

"I try not to."

She liked how he eluded the subject. "How do you pay your bills?"

"Bills?"

"Yeah, you know, the papers that come in the envelopes through the mail. They usually have numbers on them. Large numbers, often. Sometimes bills come via email, too, but I'm pretty sure you probably don't have email," she teased.

"Oh, those. I don't have many, just electricity, water, phone and internet. What else does a man need?" he inquired. "And what is email?" he joked.

"What about a mortgage?"

"Nope. My parents left me these houses."

"What about a cell phone?" She knew the answer but she wanted to tease him again—Mitch Quinn, the only man alive without a cell phone.

Mitch smirked. "I live a simple, boring life according to the average American citizen."

"What about a credit card bill?"

"I only use cash."

She'd heard that, too. Or read it, actually. "Really?"

"Why do I need a credit card?"

"So you can have five bills and a higher credit score?"

Mitch laughed. "My credit score is zero."

Addison furrowed her brow. "What? Zero. I've never heard of anyone with a zero credit score."

"Now you have."

"I don't believe you." From what London's memoir said, Mitch had plenty of money. Although if she hadn't read the book, she wouldn't know it. Either way, it didn't really matter to her. Money had never been that big of a deal. Maybe he'd wasted it all away in the last year or donated it. From what she understood, people with low credit scores were typically in a lot of debt on delinquent accounts.

"The only way to obtain a high credit score is to borrow money. Why would anyone want to borrow money just so that they could raise their credit score just to borrow more money? Realistically, all a high credit score means is that you've had a lot of debt and that you're pretty good at paying monthly payments and typically lots of interest."

Addison had never really looked at it that way, but it made sense. "What about doctor bills?"

"I pay with cash at my visits."

She racked her brain. "Oh, a car payment. Everyone has a car payment."

"My trusty old Jeep is paid for, thank God."

Addison perked up. "Speaking of God," she suggested, "let's go to church."

Suddenly a lull took hold of a conversation that had been steady since the two of them had woken up together this morning.

Church . . .

24

Pastor Kenny smiled when he watched Mitch Quinn step through the large, wooden and wide open church doors with a beautiful woman. The church always left the doors open, whether a Sunday morning or a Tuesday afternoon, as long as a staff member occupied the building. The simple gesture symbolized the message of Jesus. People were also welcome here just as they were. It didn't matter if they'd been drunk last night, argued with their spouse this morning, or dressed in ragtag clothes. If any church member had a problem with any of this, Kenny preached that they had a problem with the Bible. *Read it*, he would say. *Don't just believe what other people tell you is scripture. Don't even believe what I tell you is scripture. Don't get so caught up in following tradition that you miss the point of grace. Double check the facts. Jesus dined with sinners. He talked with prostitutes. He even befriended tax collectors and murderers. And no, I'm not comparing tax collectors to murderers.* This was the message he'd been sitting at his desk all week preparing for this morning even though he knew the words on paper would come out differently once he settled into the pulpit. They always did. Hopefully, the congregation would laugh at the tax collector remark. He liked to tell a few jokes at every service, just to loosen up the tension that so many people seemed to bring to church. Everything in church didn't have to be so serious, he liked to remind folks, which was another part of his message today. *I think when we get to Heaven, God is going to tell us that we worried way too much about things that didn't really matter. We judged way too many people for their words and actions. There's a verse about taking care of the plank in our own eye before concerning ourselves with the speck in our brother's eye.*

"Mitchell, how are you buddy?"

Mitch had always been quite fond of Pastor Kenny even though he liked to call him Mitchell. He didn't come across high and holy like so many other preachers Mitch had come in contact with over the years. He would admit to sinning, and not just before he became a Christian. In everyday life the man made mistakes, just like the people who sat in the pews. Mitch liked that about him.

"I'm well," Mitch replied, responding to the firmness of the handshake Kenny offered. He motioned toward Addison, wearing a light green summer dress cut just above the knees, similar to the one she'd worn yesterday but this one had a pocket. "This is my friend, Addison."

Kenny squinted his eyelids and moved his lips back and forth. Addison had to restrain the humor in the moment as she studied the quirky facial gestures of the fifty or so year old man with more wrinkles than most preachers his age. She could tell the movements mirrored the mental waves going through his mind, and she started to worry a little.

Then he asked what she hoped he wouldn't. "Have we met before?"

Addison hated the thought of lying in a church. She could kick herself for not seeing this coming. She should have known that Mitch would take her to the church where the man who'd spoken at London's funeral preached. The truth of it was that they *had* met previously, although only briefly. There had been a lot of people at the funeral. She was surprised that he remembered her face. Hopefully, he wouldn't connect the dots. Addison hadn't even thought about the idea of chatting with a preacher this morning. The church she attended in Silver Spring was large and people only talked to the pastor if they chose to seek him out. She'd met with her pastor on several occasions for counseling after James left her. He'd given her some really helpful advice that she'd been able to apply to her life.

"I just arrived in town for work a few days ago," Addison stated, avoiding a direct answer. "Maybe we've crossed paths on the island somewhere this week. I've visited a lot of places."

"Well, I'm glad you're here," he said, leaving it at that then turning his attention back to Mitch. "You, too," he added. It didn't matter to Kenny what it took to get Mitch back to church, he was just happy to see him here, and he noticed that Mitch seemed happy, too.

Mitch and Addison found a seat three rows from the back door. Addison fixed his collar poking up on the edge of his cream colored button-down shirt. She noted again how well the dark brown pants looked with it, untucked and comfortable. She watched Mitch stretch his hand toward the rack on the backside of the pew in front of them and then realized she hadn't seen a hymnal like the one in his hand in ages. Several people introduced themselves before the service started, and most of them seemed really genuine. Addison was quite surprised about the amount of people who could fit into the quaint white building filled with wooden pews. The congregation sang several songs before the message began. The guy who led the music, which consisted of an ancient piano and a guitar similar to the one Mitch had in his hands a couple days ago, welcomed all the guests in town for the fishing tournament along with the regulars. She thoroughly enjoyed the easy way Pastor Kenny preached the sermon, which he titled: Tradition vs Reality. When they'd first arrived, she'd been surprised to see a minister wearing a pair of jeans and a t-shirt, but now she realized that it seemed to fit his style and his message.

After church, Mitch took Addison on a day trip to Morehead City, which he called "the mainland." As they passed by thousands of loblolly pines and hundreds of vehicles headed to the beach, Mitch and Addison both took a turn talking on her phone with Hannah. Hannah seemed to be having a good time at Doc's friend's house—riding golf carts, shopping, and eating ice cream—but she still seemed confused as to why they'd had to leave so abruptly. "Doc had a last-minute invite to visit an old friend, and he didn't want to go alone" is what they'd told her, but Mitch wasn't sure she'd bought into it. "Then why didn't I bring my suitcase?" she'd asked. It was a great question. "Doc wanted to treat you to a brand new wardrobe" was the group answer for that one. Just like an adult, Hannah was stringing together clues, he knew.

"El's Drive-In is a local favorite," Mitch promised Addison just after she asked if there was anywhere they could get a delicious hamburger.

A small yellow-bricked building sat in the corner of a parking lot with cars scattered all about. There didn't seem to be any rhyme or reason to the parking pattern, Addison noticed. The menu stretched across the full length of the top of the building, and car-hops were skipping from one vehicle to the next before hustling back into the restaurant with orders.

"There's no seating inside," Mitch said.

"This place is amazing," Addison noticed. She was surprised her family had never stopped here on any of their summer vacations, but she was glad because it made it more special to be here for the first time with Mitch.

"I told you," Mitch said proudly.

"This makes me wish I lived back when drive-in restaurants were popular."

Her comment reminded Mitch of the times he and London had come here and she'd said the same thing. London would also mention how she'd always wanted to go to a drive-in movie theater but had never been. "I've thought the same thing plenty of times," Mitch said, pausing for a moment to enjoy the fresh air dancing through the Jeep. Addison had insisted that they take the top down for the ride. It turned out to be a great idea, and Mitch liked the way she looked with a ponytail, touching the back of her neck just above the circle of her dress. "Do you want to eat in the Jeep or over there on the picnic tables beneath the trees?"

Addison glanced to her right. A group of massive oak trees lined the side of the parking lot. "I'm happy right here," she said, as the carhop greeted them with a smile.

"Welcome to El's, y'all been here before?" the lady said in one breath.

"He's a regular but this is my first time," Addison offered since the woman had shown up on her side.

"You're in for a real treat," she promised.

"That's what he says. What's good?"

The carhop's eyes widened, and she glanced toward the restaurant where a thin cloud of chargrilled-smelling smoke was rising from the vents on top of the building.

"You see that menu up there?"

Addison followed the direction of her finger. "Yes."

"Everything on it is amazing," she said proudly. "And they don't pay me to say that," she added with a wink.

Mitch had said the same thing on the ride here. "Then I'll take the burger and a root beer."

The carhop asked a few questions concerning preferences, wrote down the answers with a wooden pencil on a small flip top order pad, and then looked at Mitch.

"I'll take one of everything," he said with a smile.

She pointed the eraser end of the pencil at him. "I remember you. You said the same thing last time." She tapped her bottom lip with the pencil and touched Addison's forearm. "Don't worry, honey, he wasn't here with another girl." She smiled then shifted her feet. "Well, actually, he was here with a girl, but it was a little girl." She held her hand out flat to guestimate the height.

Addison rotated her head to look at Mitch. "Hannah?" she asked with a smile, her legs crossed. Mitch noticed she'd picked up a thin layer of sun from the time they'd spent at the beach yesterday.

"Of course."

The waitress chimed in. "She ordered a hamburger and a root beer, too."

Addison smiled. It was kind of sweet that she and Hannah liked the same thing. "You actually remember their order?"

"I remember just about every order. I have a photographic memory. Plus I've been doing this for as long as you've been alive, darling." She chuckled at her own comment. "You want the regular, hon?" she asked Mitch. He shook his head. "It's a shrimp burger with a sweet tea, correct? And you want to share a fry with your new girl?" she added for the price of a couple laughs.

"Sure thing," Mitch said.

It took a little longer than most places for the food to come out, but Mitch insisted it was because the food was fresh, not frozen like so many fast food joints these days. Plus the parking lot was overflowing with an eclectic group of people—surfers, church goers, hippies; young people, old people, teenagers. While they waited, Addison enjoyed watching drivers pull in and try to figure out where to park. She also found real interest in the conversations that she and Mitch shared, the easy flow from one topic to the next. They started out talking about how El's had been around since 1959. At least that's what the sign said. That led to how church had changed since that era. Then Mitch told her that he hadn't been to a service in over a year. It didn't surprise her because she'd taken note of him previously mentioning that he and God didn't see eye to eye these days. She figured all of that must have something to do with London, but she didn't pressure him on any of it. What did surprise her is when he thanked her for talking him into going to church today. It hadn't really taken much convincing, she reminded him. She'd just said something to the tune of "let's go to church today" and he'd said "okay."

The burger ended up thoroughly satisfying her taste buds and the fries were okay, although Addison didn't share the rating with Mitch. At least not until he asked. He shared a bite of his shrimp burger with her, which was deliciously messy, and some of the ketchup and coleslaw ended up in her lap. They laughed it off as Addison stepped out of the Jeep and shook it off onto the blacktop. "The seagulls will eat that," she said, thankful that they had dodged all the aerial missiles. "If they don't get run over first," Mitch laughed, and then he talked her into ordering a milkshake for the road, which they shared through a single straw as he gave her a tour of Morehead City. She remembered many of the places on the main road, tourist traps for the most part. Then he took her off the beaten path, showing her the baseball field where he'd played Little League All-Stars, then a small stadium where a local team made up of college guys played summer league baseball. "We should watch a game while you're here," Mitch suggested. Addison thought the idea sounded fun, and they decided to pick up a schedule when they visited the downtown shops on the waterfront.

Hundreds of boats filled the slips at the docks, many of them belonging to the fishermen who were in the area—the Crystal Coast, the official name—for the big tournament. He mentioned that it was normal, though, in the summertime for the boat slips to be filled with anything from rusty old sailboats to pontoons to million dollar yachts. People from all walks of life mingled here, shopping, fishing, dining, and listening to local bands with hopes of making it big.

"Who was the band playing on No Name Night?" Addison wondered aloud.

"That was Bryan Mayer," Mitch said. "He lives in the area, and he's actually very popular. He has a few songs that are playing on the radio, and he signed a deal with a label in Nashville about a year ago."

"He's really tall," Addison noted.

"Yeah, he looks more like a basketball player than a country music singer. I think he's only a few inches from being seven foot."

"Hey, it's a memorable trait, which helps in the music industry." Addison stepped over a lump in the sidewalk. "Too bad Donald isn't that tall," she added.

"Why do you say that?" Mitch quizzed, kind of surprised that Donald's name had come up out of the blue.

"I've had my eye out for him all day," Addison admitted. "I keep worrying that we're going to run into him somewhere."

"I've been a little more cautious, too," Mitch divulged, "but I don't think we need to worry about him over here."

Addison wondered if that's why Mitch had brought her to "the mainland" today. As the thought circled her mind, she felt his thick fingers trace her wrist to her palm and then connect between her bony fingers, like two puzzle pieces settling in just the way they were meant to. She loved the safe feeling of holding his strong hand. Loved the twinkle in his eye every time he touched her skin.

"All afternoon yesterday I kept finding myself checking in every direction, especially when we ended up back down at the beach after the run-in with Donald at the house," she confessed.

Mitch had been the one to suggest that they leave the house and relax at the beach once the police car backed down the gravel drive. He figured the idea of Donald returning was the reason Addison hadn't wanted to sit in the beach chairs. They'd stood around and watched waves roll for a short period, but Addison kept thinking every white cap was a shark's fin. Then they'd taken a stroll down the shoreline in the opposite direction from where the accident had taken place. After a couple miles of exercise, they'd picked up Hannah's toys and the rest of the beach gear and then loaded it back into the shed that smelled like plastic. They'd taken separate showers at Mitch's house before heading over to the other house when they'd gathered Addison's things and secured the place as best they could.

"He's probably moved on to different things," Mitch suggested, "like getting drunk with his buddies and being a nuisance to other people. Honestly, he probably wouldn't even remember you if he saw you again."

Addison knew Mitch had said that just to try to calm her down. Donald obviously knew her face; she knew that to be certain because he had made mention of her staying next door to Mitch.

"We'll just stay in Morehead City the rest of the evening if you think that will help ease your mind."

"I'd like that," Addison acknowledged. She was shocked that she hadn't dreamed nightmares last night. She'd basically lived out an entire horror movie in one day. First, she'd been overwhelmed by the site of the girl bitten by a shark and the image of the girl's boyfriend diving onto the shark. Thank God he hadn't been bitten as well. Then Donald caused her nerves to reach a new high. She'd gone from thinking he was going to kill her to thinking he was going to rape her then kill her. Lastly, her face became a magnet for guns. All of this would make for interesting television, she knew. *Oh crap*, she thought suddenly, realizing she hadn't called Tara. Typically, she tried to check in with the office every day when on assignment. "Can we make it home before dark, though?" she requested before acting on the latter thought. "I'm not sure I can handle walking up a dark driveway and into a dark house with all of this on my mind."

"Sure," Mitch said as they continued to walk along the waterfront, dodging people every few steps.

"I need to make a quick phone call to the office," Addison shared.

Mitch sat patiently at a square picnic table beneath a cluster of shade trees between a restaurant and a souvenir shop as Addison chatted with Tara. As she expected, her boss/friend was overly dramatic about the shark attack. If Addison didn't know better, she would have thought that Tara had been the one to witness all of the blood and fright and uncertainty about sharks and people and swimming in water with creatures that didn't understand our purpose in their natural environment. Addison shifted the conversation to a round of questions about why Tara had been at the hospital earlier in the week. Along with everything else that had been going on since she'd arrived in Emerald Isle, Addison hadn't been able to keep from worrying about her friend. Had she been in some type of accident? Had a friend been really sick? Had Tara found out she had cancer? In Addison's mind, all medical-related concerns now seemed to lead to cancer. As Addison probed, Tara wouldn't budge on the reason for the visit. But then, in the most random part of the conversation, a name slipped out.

James . . .

25

It was killing Addison not to know more about what was going on with James. After the phone call, she and Mitch had meandered through the general store and even stopped to watch an artist painting an exquisite portrait of a lonely wooden row boat anchored near the shore. On any regular day, Addison would have been completely drawn in by the art. The way it came to life on the canvas would have made her want to know the boat's story. When had it first been crafted? Who had sat on the small seat and worked the oars on either side? A young man, fifty years ago? Had he taken the love of his life out for a romantic stroll down the Morehead City waterfront? Had they fished or kissed or just enjoyed the scenery? Where were they now? Why was his vacated boat floating to the songs of the sea? But these thoughts had shot through her mind like a bullet train instead of softly settling in like a smooth and subtle ride in a hot air balloon. She and Mitch had held conversations, but she remembered very little of what he'd said or how she'd responded. Was James okay? In a way, she found herself boiling for even caring. Why should she? Because she was human, that's why, she kept reminding herself. She'd been married to the man for years. He might be a chapter in the past, but he was still a chapter. What bothered her more was the way Tara had tried to cover up her being at the hospital with him. It didn't surprise her that Tara would know about whatever it was that had happened to James. They all had mutual friends. But why would *she* have been at the hospital with him? And why wouldn't Tara tell her what happened? Addison had demanded to know, but Tara had threatened to hang up. Threatened not to answer if she called back. Tara demanded it was something they'd have to talk about face to face. "Do I need to come back now?" Addison had asked. If James was hurt badly or extremely sick, she'd want to be there. Not to pry into his life, but nonetheless she'd want to stop by and see him. Bring the flowers and card that he hadn't brought to her when she'd needed it from him. Not with the intention of showing him up, either. Just to show that she cared. That she was a big enough person to put the past behind her and still care about him. "Just tell me if he is okay?" Addison had finally demanded, numb to the idea of Tara hanging up on her. "Yes, he's out of the hospital," Tara said. The next question had slipped out of Addison's mouth just like the name James had slipped out of Tara's mouth. "Then why were you there with him?" Addison needed to know. Did they have something going on behind her back? Tara had always been a few notches on the belt from earning the tramp title, but Addison didn't think her best friend would stoop so low as to start dating her ex-husband. Not after Tara had sat with her into the wee hours of countless mornings, handing her tissues as she cried about the divorce. Not after all the horrible things that Addison had told Tara that James had said to her. All the times that he'd told her how to live her life. Not to drink the milk. Not to wear a bikini. Not to have a beer if he wasn't with her. There had to be another explanation for why Tara had been at the hospital. Probably something as simple as she had gone to see a friend and ran into another friend that knew James was there for whatever reason. Maybe he'd attracted a sexually transmitted disease, Addison considered, at random, in the midst of a million thought bubbles floating through her mind. Herpes or gonorrhea. Maybe that would serve him right.

But what about her? Who was she to judge James? She'd had sex with Mitch Quinn, a man she barely knew. What if Mitch had one of those STD's? *Oh, God no. Please no. Don't let me find out that I have an STD.* She made up her mind in that moment to make an appointment with her doctor to get checked the moment she made it back to Silver Spring. "Stay there and do your job," Tara had said just before she hung up on Addison.

"Addison . . ."

Mitch touched her shoulder and said her name for the second time. "Addison."

Addison thought she'd heard Mitch say something, but she wasn't sure. The water was slapping against a nearby dock and the sound of a boat engine was whining in the background, but she hadn't heard those sounds either.

"Huh?" she probed, absent-mindedly.

"Are you lost in the painting?"

Addison glanced back at the painting, then at Mitch before turning her gaze to the painting again. "Yeah, I had my mind on something else."

Mitch had noticed that she'd been acting funny ever since she'd gotten off the phone with her boss. He wasn't sure if it had something to do with work or the conversation they'd been having earlier about Donald, or something else altogether.

"Do you want to go somewhere quiet to talk?" he asked.

Mitch led Addison to a short dock about a quarter mile past the busy downtown area. He'd been there a handful of times, and he knew it had always been a reliable place to settle his own thoughts.

"What's on your mind?" he finally asked.

Addison didn't know what to tell him, so she told him everything. About her marriage, some of the good and some of the bad, although leaving out her ex's name and significant dates. She talked in detail about the divorce and what had happened to cause it. She enlightened him on the fact that her boss had just told her that her ex-husband had been in the hospital. That she was afraid her boss might be sleeping with him. She went on for at least fifteen minutes, her head down and toes touching the surface of the water. Her shoes had found a resting place next to Mitch's. His feet were completely submerged in the water as they sat at the edge of the tattered wooden dock, stained black from years of weather and neglect.

Mitch had heard every word she said. Processed it. Processed it again. And still the only thing he could think to say was, "I'm going to need a moment to process everything you just said." He felt like a 1980's computer.

"I'm sorry, I shared way too much," she said.

"No, absolutely not," he assured. "I just don't want to say the wrong thing," he openly admitted.

She wasn't sure if she'd ever heard those words come out of a man's mouth. They sat together quietly for a moment. He hadn't reached for her hand like she thought he might at some point in her sob story. He hadn't wrapped his arm around her or told her it would be okay. He'd just listened, intently.

"Is this what has been bothering you all week?" he finally asked, not sure what all she'd found out today and what all she'd already known. She hadn't really clarified that part.

Addison had expected a lot of questions but not that one. "Um . . ." She looked away trying to think of a proper answer. Across the sound, she could see the town of Atlantic Beach. Beach houses, marsh grass, and docks lined the shore. In that moment, she felt like all of this had happened for a reason, like she was meant to be sitting here with Mitch Quinn having this conversation at this very time in her life. Like if she had been back at home or off in some other place on an assignment, she'd be totally flipping out right now. Somehow he and this place kept her calm. Or as calm as a woman in her shoes—correction, her bare feet—could be right now. "I'd be lying if I said some of this hasn't been on my mind, Mitch," she explained, hoping that he'd find that answer to be sufficient.

"This is probably the wrong time to ask this, but you know that I kind of just say what's on my mind." He paused, wanting to word his thoughts appropriately. "I completely understand that you care for your ex-husband. That makes sense. I mean, you were married to the man. So if you didn't care about him being in the hospital I think I'd be more worried about you than knowing that you do care about why he's in the hospital." Mitch held Addison's gaze for a moment. He preferred to look a person in the eyes when having a serious conversation. A person's eyes, he'd learned, were almost always honest. "Are you thinking about trying to work things out with him? Is that why you told me that you just wanted to be friends?"

Addison stared straight into his baby blue eyes. "No," she guaranteed. "Ja . . .," she started but abruptly stopped, realizing she'd just made the mistake of starting to pronounce James's name. Thankfully, she was able to stop at the first syllable making it sound like his name was *Jay*. With the pause, she knew she needed to start the sentence over again. "Jay is definitely not the reason why I told you that we just needed to be friends."

"Okay." He figured he would leave it at that for now. This wasn't the time to pry anymore about that whole ordeal, so he shifted his focus back to the topic at hand. "Before this week, have you ever had any reason to believe your boss might have something going on with your ex-husband?"

"No."

"Then chances are it's nothing. Like you said earlier, it's probably just some weird coincidence."

"That's what I keep telling myself, too, but there has to be more. I mean why would she just not tell me what was going on? It's like she's covering up something."

"Maybe he asked her not to tell you."

"Why?"

"Maybe he knew you would worry about him."

Addison hadn't considered that perspective yet. "But she's my best friend, not his."

"True." Mitch wasn't sure how his fingernail got into his mouth. Normally, he wouldn't try to play detective with a woman he was falling more and more in love with by the moment, at least not when it came to her ex-husband, but he could tell that Addison really wanted him to help her work through this. She didn't seem to just want him to listen. "It could possibly be that something terrible has happened." As soon as he made that statement, Mitch shook his head. "No, it's not that," he was sure of all of a sudden. "If something really bad had happened, she would have asked you to come back, right?"

"I think so," Addison responded. "I mean she's a workaholic and she always expects me to be just like her, but I don't think she would put the story over Jay being in the hospital unless there was something more to it."

"I think this is the question we need to ask: What does your gut tell you?"

Addison contemplated the question. She'd already contemplated the same thought in her mind at least five times. "My gut says that something is going on between them."

"Fair enough. Something going on between them could be several things. On the optimistic side of the scale, maybe they've just become better friends than what Tara thought they would. You did say that you all were really good friends prior to your divorce. Maybe it's harmless." Mitch paused, knowing that Addison already knew the pessimistic side of the scale. "Or it is possible that she's sleeping with him or dating him or whatever. I hope not. I know you hope not, but things like this do happen. People who are not supposed to fall in love do sometimes fall in love."

Addison furrowed her brow. Mitch wasn't sure why he'd just said what he'd said. Maybe it had a double meaning since for some reason Addison didn't seem to think she should fall in love with him. Regardless, he wished he could take it back. "Why would you say that?" She gave him an ugly look. "It sounds like you're trying to stick up for them."

Mitch shook his head. "I'm not. Definitely not your ex-husband. I have no mercy for a man who cheats on his wife." He waited for Addison to respond, but when she didn't, he chose to search for some humor in the situation. "In fact I've been sitting here thinking that I'd like us to run into this man in a bar so that I can put him in a choke hold and make him apologize over and over for hurting you while he cries."

It worked. Addison cracked a smile then let out a muffled snicker. "Would you do that for me?" she asked, twisting a string of hair between her fingers.

"I've done it once for you; why not twice?"

She laughed a little more. "I was just thinking that your idea seemed awfully familiar." Her smile seemed to fade as fast as it had come on. "But if she is with him, I'd be devastated. Not because I want him back or anything like that but because she is my best friend."

"If she is, I'll teach you the choke hold, and we can tag team those two."

"Why do you keep trying to make me laugh when you know I'm mad?"

"Because . . ."

Addison punched him in the arm before he could finish his thought. "Don't even say something cheesy like 'Because you're prettier when you smile' or 'You're ugly when you're mad.'"

"How about I just tell you the truth, then?"

Addison watched the expression on his face become serious all of a sudden. She'd glanced down at the ripples her feet were making in the water, but then she caught his gaze out of the corner of her eye.

"You're just as beautiful when you're mad as you are when you smile," he said.

That moment was the moment that Addison forgot all about James and Tara and shoving a high heel in each of their stomachs. Her lips met Mitch's lips, and she found herself halfway on top of him at the end of a dock in broad daylight. If it were dark outside and the Carolina moon had been hanging over their heads again, she knew she would have made love to him right then and there. Maybe later, she thought. Maybe not. She'd never in her whole life been so confused about life.

26

Mitch and Addison remained at the dock for two more hours, talking about life and all the changes that each of them faced. Mitch hoped they could continue to face them together. Addison felt the same way. But neither of them talked much about their future together. Too many walls had been put up, which made it easier to just talk about the present. Mitch was eager to see where the present would lead. Addison was afraid of where the present might lead.

Mitch took Addison out for dinner at Floyd's 1921, a beautiful restaurant inside one of the town's most historic homes. When they pulled into the gravel parking lot adjacent to the restaurant, Addison marveled at the exterior: white wood panels, black shutters, a green roof and matching red-brick chimneys on either side of the structure. It reminded her of an old farm house that she would have loved to live in. She imagined what life around this place might have once looked like, a hundred or so years ago. Massive oak trees, a tire swing, and fields surrounding it as far as the eyes could see. Maybe a long sandy path that led to the Bogue Sound.

When Mitch had begun to feel hungry earlier and brought up the idea of dinner, Addison requested somewhere healthy after having burgers and fries for lunch. She told him that she didn't want to go anywhere fancy since she'd only been able to freshen up in a tiny bathroom at one of the local antique shops. "This restaurant offers the best of both worlds," Mitch guaranteed.

As Mitch had mentioned, the hostess led them to a round black table on the patio. Addison had to admit that she felt a little special when Mitch had called the owner from her phone earlier to see if he could secure a last-minute reservation. On the way in, she'd noticed the sign out front about reservations and she'd overheard one of the other hostesses telling a couple that tables for this evening had been booked for two days.

"How do you know the owner?" Addison inquired. The place was absolutely packed. Inside she had noticed men dressed in suits and ties and women in elegant dresses, like Mitch said there would be. The atmosphere outside proved to be a little lower key. Most of the men were dressed in khaki shorts and a polo shirt. Some of the women were wearing dresses similar to hers, and others were wearing nice pants or skirts with an attractive top. A band, set up in the corner of the brick patio, was playing a Bob Dylan tune.

"I took photographs for his marketing materials just for fun."

"That was mighty kind of you."

"Well, I knew there might be some perks involved, like being able to have dinner with you here tonight on a whim," he mused.

Addison expressed her appreciation in the form of a cute grin. The band continued to play while Mitch and Addison placed their order. They both decided on fish. Addison ate the salmon while Mitch savored the taste of grouper. They each had one glass of wine with their meal and Mitch made sure to leave a generous tip along with a handwritten thank you note for the owner. After dinner, he and Addison journeyed back to the sidewalks of downtown

Morehead City and came to a halt when they reached the weigh-in station for the fishing tournament. Addison had inquired about it earlier, and Mitch had suggested that they come back for the action. Now, a rather large crowd had gathered around the attraction. As they'd been walking up, the two of them had spotted a large Blue Marlin about to be hoisted for show and weight from the back of a boat.

"How much do you think it weighs?" Mitch asked Addison.

"I have no idea," she shrugged.

"Just make a guess; it will be fun."

"You guess first," she insisted.

"That's fair." Mitch squinted as he tried to measure the size of the fish in his mind. "I'm going to say 350 pounds."

"Really? Wow!" She didn't expect Mitch to guess a number that high. "Then I'll go with 315 pounds."

Addison felt a surprising rush of adrenaline as she watched four fishermen, standing in the back of their boat, work together to steady the massive fish and slip a knot around the tail area. Once secure, a pulley system powered by two additional men on the dock, each with a separate thick rope in his hand, began to lift the fish into the air. Mitch wondered which of the six poles protruding out the backside of the boat had been the lucky one.

Multiple television station cameras were set up, reporters standing nearby to catch all of the action. Many of the bystanders had pulled out their cell phones to take photos. Others had nice digital cameras. Flashes were going off all around. Addison began to realize just how big of a deal this tournament was in this area. It reminded her of the night when she arrived and couldn't find a room to save her life. Looking back, she still couldn't believe how the last few days had turned out. How she'd ended up here in this moment with Mitch Quinn. Never in a million years would she have guessed that this could have happened to her.

When the final weigh-in rang out over various loudspeakers—announced by a man who had been standing near the boat with a microphone, commentating the entire scene—the crowd gasped.

"301 pounds," he said excitedly.

Addison threw her fists toward the blue sky, celebrating her victory. The crowd clapped and the fishermen were high-fiving. Mitch cringed as one man nearly fell on the slippery dock. He imagined it might also have had something to do with a few too many alcoholic beverages out on the water today.

As soon as one boat pulled off another would back up to the dock. Mitch and Addison watched this routine play out over and over, each time making a guess on the weight of the catch. Addison even pulled out her cell phone to keep track of the friendly competition.

As the sun began to sink over the water, creating a cotton candy colored skyline, Addison put her arm around Mitch's waist. "Don't butter up to me now," he said, just after she mentioned the score, 10-6, in her favor. She pointed out the pink and blue hues in the sky, noticing their reflection on the lazy water. Mitch smiled, happy that they were here together.

So far the heaviest fish weighed 412 pounds. Addison and Mitch had overheard someone nearby say that the winner last year weighed in at over 500 pounds.

"We better head back to the house soon," Mitch said, realizing that it would be dark in less than an hour.

﹋ ﹋

When they arrived back in Emerald Isle, there was just enough daylight to make the house and everything around the perimeter visible. The sound of the Jeep doors shutting echoed beneath the trees. Mitch had put the top on before they left Morehead City. He didn't expect Donald to be waiting on them, and he wasn't. Once inside,

Mitch flipped on a few lights and double checked all of the rooms. Addison noticed that when he'd asked her to check to make sure all of her belongings were still in Hannah's room, he scurried down the hall into London's room. She wondered how often he went in there and how much time he spent looking at the photographs. This time, she assumed, was probably his shortest visit ever. She heard the door shut less than fifteen seconds after he'd walked away. She'd already decided that she wouldn't come out of Hannah's room until Mitch came back out. She didn't want him to feel like they had to talk about the secret room. To this point, he'd made absolutely no mention of it. Maybe Mitch just assumed that she thought it was a closet, she considered.

"Do you want to watch a movie or play a board game?" Mitch queried.

"Either sounds fun to me." A movie would be romantic and peaceful, she thought. A board game would probably bring on conversation and laughs. Whichever they chose, Addison had already decided that afterward she would spend some alone time in Hannah's room. She only had a few chapters left to read in London's memoir, and she'd been dying to read more ever since she set it down last night. So that Mitch wouldn't become curious about why she wanted to be alone, she'd just play it off on work since she did need to think about her next steps. "What board games do you have?" she asked, realizing that snuggling on the couch during a movie might make it more difficult to pry herself away from Mitch.

"Monopoly?"

"Monopoly is no fun with just two people."

"Life?"

"We've been playing that all day," she laughed.

The saying *Third time is a charm* rang true. The next game Mitch mentioned was Yahtzee.

After Mitch called Hannah to whisper goodnight through a telephone line, which Addison thought was absolutely adorable, the two of them ended up rolling dice for the next two hours. As she expected, they talked and laughed amid the sounds of clanking dice on the kitchen table. What Addison appreciated most is that once again Mitch found a way to get her mind off all the other distractions in her world. When it came time for them to go to bed, she kissed him goodnight and they walked in opposite directions. Just as she had last night, she locked the door to Hannah's room and slid beneath the covers. With the lamp shining on the pages of the memoir, she wondered if this would be the last time she would open this book.

I never made a bucket list, but there were some things I wanted to do before I left for Heaven. Not anything crazy, like climb Mt. Everest, skydive, or be proposed to at the top of the Eifel Tower. Just simple things.

Mitch had always had this keen sense of picking up on all of the little things I'd mentioned since the day we met at the bowling alley. Even before he found out I had cancer, he'd been making my dreams come true. I once mentioned to him that I'd never swam in the rain. Then one night at his house when we were watching a movie, out of nowhere rain began pounding on the tin roof. I'll never forget what Mitch said next: "You haven't lived until you've felt sand between your toes, rain drops dripping off the end of your nose, and sweat pouring off your clothes." Without hesitation he took my hand, and at this point in our relationship, wherever he led I would follow. We ran out the back door, darted through the sand, and disappeared into the dark, massive, and mysterious Atlantic Ocean. We swam in the rain for nearly an hour. It was one of the most memorable nights of my life, and not just because Mitch's air conditioner had been broken that evening—hence the meaning behind 'sweat pouring off your clothes'.

One day not too long after Mitch had found out that I had cancer, I found myself resting in bed with nothing more to do than think about being sick. Mitch mentioned he had an errand to run, and when he returned he set a stack of books on the bed. I rolled over and studied them one by one. I couldn't believe that he'd remembered every book I'd ever mentioned wanting to read. He even brought one title that I'd forgotten all about. He reminded me that I'd pointed it out in a bookstore one day when we'd had nothing better to do than sit, drink coffee, stare into one another's eyes, and talk about the classics. I made sure to read every single one of the books, reading mostly on the days when I didn't feel like getting out of bed. The stories helped me escape from my own. A love story, although epically tragic, I foreshadowed.

I could go on and on about the things that Mitch did for me that outweighed any bucket list that any person has ever created, but there was one thing that meant more to me than anything any human being had ever done for me. I came to a point in my battle with cancer that treatment just wasn't working. I wanted to live the days I had left without being sick from all of the medicine. I felt too weak to go anywhere or do anything that involved effort, and I knew there was a place that Mitch had always wanted to take me. A place I'd mentioned several times, but it had never worked out. Honestly, I had given up on ever being able to watch a movie at a drive-in movie theater. It made me sad in a way that a kid might be sad if she found out she'd never be able to visit Disney. Mitch knew that I couldn't make the trip to Henderson, North Carolina, the closest drive-in on the East Coast, so Mitch did what Mitch does. He brought what Henderson had to me.

As I write this line I'm crying and I'm smiling. You see, he carried me in the dark from my bed in his house—where I'd chosen to spend the last days of my life—and gently sat me in the front seat of a 1961 Chevrolet Corvette convertible. He'd pulled it right up to the front door. I instantly noticed that the night was calm and Mitch Quinn was a complete gentleman. We took the shortest ride to the most romantic place in the world. I hadn't asked him where we were going, I just watched him maneuver the gear shift and turn the steering wheel ever so slightly. We coasted slowly around the side of his house and ended up in the backyard beneath a clear sky with endless stars. We parked facing the ocean, but all I could see was what looked like a large, white, homemade movie screen tied to trees on either side. Tears filled my sleepy eyes. It must have been over 1,000 inches in diameter.

As we sat holding hands, a projector played my favorite movie, the most romantic movie ever filmed: Pride & Prejudice. My sister had always said that I looked like Keira Knightley. I'd always said she resembled Natalie Portman, and I'd always thought these two actresses could pass for sisters. I missed Harper so much and I felt awful about not letting her know that I was dying of cancer, but I just couldn't fathom the thought of her having to suffer with me. I wanted her to remember me healthy and full of life.

Mitch had thought out every single detail that makes a drive-in movie romantic: Popcorn. Drinks. Candy. Blankets. Citronella candles. Tissues. He even had a small speaker set up on either side of the car playing the audio. Even though I didn't feel much like eating, I appreciated that he had made the experience real. I can't imagine that going to an actual drive-in movie theater could have been any more perfect.

I rested my head on Mitch's shoulder, and we watched our last movie together.

Addison had to stop even though she hadn't quite finished her sister's memoir. She couldn't take anymore. Now she knew exactly why London had picked out the cover on the front of the book. It was the scene from the backyard drive-in movie theater Mitch had created for her. It was one of the most romantic stories Addison had ever heard, more romantic than *Pride & Prejudice*. She wanted to waltz into Mitch's room right then and tell him how much she loved him. Not in the romantic way that she'd come to love him during the days they'd spent together this week, but in the way that a sister loves a man for making her dying sister's dreams come true.

As tears continued to slide down Addison's face, she walked into the living room, tasting salt and fighting shadows. She'd thought that she might find Mitch on the couch again, but he wasn't there. His bedroom door was wide open, and as she stood in the doorframe she watched his head lift from his pillow.

"Addison," he called out.

She imagined him squinting since he sounded half asleep, but she couldn't see him all that well. "Mitch," she replied, the sound of her breathing—heavy and fast—making its way to his ears.

Neither of them spoke another word that night. Mitch simply lifted the covers for her to climb into his bed. She scooted up close to his body and wrapped her arms around his waist. She just wanted to hold him. Wanted him to hold her back. She didn't want to kiss him or make love to him or do anything other than feel the warmth of the man she loved in more ways than one. Somehow, Mitch Quinn seemed to understand that, she realized as they drifted off to sleep to the sound of the nighttime critters outside his bedroom windows.

27

Another shark attack happened early Monday morning. This time the victim was a fifty-five year old swimmer. Addison got the phone call with the news from Officer Pete just before eight o'clock. She and Mitch had only been awake for about thirty minutes. They'd just been lying in bed talking like she'd grown up imagining happily married people would do. It's what her parents had always done on Saturday mornings when she'd get up to watch cartoons. James had never wanted to lie in bed with her and talk at night or in the mornings. If they were in bed doing anything other than sleeping, he'd wanted their clothes to be off.

Addison changed into a fresh pair of clothes, brushed her teeth, and put her hair into a ponytail in less than five minutes. "I'll be right there," she had told Pete. He had really taken to the idea of the television station she worked with doing a story on the shark attacks in Emerald Isle. She could tell that he'd really believed her on day one when she promised him that this story wouldn't be about scaring people away from the beach. *It would be about safety, not just for people but also for sharks,* she had said. *After all, the ocean is their natural habitat.* It would draw attention to the science behind why shark attacks happen, where they are most likely to happen, and how humans can minimize risks. It would cause scientists to study the patterns of these attacks and learn how to predict such occurrences. Shark migration patterns might also be involved in the recent attacks, she'd recently discovered during some of her research.

"Do you want to come with me?" Addison asked Mitch.

"No, thanks," he said, yawning. "I think I'll eat some breakfast, read the newspaper, and call Hannah. I really miss her."

Addison smiled, then planted a kiss on his lips, ran to Hannah's room to grab her purse—stuffing the memoir down deep inside—and headed to the address Pete had provided.

"Hey, Harper," Pete said as she walked toward him.

"Hello, Pete," she smiled. "By the way, you can call me Addison," she said nonchalantly. "It's my middle name," she clarified, knowing that a man in his profession was inclined to question everything, although she figured he probably recalled seeing her middle name on her license as well.

"Addison it is," he replied without hesitation then moved on to dialogue about the shark incident. "I talked with the victim's wife earlier," he mentioned. "They live in the house right behind us." His eyes darted in the direction, but he didn't turn his head.

Recognizing Pete's hesitance to turn, Addison glanced carefully. Out of the corner of her eye she could see the wife standing on a second story balcony. If she hadn't known better, she would have imagined that she was enjoying the way the wind was blowing her hair. Addison had noticed on her walk from the street that the sand seemed to be kicking around much more than normal this morning. It was a good thing she'd put her hair up, she thought. Her baggy pants were flapping against her legs and the flares on her sleeves kept catching the wind. "How did it happen?" she asked. "And why isn't his wife at the hospital with him?"

"The wife watched it happen from the balcony," he confirmed. "She called 911. Now she's in shock, as expected. She said that her husband has been coming out here every morning in the summer for the past ten years to swim laps. Said she'd warned him about the sharks, but he'd told her that when it was his time there wasn't anything he could do to stop it." Pete pursed his lips and shook his head. "The bittersweet part is that she normally swims with him, but after the attack the other day she decided to hold off for a little while. She said they'd swam together every single day since the day they met at swim team practice in college."

Addison let that sink in.

Pete didn't say anything for a few moments.

"Once she found out he was going to be okay, she started being mad at him again for swimming. When they loaded him into the ambulance, she told him that she wasn't going to go to the hospital with him, but that he could call her when he was ready to come home."

Addison grinned.

The scene today looked nothing like the scene from the last shark attack. This part of the beach was remote, a little further down the island and away from public beach access. No crowds were gathered. The emergency vehicles had come and gone, and now only one Coast Guard boat was patrolling the area, and a few of the residents were standing around talking.

"I told her I would come up to let her know when we were finished," Pete said referring to the wife.

"You want me to come with you?" Addison asked.

"It's entirely up to you."

"Well, I'd like to, actually." Addison felt bad for the lady. "But I don't want to go up there and ask any questions or tell her what I'm doing in Emerald Isle. I just want to give her a hug. If that was me standing up there, I'd want someone to give me a hug."

"I think that's a fabulous idea," Pete confirmed.

Pete knocked on the door. The wife wore a designer pants suit, and her makeup had smeared in so many directions that it looked like a child had finger painted her face. Just the mere sight of this woman, helpless and lonely, made Addison want to cry. One minute her life had been peachy, and the next—this. She led the two of them to the balcony. "I just want to be out here," she said. "Even though he's not there, I can still see him swimming in the ocean. I can imagine all the great times we had out here together."

Addison noticed how the woman talked like her husband hadn't made it. She hadn't had to offer the wife a hug; the lady had actually been the one to hug Addison as soon as she walked into the grand room, a staircase leading up either side of an opening that provided a wonderful view of the ocean. The three of them talked on the balcony for about fifteen minutes while Officer Pete asked a few questions to finish up his report.

The weirdest thing happened next.

"I really don't want to talk anymore," the wife said.

"I understand," Pete responded respectfully. "We'll just be on our way."

"Darling," the lady said, touching Addison's arm. "Will you stay with me for a little while?"

Addison couldn't think of any response other than, "Yes, of course."

Pete walked himself to the door where he'd introduced Addison to Donna. He'd simply told Donna that Addison was working with the local police department on a special assignment.

"Addison, I meant what I said when I told the officer that I didn't want to talk anymore."

Addison clinched her brow, wondering then why Donna had asked her to stay.

"Would you just sit with me on the balcony? My husband and I would always sit on the balcony and read after our morning swims. I just don't think I can sit out here by myself."

"Sure, I'd love to."

"Oh, thank you, honey." Another tear fell from her eye. She wiped it with a handkerchief that most likely belonged to her husband then sat in one of the two chairs overlooking the wavy blue water. "You can sit in my chair." She gestured to the only other chair. "I'm going to sit here in his."

Addison sat and the air grew silent, aside from the wind and the birds and all of the sounds of the beach on a Monday morning in June. She watched Donna pick up a book and remove a bookmark about halfway through the thick pages.

"Where are my manners?" Donna eventually said, a few pages later. "I didn't offer you a book. All I read is mythology. Do you like mythology books?"

Not really, Addison found herself thinking. Even if she did like the genre, there was no way she'd read any other book before finishing London's memoir. So instead of reading mythology or reaching into her purse for *Mitch & Me*—this just didn't seem like the proper place to finish the book—she just sat with Donna until she received a call from the hospital.

When Donna headed to the hospital, Addison went to the pier and sat at one of the tables with a glass of wine and the memoir wide open. She'd decided this was the perfect spot to finish her sister's book.

This is the last chapter of my story. My love story.

My lungs are becoming weaker. My bones frailer. My will to live more distant. If I could, I would write until I breathed my last breath, but I want to be the one to decide where my story ends.

Today I've decided that it will end on a good note because today was the best day of my life.

Mitch Quinn would gain nothing by marrying me, but it didn't stop him from asking. I had often wondered if he would ask me to marry him even though we both knew a wedding and a honeymoon were out of the picture.

When my first ever drive-in movie came to an end, I already had tears in my eyes. Then, I looked at Mitch to see if he had teared up also. Mitch had never been a softie, but that didn't mean he didn't have a soft heart. He did. When our eyes locked, I could see the glassy look swirling around his gorgeous blue eyes, but I knew he wasn't teary eyed because of the movie.

Mitch didn't drop to one knee. He didn't say anything super romantic. He just said exactly what I needed to hear.

"London Adams, you are my soulmate. My Northern Star. My first true love. My last love." I let the words sink in with a gulp, then I watched him pull a small wooden box out of his pocket. It had been there the entire movie. I knew he must have been nervous. That was my fault. Ever since the day we realized I would never be able to adopt Hannah and that the three of us would never be able to have a family, I'd begged him not to ask me to marry him. Honestly, I thought he had listened. I thought that if he was going to ask he would have asked much sooner, but Mitch Quinn doesn't follow normal expectations. He lives life to his own music. "Will you marry me?" Mitch asked.

By now, tears were streaming recklessly down my face. The main reason I didn't want to marry Mitch was because he deserved someone he could spend the rest of his life loving the way he loved me. Someone he could kiss and touch and make love with on warm summer nights in Emerald Isle. I knew he would always love me, but I also knew I wouldn't be there to love him back. I wouldn't be there for the most difficult days of his life, like the day I would leave him here alone or the day when he reads these words for the first time. That's why I knew I had to say no. "Mitch . . . ," I whispered—I was just about to give him the answer when he interrupted me.

"I'm not asking you to walk down an aisle and meet me at the end. I'm not asking you to say 'I do'. I don't want us to sign a sheet of paper that will be locked away in a file cabinet for years to come. I'm not asking for a honeymoon or even one passionate night

of lovemaking." He paused, letting a single tear slip down his cheek. It hung there as he spoke. "I'm simply asking you to wear this ring to Heaven." He pursed his lips and his nose twitched. I could see that he was trying not to let the rest of his tears escape the walls of his eyelids.

Stating that Mitch's words weren't super romantic was somewhat misleading. They were, but then came a twist. A moment when romantic words turned into the reality of infinite love. "To wait on me there," he finished.

My brow furrowed. "Mitch, you're young . . . ," I started. I went through the whole spill that had just danced in my mind. To me, his love had been a blessing. Suddenly, I felt that my love, to him, would only end up being a curse.

Again, he interrupted.

"London, you don't understand because I haven't been completely honest with you."

My face began to tremble, then the rest of my body followed suit. Not because it was cold outside, although I had been known to get the chills in hot weather lately, but because Mitch Quinn had always been honest with me. I didn't want this to happen. I didn't want to hear what he had to say. I wanted to die knowing that he was my soulmate. Thinking of him as perfect as grace itself. "Why are you doing this, Mitch? Why are you asking me to marry you when I'm dying?"

I'll never forget what he said next.

"Because I'm dying, too."

A lump filled my throat.

What did he mean? Was he being philosophical in some way? Stating that a part of him was dying with me? I think I could have understood that. Or maybe he meant dying as in the way that some people say they're closer to dying with every breath they take. There is truth to that. But that's not what Mitch meant.

"I have cancer, too," he admitted.

"No, Mitch," I screamed. "You don't have cancer. You can't have cancer." I wanted to be right. I wanted him to be wrong, but he wasn't. It all made sense now. In one single moment, I saw everything as clear as the night sky above our hairless heads. He hadn't been at the bowling alley just to take pictures. He hadn't just shaved his head so that he would look like Hannah and I. He hadn't just been sick because he was worried about me. He hadn't been leaving just to run errands. He had been dying just like me.

"I thought I could beat it," he said. "I thought you could, too, but fate had something else in store for us. I wanted to tell you, London. I wanted to tell you every moment of every single day but I couldn't. I had to be strong for you. I had to take care of you."

"But, Mitch. Who took care of you?"

"You did." He started crying more. "You kept me going. You showed me how to . . ." Through the pain and tears and pinned in emotions he couldn't finish his sentence.

I shook my head. I was angry. Not at him, even though I knew I should be. I wanted to be, but I couldn't be. I didn't have enough time left to be mad at Mitch. "I showed you what, Mitch?" I paused. "How to die?" I cried.

He nodded his head. "London Adams, the only thing you've ever shown me how to do—is love."

In that moment, I wrapped my arms around him and spoke the only word that mattered: "Yes." I knew exactly why he hadn't told me until this moment. I knew he'd waited until he thought this might be his last chance.

Mitch furrowed his brow.

"Yes," I answered again, "Mitch Quinn, I will absolutely marry you."

He smiled the biggest smile I'd ever seen on his suntanned face.

I suddenly found it hard to fathom that Mitch Quinn would never have all of the things I wanted him to have in life. A real wedding. A picket fence. A newborn baby. A love story that would last fifty years. I had actually imagined him marrying someone like me but healthy. Someone like Harper. Of course she was already married, but when I thought of the perfect wife I always thought of my sister. So I imagined a woman like Harper helping Mitch raise Hannah, who my heart suddenly broke for at the realization that neither Mitch nor I would be around for her much longer. I knew Doc would find a way to take care of her, but I knew that Mitch and I already loved her like our own child. Ultimately, I knew I had to trust God. I didn't have time to worry. I knew my time would soon come to an end. I could feel it. And if Heaven was better than this, if Heaven was more than this moment, I knew I wanted to be there.

That night Mitch Quinn carried me into our room with an engagement ring on my finger. I fell asleep with my fiancé, not knowing if I would ever see him on Earth again but hopeful of our wedding day in Heaven.

28

Mitch had been putting together puzzle pieces since the moment he'd met Addison. Why hadn't she wanted to tell him her real name? Why had she not been forthcoming about where she lived? Why had she flipped out on him? Just wanted to be friends? Said that she would tell him something that would blow his mind, but not until the day she left? Suddenly, he didn't want to wait for all of these questions to be answered. He wanted the truth even if that meant he had to search for it. But then there were more than just questions, there were also facts. He was almost certain Officer Dunlap had called her Harper. Pastor Kenny had recognized her, and when Addison had told him that she'd been married, she started to say a man's name, but it seemed she stopped short.

Mitch walked from his bedroom to Hannah's door. He stood in front of it for a moment. The only door he wanted closed in this house was the one at the other end of the house. He reached for the doorknob, knowing that if he went in this decision might change his entire life.

—◆ ◆—

Addison didn't know whether to knock on Mitch's front door or just twist the knob and walk in. She decided to knock just to let him know someone was there, then she opened it.

— —

At the sound of the front door, Mitch's head jumped. He'd had no idea when Addison would show up, but he knew that she probably wouldn't stay long.

Addison stopped in her tracks when she saw Mitch sitting at the kitchen table, but not alone. She hadn't seen this coming. She'd expected to march in here and ask him why he hadn't been honest with her. Why he hadn't told her that he had cancer. She figured it would also be the perfect time for her to come clean with him. They could face facts together, but then she realized it was too late for her to be the one to expose the truth.

"Where did you get this?" Mitch demanded to know.

Addison's eyes darted between Mitch and Snuggles. He had both hands on the bear, propping it on the table like a newborn baby, fragile and priceless.

"Mitch," she started but then stopped, not sure what to say.

"Addison," he said. "Or is it Harper?" He shifted his eyes from Snuggles to her. "Who are you?"

In that moment Addison became Harper again, and all of a sudden she felt helpless. She had wanted to be the one to initiate this conversation. She had never imagined that Mitch would find Snuggles, which meant that he'd gone through her suitcase. Meant that he had snooped in her things just like James. "Who are you?" she interrogated. "Who are you to go through my personal belongings?" she said, slamming her purse onto the kitchen table and glaring across at Mitch.

Mitch stood to meet her eyes, and the chair beneath him suddenly flung into the wall behind him. The whole table shook, and a bowl fell and shattered into pieces all over the floor. The sound of broken glass echoed within the walls and Harper jumped.

"I didn't go through your stuff," Mitch clarified. "I was going to, but I didn't. I went into Hannah's room and found this on the bed," he said holding Snuggles tightly. Harper could see the veins popping out in his forearms. Mitch shook his head in disbelief.

Harper slapped both of her hands on the table. How could she have been so stupid? She had been so careful this whole week to keep Snuggles and the book hidden, but somehow in her haste to leave this morning, she must have left Snuggles on the bed, which meant London's bear had been there since she'd left the room last night. She suddenly remembered the last time she'd had him—just as she'd finished the next to last chapter in London's memoir. Then she'd stuffed the book away but had completely forgotten that she'd left Snuggles with the other stuffed animals on Hannah's bed.

"Then I guess you know who I am?" Harper admitted.

"I shouldn't have had to figure out who you are," he insisted. "You should have told me. The moment we met you should have been honest with me."

Harper's mouth was gaping. She doubted that anything she could say now would change the inevitable. "I never meant for this to happen," she admitted.

Mitch's nostrils flared. "Meant for what to happen? For us to have sex and fall in love and spend four amazing days together? You never meant for that to happen?" He paused. "Well, it did, Addison or Harper or whoever you are."

"Yes, I'm Harper Addison Adams." She shrugged her shoulders, knowing her real identity had cost her an amazing man, "which makes me London's sister."

"Thanks for letting me know," Mitch said, sarcastically. "You're also a liar."

Those words hurt, but they were true. "I guess I am," she admitted.

"Why?" Mitch begged. "Why would you do this to me?"

"I tried to tell you, Mitch. I tried to tell you so many times, but one thing kept leading to another, and I was afraid that the moment I told you, this would happen."

"Well, now it has happened. So now you can just leave. You can go back to wherever it is that you live so that we can both go on with our lives." Mitch waited a short moment for Harper to respond, but she didn't. "You don't have to pretend like you're here for work anymore," he finally added.

"Fine," she said. "If that's what you want, then fine." Sure, she'd lied, but not everything had been a lie. "Actually, I was here for work," she clarified. "But I have enough information for my story now, and I'll be out of your way as soon as I can get my things packed," she promised. She paused, wondering what to say or do next. She thought Mitch might question her response about work, but he didn't and she didn't see any need to explain the difference between being a reporter and a scout. He just stood there glaring at her, making her feel like a piece of dirt on the floor next to the shattered glass. She then realized that this might be the last chance she would get to say a few things she'd had on her mind since finishing London's memoir. "But don't stand there and act like you've been completely honest with me," she said reaching into her purse. Her hands were shaking, and her heart was beating as fast as it had all week. "Here's another surprise for you. London sent me here to check on you."

Mitch furrowed his brow as he watched a book swivel across the table, coming to a rest at the edge nearest to him.

Harper continued. "She sent me this in the mail just recently. I actually finished reading it thirty minutes ago. London wanted you to be the next person to read it."

Mitch picked up the book and studied the cover. He knew London had been writing a lot toward the end. She'd always had her laptop with her, but he had no idea how she'd managed to publish a book without him knowing. It had to have happened since he'd met her—the title, *Mitch & Me*, gave that away. He wanted to ask Harper a hundred more questions, but more than anything he just wanted her to leave.

"And for the record, I didn't have any idea that you were Mitch Quinn until the moment I woke up in your bed that first morning."

Harper wanted to say more. She wanted to talk through this with Mitch, but what he said next made it obvious that he had no interest in a conversation. "I'm going somewhere," he said, "and when I come back I don't want to even know that you were ever here."

Harper stood motionless in the kitchen as Mitch headed for the door that led to London. When he disappeared, she quickly gathered her belongings, and in less than five minutes she made it out the front door.

Sitting on the floor, surrounded by London, Mitch couldn't see out the window, but he heard the sound of tires crunching in the driveway and imagined the red haze coming from fading taillights.

Harper didn't spin out of the driveway or squall tires on the pavement, she just left. When she needed advice the most, she felt that she had absolutely no one to turn to. London was gone. Tara was most likely sleeping with her ex-husband. Her mother wouldn't understand, and now Mitch Quinn hated her.

29

esterday, Harper had set her trip odometer as she backed out of Mitch Quinn's driveway, and she had forced herself not to look back, not to turn back, not to think about what could have been, or maybe even what should have been. The latter part of that equation had lasted until she crossed over the high-rise, the same one that she remembered crossing over on the way in just last week. In some ways, her trip to Emerald Isle felt like a blink. In other ways, it seemed like an eternity. For some reason, that's how long she felt like she'd known Mitch Quinn. Driving away from whatever it was that they'd had together seemed eerily similar to the way she felt when James left her. Although with Mitch, she couldn't be mad at him for cheating on her or treating her like a child.

One thing she had decided for sure is that she wasn't going to let what happened between her and Mitch knock her off balance the way losing James had, which is why she'd decided to lace up a pair of sneakers this morning and head for the park instead of cozying up on the couch with a pint of ice cream. In front of her, a one-mile trail with small hills winded through Bradford Pear trees. The dirt and grass didn't bother her knees like running on asphalt. When she made it back around to the park bench where her run had started, her long legs felt like jello. Nine minutes and two seconds ago she'd taken her first stride, she realized checking the app on her phone. Not a record, but not bad. Running times were relative. Her goal had always been to beat her last time.

The next day, the same park bench came a few seconds quicker, and Harper's breaths were a little more spread out. On the third day, she shaved off five more seconds, but midway into her second mile she found herself buckling over near an old stump. She knew she needed to stretch to drive the cramps out of her stomach, but it took a moment for her to force the action. Each day she ran three miles, which meant three laps.

When she finished running each day, she would wander to a nearby grassy field and unroll her purple yoga mat. In the middle of her downward dogs when she knew her mind should be relaxing, she'd thought over and over about how she would approach Tara today. She knew what she wanted to do—slap her across the face and throw the report that she'd been working on the last two days at her feet. At least she'd cleared her mind enough to make the decision not to meet Tara at the office, just in case she ended up doing something unprofessional.

It was Friday, and she noticed the soles of her shoes tapping the dirt as she waited, her fingernails tracing lines in the bench frame. She and Tara had run this trail together a hundred times over the years. But this time, when she spotted Tara in the distance, fake smile and fake boobs, she wanted to puke. It was amazing how quick your best friend could turn into an enemy, she thought to herself.

Tara, sporting a tight, black spandex suit, jogged up to the bench. Harper stood, her knees knocking.

"Hey, babe," Tara called out. "I've missed you."

Harper offered a fake smile of her own. "Hey, Tara."

No one else was around which was good. Harper had decided that she was going to jump straight to the point. No small talk. No more being fake or pretending that they were friends.

"When did you get back?" Tara inquired.

Harper figured that might be Tara's first question. When she'd sent Tara a text message, it had been simple and to the point: *Will you meet me for a jog at our park on Friday?*

"Are you sleeping with James?" Harper asked bluntly.

Tara's eyes bulged. "I can't believe you would accuse me of having sex with your ex," she exclaimed.

"Answer the question, Tara," Harper demanded. "Are you sleeping with James?"

"No," she replied forcefully.

She quizzed further. "Are you dating James?"

"No."

"Well, I should have known that if you weren't sleeping with him then you weren't dating him."

"That was a low blow, Harper."

"Well, it sure seems like there's something going on between the two of you that you're not telling me," Harper suggested.

"James and I are just friends."

"Friendly enough to be the one with him at the hospital?"

"You know you're being irrational, Harper. Instead of your first question being 'Is James okay?' you accused me of sleeping with him."

"I don't care if James is okay." That was a lie.

Tara furrowed her brow. "Well, just so you know, James *is* okay."

Harper fired her backup question. "So why were you at the hospital with him?"

"Because he called me, asking if I would get in touch with you."

Harper stepped back, literally and emotionally. This angle had never crossed her mind.

Tara continued. "He tried calling your home phone, but he didn't get you. Then he tried your cell phone, but, of course, we both know why he didn't get you there either."

A couple months after James had left and Harper hadn't heard a peep from him, she'd decided to change her phone numbers, which in hindsight made no sense. It wasn't like he was stalking her. It was the opposite. He wasn't calling or coming around at all. He'd just up and left.

"What happened to James?" Harper finally asked.

"I thought you said that you didn't care," Tara snapped.

"Of course I care, Tara. We were married for years."

"He got into a car accident and had to spend a couple days in the hospital. But he's fine now."

"What did you tell him when he asked you to get up with me?"

"I told him that you were out of town."

Harper felt like a complete idiot now. "Thanks," she uttered.

"How about we run off some of this anxiety?" Tara suggested.

Harper thought about declining. Calling it a day and heading home for the ice cream she'd been holding out on these last few days. But if Tara was willing to stick around after the accusations she'd made, she felt like she owed it to her to follow through on the plan to jog.

Before beginning the laps that Harper had never expected would actually happen, they walked to Tara's car to put away the shark attack report. "I'll read this at the office later," Tara mentioned. "I'm sure you did a great job."

When Harper and Tara found their stride, Harper felt herself beginning to loosen up, physically and emotionally. As usual, Tara had a way of making her laugh even in stressful situations.

"Do you remember that time when the stripper jumped out of your cake?" Tara asked out of the blue.

Of course she remembered it. The image of not just one, but two male strippers exploding out of the largest cake she'd ever seen, wearing overalls and oil, had etched itself into her brain. "Yes, how could I forget?" she replied, rolling her eyes.

"Someone has a birthday coming up," Tara reminded her. Then, she watched Harper shake her ponytail repetitively. "I'm just saying . . ."

"You are not allowed to throw me a party ever again," Harper reminded Tara, giggling. "I asked you not to do that when I got married, and James gave me a hard time for weeks after I told him about half-naked men trying to give me lap dances."

"Don't worry, I wouldn't waste my money again. I spent five hundred dollars on those Chippendales and then the bride-to-be walked out."

"It wasn't like it took the excitement out of it for you," Harper recalled. "If my memory serves me correctly, you showed up the next morning with Chip, or was it Dale, on your arm?"

"I still felt bad. I always do stupid stuff like that and then regret it when it is too late. I did apologize though."

"And I forgave you like I always do."

"This time I forgive you, Harper."

"For what?" she asked between breaths.

"For thinking that I was sleeping with James."

Tara spent the next two miles filling her in on how the car accident had happened. She told her about James's broken arm, bruised ribs, and scraped up face. In a way, Harper felt like it served him right, but she also felt bad for him. Ultimately, she was glad that he would be okay and even more relieved to find out that Tara wasn't sleeping with him. If he'd called Tara looking for her, it meant that he'd probably left the woman that he'd left her for.

"You want to slow our pace down to a walk?" Harper asked after they finished the fourth mile. Tara had always been better at running than she, and Harper could tell that the extra mile was taking a toll on her body.

"How about you rest at the bench while I run one more mile, then we can walk a couple together and you can tell me all about Emerald Isle."

Harper plopped down on the bench and watched Tara's perfectly rounded cheeks bounce as the soles of her shoes carried her into the distance. Then, she smiled as a group of men jogging toward Tara became trapped in her features. When they passed Tara, Harper noticed how it appeared as though each had a perfectly aligned spring that caused his head to turn back. She laughed as she caught them studying Tara's butt. Then, as the cheerful runners neared the bench supporting her own backside, Harper couldn't help but take advantage of the situation. "Like what you saw, guys?"

Busted. Their faces turned red and their legs began moving at a quicker pace. None of them said a word, and the thought kept Harper entertained until Tara made it back around. Harper had spent most of her time stretching as she waited. Tara slowed her stride as she neared, and the two picked up the same walking pace almost instantly.

"Tell me about Emerald Isle," Tara suggested. "Not the work part, the fun part."

Harper figured she'd start from the beginning. She knew Tara would laugh about the first motel where she had almost ended up staying. If it wasn't for Mitch, she still had no idea where she would have stayed. Harper thought about leaving Mitch out of her story, but then she realized that Mitch was the story.

"If I tell you something do you promise you won't tell anyone?" Harper asked, finding her rhythm again, not just on the hills but in her conversation with Tara. She'd always been able to talk to her about anything and everything. Bottling this all up had been eating at her constantly the last few days.

Three miles later, Harper had no idea how many laps they'd walked, but she knew she'd poured out her entire heart. Tara now knew pretty much everything that had happened between her and Mitch Quinn.

"Have you called him?"

Harper wrinkled her brow. "I'm not going to call him."

"I realize that you just spent twenty minutes explaining to me how stupid what you did was, but the entire time you talked about how much fun you had with Mitch. How much the two of you have in common. How you wished the circumstances were different."

"Yeah, all that is true, but the circumstances aren't different. They'll never be different."

"Listen, Harper. You're not like me. You don't just sleep with a man the first time you meet him."

"But I did."

"Exactly, which means you had some type of real connection with Mitch." Tara veered off the path and Harper followed her to a cluster of trees overlooking the spot where Harper had been practicing yoga the last few days. They sat on a protruding root system as Tara told Harper the truth. "You're an attractive woman. You've had countless opportunities to have meaningless sex with hot guys. I know this first hand. Remember, we were in college together. Frat parties. Dance clubs. You've probably had more men hit on you than I have, and I walk around asking for it. I mean, I kind of even paid for it," Tara mentioned, motioning to her breasts.

"Thanks for cheering me up, Tara, but what happened between Mitch and I isn't going to amount to anything. Maybe in another time in another world it would have. But reality is reality. We can't go back and change what happened."

30

The day that Harper had walked out Mitch's front door with her bags packed, he spent the entire afternoon and evening surrounded by memories of London. He felt like he had cheated on his soulmate. Felt like he had lost a part of her that he could never get back. He felt like he owed her an apology, too. He'd never imagined being with anyone else. He'd only imagined dying and spending an infinite life with her in Heaven. Hoping that God would allow marriage there. Honestly, he didn't know what the Bible had to say about that subject. His dad had once argued with a preacher for hours over whether dogs went to Heaven. Mitch wasn't really sure that it mattered. What mattered is that he wanted to touch London again. Hold her in his arms and make love to her for the first time. But instead, he was still here—on Earth, where instead of making love to London, he'd made love to London's sister, and he'd actually enjoyed it. More than enjoyed it, he'd fallen in love with Addison—or Harper. Not knowing which name to call her made him feel even more guilt, but he'd decided he'd think of her as Harper since Addison had been a lie. Now he figured he'd probably end up in hell for what he'd done. What purpose did

Heaven serve now anyway, he contemplated? God had never come through on his end of the deal—the deal that Mitch had made with him over a year ago. Once London died, he was supposed to die, too. He wasn't supposed to be alive one year later, meeting her sister and falling in love again. He realized that he was probably the only cancer patient in the world who hadn't prayed for a cure.

Mitch had started reading page one of London's memoir before Harper made it over the high rise bridge. He completely lost track of time as the story pulled him into a life where only memories existed. There had never been a need for a clock in the room where London had spent the last days of her life. The room was as timeless as the photographs that now filled it. When darkness took over the room, Mitch found indentations on his hands from holding the book. His neck was tired from holding his head over the pages as he flipped them to the sound of a swish. His eyes were weary. He needed a beer.

That night, he had one at the bar where he'd met Harper. He thought if he went back there he could quit thinking about her by making a more recent memory of the place. He wanted to only think about London, about their life, their love story. The one that had meant so much to London that she'd written a book about it. When he made it home at two o'clock in the morning, he brushed his teeth and watched the bitter taste circle into the drain pipe, wishing he could disappear with it and wishing he'd never gone back to the bar.

He called Doc the next day and suggested that he and Hannah spend a little more time away. "I've seen signs that Donald is still around," he lied. It wasn't that he didn't miss Hannah or want her to come back home, he just didn't want her to see him like this. He needed to pull things back together. When he spoke to Hannah on the phone, he remembered why he wanted to live. Life now was about more than just him, which is why later that day he felt bad when he picked up a twelve pack at the grocery store. Being there reminded him of the time when he and Hannah had run into Harper. It also reminded him of all the times he and London had shopped there together. He battled back and forth between memories of the two, and he hated it. When he got home, he sat the beer on the boards by his feet as a cool breeze blew beneath the covered porch, dancing with the swing he occupied. Each time he went inside he left the cans in a cooler outside. By the time the sun went down, six of them were in his recycling bin. He'd always preferred to drink alone, at least if he was going to have too many. That way he couldn't do anything too stupid or say anything he would regret. The strings of curse words that flew out of his mouth were between him and the moon. He tried to play his guitar and sing, but he just couldn't. It hurt too much.

On Thursday, Mitch finished his last beer and decided that he wouldn't be going back to buy more. Instead, he called Pastor Kenny.

"Thanks for coming over on short notice," Mitch said when he arrived.

"Of course, that's what friends are for," Kenny responded, meaning it. He'd always believed that God showed up in the every-day lives of friends just as much as he showed up in a church service on a Sunday morning. "What's on your mind?" he asked when he realized Mitch seemed quieter than normal; a bit tense, too.

"A lot."

Kenny just nodded his head in understanding. In situations like this, he hoped to listen more than talk.

Mitch stared at the boards beneath their feet. Just yesterday he'd been sitting here half drunk, sharing a beer with no one. Now he was sharing a swing with the pastor. "I don't think I believe in God anymore," Mitch admitted.

Kenny thought in silence for a moment. He could say some-thing preachy like, *God still believes in you*, but what good would that do?

None, most likely. Or he could tell Mitch all the reasons why *he* believed in God, but that probably wouldn't get them very far either.

"Fair enough," Kenny finally said. "Why not?" he asked, nonchalantly.

"If God is this magnificent, powerful, loving being, then why does he let bad things happen to good people?"

"Ah, the age-old question." Yet another chance for him to get preachy. *Well, Adam and Eve chose this path for us. They chose to disobey God and let evil seep into our world.* Or he could paraphrase a verse like: *All things work for the good of those who love God.* "I'm not sure, Mitch," he said honestly. "I mean, I know what the Bible says, but I don't think that's what you want to hear right now."

Mitch shrugged. "If I don't believe in God then I guess I really don't believe the Bible either." His hands were folded but not for prayer.

"That makes sense." Kenny paused for a moment. "What bad things are we talking about here?" He had an idea, but he didn't want to assume.

"Why did London have to die?"

Kenny had never been able to answer this question for himself, so he knew he couldn't answer it for Mitch. "Mitch, you know I don't have an answer for that question. God knows I miss her, too. She was a special person that touched a lot of lives." Maybe that was the answer, maybe it was that simple and that complex at the same time.

"I was supposed to die of cancer, too, Kenny."

"What?" he asked, stunned.

Mitch studied the ridged bark on a nearby tree as he spoke. "When I found out London was dying of cancer, I was just about to start treatment for my own cancer. The doctors didn't seem hopeful about the outcome in the first place, so I decided to let nature take its course."

"Mitch, I had no idea." He wished he had known so he could have prayed for him. Talked to him. Loved on him more.

"Not many people did. I kind of kept it to myself."

"But, Mitch, most people who think they are going to die from cancer but end up living would see that as a miracle."

Mitch agreed with a nod. "Not me. I felt more like God was punishing me."

"How can a God you don't believe in punish you, Mitch?"

Ouch. That one dug deep. Mitch took a moment to think. "That's just one more reason I don't believe in him. If he were real, he would have let me die."

"Why? So that the rest of us could sit here and beg God for answers about why another great person died?"

"I'm not a great person, Kenny."

"I disagree."

"Great people don't have sex with their soulmate's sister on the one-year anniversary of her death."

Kenny was beginning to put the pieces of Mitch's shattered puzzle together. The lady he'd brought to church, that's where he remembered her from, London's funeral. Harper Addison was London's sister. It all made sense now, except for Mitch having sex with her, although Kenny did appreciate the honesty which he had come to expect from Mitch. Mitch had never been one to dance around the truth.

"Mitch, great people make mistakes every day."

"She lied to me."

"London's sister?"

"Yes."

The swing was as still as dust in an abandoned house. "Why did you bring her to church?"

"I didn't."

Kenny furrowed his brow.

"She brought me to church," Mitch clarified.

"Was that a mistake?"

"I don't know." Mitch tapped his feet on the flooring. "At that point, I didn't know about her lie."

"If I'm going to be of any help you're going to have to give me a little more information."

Mitch spent the next five minutes confessing to the pastor. As he spoke, he didn't feel judged one bit, never had by Kenny.

"Great people make mistakes every day, Mitch," was his response.

"You said that already."

"Yes, but this time I'm talking about Harper."

"So are you saying what I think you're saying?"

"That depends. What do you think I'm saying?"

"That I shouldn't have any problems forgiving her and continuing a relationship with London's sister—who lives two hundred miles away."

"I'm not saying that, Mitch, but I'm also not, not saying that."

"Then what are you saying?"

"I think you should forgive her. What you do after that, well that's up to you." He waited for a response from Mitch, but one didn't come. Mitch just sat there with his face in his hands. "As far as you not believing in God, I think you need to close your eyes."

"Don't you mean open my eyes?"

"Nope, close them."

"Oh, you mean pray." Mitch shook his head side to side. "I'm not in the mood to pray to someone that doesn't exist."

"That's not what I'm saying, but it's not a bad idea. What I'm saying is you're only seeing what you want to see. So, close your eyes and see reality. Sure, London died from cancer. Sure, that sucks. You didn't die. In my eyes, closed or open, that's a miracle, but I can see why you don't see that. But you have to see the other miracles in your life as well."

"Like what?"

"Hannah is alive. Cancer could have taken her, too, but it didn't. The two of you have each other. You're her dad now, Mitch. You're the best thing she has in this world."

"Doc is the best thing she has in this world."

"Then why did Doc let you adopt her?"

Mitch shrugged his shoulders.

Kenny went on. "You must have wanted to live if you ended up having chemotherapy or radiation."

"I didn't."

"Then if you didn't want to live, why did you decide to have treatment?"

"Like I said, I didn't."

On Friday, Hannah came back home and Mitch greeted her with the biggest hug he had to offer. Her shoes were three feet off the ground, her legs dangling loosely as he squeezed her. She planted a kiss on his cheek and smiled a big smile.

"I missed you," she admitted.

"I missed you more," he guaranteed.

He needed Hannah more than Hannah needed him. He'd been looking at it the other way around, but now he knew the truth. She was the girl in his life. She was his miracle—the reason for all of the miracles he'd been staring at with his eyes wide opened but too blind to see.

31

The next few weeks of Harper's life moved slowly, like a ditch bank eroding over time. She continued to run several times a week at the park. Tara would join her about half of the time, and the two of them had been able to glide right past the misunderstanding about James. Harper thought about calling James on several occasions, especially on nights when she felt lonely, when her life felt about as exciting as a library, but she didn't want to reopen that can of worms. It meant a lot to her that he had tried to contact her after his car accident, but she wanted to leave it at that.

Even though she and Mitch had only had a brief relationship—if that word could even define their time together—she often felt a void. She didn't want to call what they had a fling either. It felt much more impactful than a fling. Even though it lasted less than a week, the taste of love still lingered within her.

The truth was, most any single woman would have slipped into bed with Mitch Quinn without hesitation, Harper figured. A man like Mitch didn't come along every day. Most women with any experience with men had learned by the time they reached the age of twenty-five that a woman was lucky to find even one like him in a lifetime. He was the type of man you want to call home about, the type of man you would want to raise your children. The added bonus came in the form of his physical appearance; Mitch was the specimen of a man whom a woman dreamed of having sleepless nights with while working on making those babies. She'd also most likely be a little selfish and just practice quite often for pleasure.

Harper often thought back to the night she met Mitch. She remembered the look in his baby blue eyes that said there was someone else. Someone no other woman would ever be able to replace. For most women, when you stumbled across a man like that, you hoped for at least one night of passion. Anything else was a bonus. Harper now knew why she'd noticed that look in Mitch's eye—London. His heart had been reserved for someone he could no longer have. In hindsight, she'd noticed how that look seemed to have faded as they got to know one another. She wasn't sure what to think of that, but she kept finding herself wishing they'd met on different terms. Wishing she'd been honest with him the moment when she found out to whom he belonged. She also wished she hadn't stolen his heart from her very own sister, but she had. The clock couldn't be turned back now. Words couldn't be unsaid. Actions couldn't be untaken. She could only imagine how he felt now. How he'd dealt with the days and weeks since he'd told her to leave. She wondered what thoughts swirled in his mind as he read the romantic story London had written about her and Mitch's brief life together. Of all the things the focus of the memoir could have been on, she'd made it about her journey with Mitch. Harper figured that he probably felt guilt even though nothing that happened had been his fault. Like her, he'd simply followed his heart. Unlike her, he'd ended it all the moment he discovered the truth.

These were the thoughts that Harper wrestled with on nights that felt like they'd never end. She'd promised herself that she wouldn't let what happened in Emerald Isle affect her this way, but it had. It was as if she had no control over it, no matter how busy she stayed. Running. Eating dinner out with friends. Watching television. Reading books. Working at night when she should be doing something fun. None of this seemed to keep her mind off Mitch Quinn. She knew that in time her heart would heal, or at least she hoped it would.

Harper also hoped that when she went to the OB-GYN all the tests would come back normal. She had no legitimate reason to think that Mitch would have passed along an STD. She doubted that he'd even had sex with anyone since London. To her knowledge, he hadn't even had sex with London. This fact bothered her nearly as much as the fact that she'd slept with London's Mitch, because not only had she slept with him, but her sister hadn't. Her sister hadn't known what it felt like to give herself completely to Mitch Quinn. To share the most intimate physical moments that two people can share. Harper knew that sex had the power to bond two people in more ways than the simple meshing of their flesh. A story she'd once researched on sex, for work, enlightened her on how the human body reacts to such a physical connection. Both parties are indefinitely connected in ways beyond what the mind can comprehend—emotionally, mentally, and physically. These are the reasons she'd been so careful not to give in to the desire to have random sex, even before she fully understood the true power of making love with another human being. It all made sense. It shed more light on the reason the Bible teaches to save yourself for marriage. Something London had done but not her. It was odd, though, she hadn't ever actually felt guilty for the actual act of having sex with Mitch. She'd felt guilty because of his connection to London. She'd also worried because of the risk of an STD.

When the doctor asked her how many sexual partners she'd recently been intimate with, Harper furrowed her brow. It took her a moment to realize that he didn't really know her. All types of women probably came to him to get checked for diseases. Promiscuous women. Prostitutes. Women like her who had only had sex with one man in the last year but were freaking out that one encounter could alter her entire life's course. When she explained this to the doctor, in more words than necessary, he didn't seem to change his temperament one bit. The office was still cold, and the air seeping in beneath the paper gown had only intensified the shivering sensation she'd felt since walking in the front door. He asked if she had any reason to think that she might have an STD. Any signs. Any information. He went through a list of possibilities that nearly made her gag. When she answered, *No*, he said they would test for the most common possibilities and perform other regular tests as well. She consented to his suggestions and felt dirty for being there for such a reason. She couldn't help but wonder if Tara had been through this before.

The next day at work she slipped into Tara's office and asked her as much.

"Of course," Tara said. "I worry a little bit every time I have sex. Even if it's with the same man over and over, you never know whose bed he's been slipping off to on lonely nights."

"Tell me about it," Harper responded, thinking of James, but simultaneously remembering the accusations she'd recently made, hoping that Tara didn't take her comment as a jab. If she did, she didn't say anything or show signs of letting it bother her. The two of them hadn't spoken a word about it since the first day when they ran in the park together following Harper's return to Silver Spring. Harper *had* heard back from Tara about the shark report she gave her that day. Tara absolutely loved the idea of sending a crew to Emerald Isle. In a way, Harper wanted to go with them, to show up at Mitch's door and pour her heart out, but she had decided that if ever a move was to be made, he'd have to make it. She didn't want to put him in an awkward position. More honestly, she didn't want to feel the sting of rejection.

"So have you ever had an STD?" Harper asked Tara.

Slowly, Tara's head nodded north and south, her lips pursed. The skin around Harper's eyelids stretched as she unknowingly visually displayed her surprise. Although she wasn't sure why it shocked her. Tara had run out of fingers to count men on during college.

"Which one?" she had to ask.

"Chlamydia."

"That one is treatable," Harper sighed. She'd taken it upon herself to perform hours of research on the subject. She now knew as much about STD's as the doctor who had run the tests on her. Well, maybe not to the degree as a medical professional in his field, but she knew enough to know that she didn't want any of them.

The subject soon changed from sexual diseases to work. Outside Tara's office, as the two of them had talked personally, the scene had been frantic as usual. A large glass window framed the everyday grind of staff members pressing to meet deadlines, making phone calls, researching online, stressing.

"Are you sure you don't want to accompany the film crew to Emerald Isle?"

"I'm positive," Harper hissed.

"Suit yourself." Tara peered at Harper for a few moments. "Mitch might have thawed out a little by now."

"Funny," Harper rebutted before shifting the subject away from Mitch. "What I actually came in here to tell you is that I received an email from Officer Dunlap this morning. There has been another shark attack. This one near Cape Lookout, North Carolina."

"Oh my goodness," Tara responded.

"The good news is that the injury is not life threatening."

"I'm glad to hear that." Tara searched her desk for a note she'd wanted to show Harper. When she found it beneath some loose papers and a granola bar, she handed it over. "I spoke to this gentleman earlier. He's a shark expert. He seems to think that the migratory patterns of the fish the sharks prey on have something to do with the number of attacks. So we're sending a team of experts down there with the crew. They'll be able to explain the science behind this phenomena."

— —

A few days later, Harper found herself sitting in a leather chair in the doctor's examining room. This time it felt much more comfortable since she didn't have to take her clothes off or be poked or prodded, but she noticed that the feeling of anxiety seemed more prominent than the day of the actual tests, which made sense. Today was reveal day.

When the doc came in, glasses perched on the top of his head, she tried to read him, but that was pointless. The man was as stoic as a statue. He'd been through this thousands of times, delivered bad news and good news. Now it was time for her news—the only news that mattered to her. She sat, knees crossed and arms folded. Now that it was time to hear the results, she wished she had brought someone with her. Tara would have come. Her mom would have come, but never in a thousand years would she have brought her mom here today. She hadn't even told her about Mitch Quinn let alone that they'd had sex and that she was going to the doctor to make sure she was clean. When the doctor shared the news, Harper pictured what her face must have looked like. Frozen. Frightened. Relieved. All at the same time. She didn't expect to hear what she'd heard, and it took a few minutes to digest the findings. All of the tests had come back negative, except for one.

32

The next three weeks of Mitch's life—after Doc brought Hannah home from Durham—ended up being some of the best weeks he had ever experienced. He felt rejuvenated, like a new leaf in his life had been turned over. He still missed London like crazy. Harper, too. It seemed as though everything that had happened during the time he'd spent with Harper had refreshed his way of thinking, even though it had taken him some time to realize it—kind of like a frozen computer needing someone to click control, alt, delete, and just restart the thing so it could start doing what it was meant to do. He'd been in hibernation for way too long.

With Hannah's help, he fell in love with photography again. The two of them began taking hundreds of pictures every day. One afternoon as the sun sank in the distance, he pulled his Jeep into a dusty field on a whim. Hannah had spotted a wild turkey. She found the creature to be both magnificent and funny. The turkey didn't seem to like the idea of being photographed which made the adventure that much more exciting for Hannah. Every step the two of them took toward the turkey, the turkey took two in the opposite direction. When they started walking faster, so did the turkey. When they jogged toward it, the turkey's scrawny limbs sped up.

Finally, everything became still, and the turkey attempted to camouflage itself in a patch of tall grass. Mitch could see its head peeking above the weeds, and he taught Hannah how to move in slowly like a mountain lion on its prey. They could have used the zoom lens and taken the same shots from where the chase had started, but Hannah wanted to get up close, wanted to feel the intensity of the moment. She had mimicked Mitch's every step, and he put her on his shoulders to capture a better view of the creature.

As Mitch hung tightly onto Hannah's legs, she snapped away. Eventually, the turkey realized his cover had been blown and he made a mad dash for a patch of woods on the far side of the field. As they watched his little limbs haul boogie, Hannah began laughing hysterically. "Look at him go, Daddy." Mitch smiled. He'd come to love hearing her say that word. He loved the sound it made as it rolled off her little tongue. He knew every child must long to call a man daddy; he was humbled that she felt comfortable enough to give him that title.

Hannah wanted to continue the chase as the turkey stopped where the trees started, but Mitch knew they had caused enough commotion in this turkey's day and he explained to her why they should retreat to the Jeep.

Mitch knew that photographing animals would be a great starting point for Hannah, who seemed to love being behind the lens. Her shots turned out very appealing for a child. It wasn't uncommon for an amateur to produce captivating shots of a furry little creature. The quality of camera didn't even need to be professional grade. Mitch had noticed time after time that when put in front of a lens, dogs, cats, and birds will do all the work for the photographer as long as a little patience is practiced. Animals always seemed to open their mouths at the right time, turn their heads to just the right position, and lift their front legs for the perfect shot.

Mitch and Hannah often walked the city streets in the mornings, searching for more challenging work. One morning they stopped at a fountain, and Mitch worked his way around as the water fell from one level to the next. He found angles that would produce reflections in the water drops, and he knew some would display the buildings in the background while others would capture images of Hannah dropping pennies and splashing her delicate hands in the water. He taught her how to take similar shots.

They ate pizza in the plaza near the fountain and then ordered ice cream from the shop across the street. Mitch enjoyed mint chocolate chip while Hannah licked around the outer edges of an ice cream sandwich. He decided to start a scrapbook of the pictures Hannah had taken, and with the ones he'd shot, maybe he would add some of them to his portfolio.

For a moment he thought about taking on a photography assignment, maybe traveling to some place he'd never been, but with one glance at the young lady holding his right hand and skipping on the sidewalk that thought faded. Even though he had no college degree mounted on his wall or even a single photography class under his belt, he had devoted his entire 20's to traveling the globe; he had simply picked up a camera at the age of sixteen and taught himself how to make art out of the simplest of objects. He vividly remembered one of his high school teachers telling him that he would never amount to anything. A teacher should never tell a student that, he realized, both then and now. He would have died to see her face when Barbara Walters interviewed him in Times Square several years ago.

Mitch's work had hung in museums from Washington, D.C. to Paris, France, and his photography graced the pages of the most prestigious magazines around the world. But there was no bus, or train, or airplane that could get him to where he wanted to spend the rest of his life. There was no one else to impress, no one to please.

Ironically, he had encountered several opportunities to meet women lately. The first, a lady at a gas station—pump number three wouldn't take her credit card, and Mitch watched as she went through the motions. Insert card. Remove quickly. A string of beeping noises. Press the *pay here with credit* button. Insert card again. Another string of beeps. Twist the card, insert and remove quickly. Beep. Beep. Beep. Push the credit button again and insert card once more.

Mitch knew the machine wasn't going to accept the card; that particular pump wouldn't take his either, he had tried. He rested his sunglasses on his head. He could tell she was annoyed. Needed assistance. Wanted an answer.

Mitch's voice echoed beneath the canopy, "I couldn't get that pump to take my card either."

She smiled, American Express in hand. "I thought I was doing something wrong. I can't ever figure out which way to turn these things. They are so aggravating sometimes."

The black suit pants and gray blouse fit her body perfectly. The matching jacket was hanging in the back seat. She'd probably taken it off to let go of a hard day at the office, Mitch assumed, which meant she wasn't in the mood for denial at the gas pump. He grinned. "I know what you mean. I'll be finished here in just a minute and you can have my spot."

"Thank you so much."

When the nozzle clicked, Mitch returned it to the pump. Her arms were crossed and resting on the top of her door, watching him. Waiting. She could have circled around to any of the other open pumps but hadn't.

Mitch smiled thinking about vultures. Not the ones with black feathers and an annoying squall, but the ones with a *you-know-what* for a brain. He wondered how many of them just this week had hit on the woman at pump three with dangly silver earrings and high heels. Wondered how many she had turned down.

It had always amazed Mitch at how men wonder why women constantly turn them down, but then they continue to use the same dimwitted methodology. The right moment is the key ingredient, and this was one of those right moments. There should be a man in a blue jumpsuit pumping this woman's gas. She deserved to relax in the car and listen to her Miles Davis CD while an attendant washed her windows and checked the tire pressure, not because she couldn't do it herself but because the smell of jasmine perfume shouldn't be tainted by even a single drop of the highest octane gasoline.

"Would you like to have dinner with me tonight?" the lady with a small red handbag in the front seat of her gold Mercedes asked Mitch.

He appreciated the offer, even felt it bring a smile to his face. "Sorry but I already have a date this evening," he said politely. It wasn't a lie, he'd promised Hannah that he'd take her to a movie. She loved watching movies at the theater—animated, of course, and eating popcorn with butter, lots of butter. She also begged to sit in Mitch's lap, so she could see better, she always said. Each time he told himself that next time he'd make her sit in her own seat, but that hadn't happened yet. Another thing that hadn't happened is Hannah making it through an entire movie without falling asleep.

— ～

A week or so after Mitch's encounter with the lady at the gas station, he found himself in a similar situation on Highway 58. This time with Hannah in her booster seat in the back. He didn't know a lick about fixing cars, but he did have a vehicle of his own, that happened to be running just fine. Her hood was raised, and like a mechanic she was leaning over the engine. At first, the wheels on Mitch's Jeep blazed right past the old Ford pickup, but the wind from his draft caught the cotton dress of a woman in desperate need of help. Her tanned legs caught his eye. He stopped just ahead and reversed on the grassy bank.

"Need some help?"

Without looking in his direction, she responded, "Please," annoyance lining her voice.

He could tell this woman was much more disgruntled than the last and he was worried that if he told her he didn't know the difference between a carburetor and a catalytic converter, she might tell him to get back in his vehicle and head wherever he was headed.

"What seems to be the problem?" He'd heard that line in a movie, probably a handful of movies.

"I have been standing here for fifteen minutes and at least ten cars have passed by but not a single one stopped, until you. I pried open my hood so someone might, but I guess what I really needed to do was lift up my dress and show a little more leg." She smirked a bit as she said it, but Mitch kept his mouth shut. That wasn't the reason he'd stopped, but this six-foot stranger did have nice legs.

"Did it just cut off on you?"

"Yeah, it began stalling out, and I was barely able to pull off the road."

He tugged on a couple of hoses and unscrewed two caps to look inside. "Your fluids look good and your pistons seem tight." The look on her face told Mitch that she had no idea what that meant, and to be honest neither did he. It sounded good, though, he thought.

"Are the keys in the ignition?"

She pointed. "Yes. Go ahead. Try it."

Mitch could tell by the tone in her voice that *she* had tried it more than once. "I need to find out if the engine will turn over. Could be the battery or the alternator." He twisted the key, listening as the engine attempted to roll over but couldn't. He studied the gauges.

Oil level looked good, the needle was right between that thing and the other thing. As he studied the other gauges on the dash, Mitch discovered a pot of gold. "I've got good news."

"Really?" she asked, walking toward the open door.

"Looks like you're just out of gas." Mitch glanced in the direction he'd traveled from. "There's a station just down the road. I would be more than happy to take you to it or bring back a can of gas if you would rather stay with your truck." He figured she knew this was his way of saying: *If you think I might kidnap you—with a little girl in my backseat.*

"Let me get my purse."

If he were on the singles market, it would appear that gasoline would be his lucky charm, he recognized, as he caught glimpses out of the corner of his eye of this young woman's hair blowing with the wind as they drove to and from the nearest gas station.

"How much do I owe you for this, Mitch?" Julia asked as he funneled the gas into the tank on the left side of her truck. Hannah had asked her name as soon as she had climbed into the Jeep.

"Not a dime," he answered. "Just pay it forward."

Every time he met a woman now, he found himself not only comparing her to London, but oddly enough, to Harper as well. The two of them had so much in common, yet they were completely different. He still wasn't sure how he hadn't picked up on Harper being London's sister sooner than he had. Honestly, he just didn't know if any woman would come along that would be worthy of a tryout to be Hannah's potential mother.

Hannah was his world now, and the two of them were turning his house in Emerald Isle into their home. She would swim with dolphins in the summer, start kindergarten in the fall, and play soccer in the spring. They would drive to Duke every year and celebrate Cancer-Free day, and it would remind Mitch of one of the happiest moments in his life—the day Dr. Thorpe announced

Hannah's going away party. She had cried and Mitch had cried, too. He would never forget the countless nights of prayers and tears it took to bring that day to fruition. He hated that London hadn't been there to hold Hannah's hand as they walked into freedom.

God had, no doubt, had His hand on Hannah the Banana, as London Adams liked to call her little blue-eyed angel, Mitch now realized. God had his hand on him, too, and even though Mitch hadn't pulled his Bible out of the drawer until the day Doc brought Hannah home from Durham, he knew God had been the one to carry him along the broken road that life had set before him. "I will never leave you nor forsake you" were the words in the first verse he found after he brushed the dust from the cover. In that moment he'd thought of Harper, wondering if she would have sneezed. He also wondered what she had been doing for the past few weeks. He wasn't the only one thinking about her. Hannah asked about Harper almost every day. At bedtime, she always asked to pray for her and London. Mitch hadn't stepped foot on the property next door since he'd told Harper to leave. The porch light had flickered out last week, and the grass was growing over the rocks in the driveway. He had thought about calling to let her know he had forgiven her. Pastor Kenny had continued to tell him that holding on to his anger against Harper would damage him more than it would her. Mitch had taken Hannah to church every Sunday since his talk with Kenny on the front porch.

Mitch also wanted to thank Harper for leaving Snuggles. At first, he had been irate when he found Snuggles, not just because that was the final dagger that linked Addison to Harper but because he'd asked the funeral home director to place it in her casket, so London could be buried with Snuggles. He wanted to know why Harper had taken it out, but he'd probably never get the chance to ask her. On the contrary, he'd kind of been glad Harper did because he'd been regretting ever putting London's bear in there in the first place.

Even if Mitch wanted to ask Harper these questions, he realized he still didn't have her phone number. Of course, he could probably get it from Doc. He and Doc had talked in detail about the memoir. He nearly lost his cool with Doc when Doc admitted to mailing the book to Harper, but then Doc told him that he had no idea what had been in the package that had been in his possession for nearly a year. London had actually initially mailed it to him sealed inside another package and asked him to send it on a specific date.

Mitch had read every word of the book—twice. The first reading took only two days. The next reading took a week and a half as he read every night after putting Hannah to bed. He found out a few things about London and Harper's childhood that London hadn't told him, like they had both been stung by a jellyfish while on vacation in Emerald Isle. He also laughed his way through a story about one of their friends in college streaking at a Baltimore Orioles game. He also found out the truth to another red flag Harper had raised, one he hadn't previously noticed—the story about her banging London's finger with a hammer. He found himself humbled at how highly London thought of him, but he knew that he wasn't half the man she made him out to be. Sure, he'd loved her with every ounce of his being, still did, but in the end he hadn't been able to fulfill his promise. That's what made the ending of the book so difficult. The words he'd spoken to London—words he thought would come true but hadn't.

Snuggles spent every night in Hannah's arms, and she assured Mitch that neither Snuggles nor she could fall asleep until he read *Good Night Moon* at least twice. Tonight was no different, and Hannah wanted him to stay in her bed with her and Snuggles. "Can you please stay again?" she pleaded.

After she'd come back home, he'd stayed with her the next few nights in her new bed—where he could still breathe in the scent of Harper's perfume—but since then he'd been trying to break the habit. She needed to learn that he had his own bed and she had hers.

"Big girls get to sleep by themselves, Hannah, and you are a big girl."

"If I'm a big girl, why do I cry when you leave?"

Wow. How in the world was he supposed to answer that question?

Mitch did his best. "You miss me, and it's okay to miss people. It's okay to cry, too."

"I miss London," she admitted, frankly. "And Addison."

"I know you do, sweetie. I miss them, too." He hadn't told Hannah that Addison's name was really Harper or that she and London were sisters. Honestly, he doubted he ever would.

"Daddy, would you be mad at me if I told you the reason I cry at night is because I know you have to sleep alone?"

Mitch wrapped his arms around Hannah and pulled her close to his chest, close enough that she couldn't see the tears building in the corners of his eyes then filing down his cheeks. She was so smart, so perceptive. Here he was assuming she'd been crying because *she* had to sleep alone.

"Snuggles will sleep with you if you would like," she offered.

"He's your bear now, honey, you keep him."

Hannah talked into his shirt as Mitch rubbed her back. "When I get a new mommy, I'll let her sleep with you."

33

itch had forgotten about Harper's birthday until he flipped the calendar on the fridge to a new month this morning. The blue ink and neatly drawn daisy in the Friday, July 3rd block reminded him of what she'd said as she drew the flower beside the words *Addison's 30th!*: *This is the day I will become an old woman.* He'd laughed, and until her abrupt departure he had planned on giving her a small present, something sentimental. Instead, he had decided that today he would ask Doc for her phone number, and he would call her to wish her a happy birthday.

In thirty-one years, he had learned that a man should never leave anything unsaid. Although he wasn't sure what the future held for either him or Harper—though he was almost certain their paths would lead in opposite directions—there were things he wanted to say, questions he needed to ask.

Mitch shifted his attention to Hannah. They'd just come in from a bike ride down the sidewalk in front of his house that stretched across most of the island. During this time of year, the bike path stayed busy. They'd passed at least twenty people within a one-mile stretch. Some walking. Some jogging. Some riding bikes like he and Hannah. On days when they had nothing else to do, the two of them would sit on the porch swing and watch people pass by.

"Can we eat on the porch and watch people?" Hannah asked.

"Sure, just let me finish making our peanut butter and jelly sandwiches." That's what Mitch had been doing when he noticed that the calendar needed to be flipped.

"Which would you like today, strawberry or grape?" he asked.

"Strawberry, please." Hannah grinned. "Can I sit on the porch and wait for you?"

"Sure," Mitch said. "Just stay on the porch and leave the front door open." He kept his ears open as he spread the peanut butter and jelly. He could hear the sound of the chains grinding on the swing as Hannah swayed back and forth, and in his mind's eye he could see her two little bare feet dangling. He finished the sandwiches and grabbed two cups from the cabinet. "Would you like orange juice or sweet tea?" he called out. He didn't know why he even asked, she almost always picked orange juice.

"Sweet tea, please," is the response he heard.

Mitch immediately raised his head. His ears perked up. Really? He had to be hearing things. He followed the sound of her voice to the screen door, then he saw her face—just as beautiful as he remembered it. The voice hadn't been Hannah's; he'd known that as soon as he'd heard the first syllable.

Her arms folded and her lips pursed, Harper was standing on the steps that led to the porch.

"Hey," Mitch said. He poked his head out the door and looked to the right at Hannah, grinning from ear to ear, then back at Harper.

"I'm sorry to just show up like this unannounced, but I really need to talk to you."

Mitch knew he needed to talk to her as well. He was shocked that Hannah hadn't run across the porch screaming her name. "How did you keep Hannah from shouting out your name and running up to you?" he asked.

"She held her finger over her mouth like this," Hannah answered for Harper, showing Mitch.

He smiled. He'd decided that when they talked he was going to be cordial, although he had imagined a conversation on the phone, not face to face. Treat her the way he would want to be treated if the roles had been reversed. They easily could have been; Pastor Kenny had pointed that out to him one day last week.

"I would like to talk to you as well," Mitch admitted.

"You would?" Harper asked, openly surprised.

"Yes," he said. "But first, would you like to have a PB&J with Hannah and me?"

"Sure, I haven't eaten since breakfast."

"I assume you've been driving all day?" Mitch glanced out at the vehicle she'd driven up in—different from the one she'd been driving last time. This one, he assumed, most likely had a Maryland license plate. Unless she was just here for the filming that Officer Dunlap had told him about when they'd run into one another at the grocery store this week, but the backseat full of stuff seemed to tell a different story. One he found himself looking forward to hearing.

"Yes," she said simply, her eyes darting back at her car, realizing that Mitch had noticed that she'd packed everything she could possibly fit into the backseat. *You should see the trunk*, she thought to herself.

Before Mitch darted back into the kitchen, he watched Hannah run up to hug Harper's leg. A few moments later he surfaced with the sandwiches, then Harper helped him bring out two sweet teas, an orange juice and a bag of chips. Mitch let Hannah and Harper occupy the swing and he pulled up a nearby chair. They chatted loosely as vehicles and pedestrians passed by. Hannah filled Harper in on the fun that she and Mitch had when watching tourists stroll the street. Mitch enjoyed the conversation—much more relaxed than he would have expected—but he was eager to talk to Harper alone.

After lunch, he convinced Hannah to play in her bedroom while he and Harper played catch-up. Hannah laughed out loud. She said, "You're going to play with ketchup? That's silly, Daddy." The three of them laughed as they got Hannah started on a story that involved her GI-Joes and Barbies teaming up to search for a lost monkey in a rain forest. Mitch wasn't sure how it all came about, but Hannah seemed to be very involved in the plot as Harper pulled her door to and followed Mitch back out to the porch.

"Harper, I'm sorry about how I reacted the last day you were here," Mitch apologized. "I should have let you stay so we could talk like adults."

Harper immediately noticed that Mitch had called her Harper instead of Addison, which was perfectly fine by her. "That's okay," she admitted. "I probably would have done the same thing if I had been in your shoes."

"I forgive you," he said, bluntly.

"You do?" Harper wore her surprise all over her face.

"Yes, I have to. It's the right thing to do."

"That's mighty kind of you," she admitted.

"I've had a lot of time to think about the time we spent together." Mitch studied her eyes, intent on what he had to say. "I decided that I think it was brave of you to stick around after you found out that I was Mitch, the Mitch that loved your sister dearly. I need you to know that she meant the world to me, Harper. No one will ever be able to replace her."

Harper hoped he didn't think that she'd ever considered replacing London. "I really did want to tell you every day," she told him. "But I was so afraid of how you would react. I was terrified that you wouldn't believe me when I told you that I didn't know who you were when we met on the pier that night." Harper paused, flashing back to that night again. The memory hadn't faded even an inkling. "I know it was selfish of me to keep the secret once I figured it out, but after we made love that night, I gave you a part of me that I've only ever given to one other person. It meant something to me, regardless of what I found out the next morning. I had to find out *exactly* what it meant, though. I had to find out if my initial attraction to you was more than just this infatuation with this incredibly good looking hero who had just saved me from some pervert." Harper let a lull take over the conversation long enough to see if Mitch would interject. To see if he was going to tell her that what had meant the world to her now meant nothing to him. But he didn't speak, he just waited to see what else she had on her mind. "Once I realized you were London's Mitch, that's when I started acting like a lunatic."

Mitch laughed. "I honestly wondered for a brief time if you had escaped from a mental hospital," he admitted.

"What?" she hissed. "You really do just say whatever comes to your mind, huh?" she teased.

"Not always," he insisted. "I didn't say it that night that you told me you had something really important to tell me, but that you weren't going to tell me until the day you left, and that it would totally change the way I thought about you. If I had, then maybe things would have turned out differently."

"It's all I could think of at the moment. That's why I said I just wanted us to be friends, because I wanted to get to know you, to find out why London loved you the way she loved you."

"And then what?" he asked.

"And just see what happened."

Mitch took a deep breath. "Do you still want to be friends?" he asked.

"I'd like that," she replied, but now there was something more that connected them, something he needed to know about.

Mitch shook his head. "You see there's only one problem." Harper furrowed her brow, afraid he might not be on the same page or even in the same book. "I don't want to be friends with you, Harper."

Harper felt her entire face tighten. Honestly, his response didn't surprise her, but she still found herself clinching the muscles in her stomach and pursing her lips, trying to hold in the tears that ignited in her heart and began working their way to the corners of her eyes. "You don't," she said like a sad little girl who hadn't gotten her way. She knew she should have just blurted out what she'd come here to tell him. Now it would be more difficult.

"I can't be just friends with you, Harper," he started. "I couldn't be just friends with you the first time you asked me to be just friends. So, I'm guilty of covering up the truth, too."

Mitch moved to the empty spot on the swing next to her. His leg rubbed against her leg. His fingers stroked her cheeks softly, and for the first time since they each knew one another's true identity, Mitch and Harper's lips met. He missed the taste of her mouth, the touch of her fingertips. He was so happy that she'd shown up on his doorstep today.

Harper finally felt a calm come over her body. She'd been tense ever since the moment she woke up in Mitch's arms and found out about London. So many things had happened since then. So much stress had taken over her body. In this moment, she felt like the weight of the world had been lifted from her conscious, but there was one more thing she needed to tell Mitch Quinn, she remembered as she slowly released his lips. This time she knew that this wouldn't be the last kiss, which made her smile. She only hoped he would smile when she told him what she'd driven two hundred miles to tell him.

"There is something else I think you're going to want to know about me; actually, about us."

His eyebrows wrinkled. She always seemed to keep him on the edge of his seat. "Okay." He waited.

"I've decided that I will never keep anything a secret from you ever again."

Mitch smiled, "I promise the same."

Harper began to summon up the courage to tell him the news. She took a deep breath. When his eyes locked onto her eyes, she took his left hand with her right hand. Gently, she slid her fingers between his and rested their hands on her stomach. "Mitch, I'm pregnant."

34

itch held Harper's gaze. His brain was processing, but he couldn't seem to force his tongue to move. She waited for him to respond, but he seemed to be in a trance. "Mitch," she finally uttered, "say something."

"Is it mine?" he uttered, confused.

Not the words she'd wanted to hear. "Yes."

"Are you sure?"

Oh, no, she thought, he's going to try to wiggle his way out of this. "Mitch, I just admitted that you're only the second man I've ever made love to."

The words he spoke next fit perfect. Harper only wished they had been his first reaction.

"It's a miracle," he admitted. As the words sank in a few tears fell out. It had to be a miracle, he decided, right then and there. He vowed to God never to look at this news any differently. God had given him a second chance at life. He'd given him Hannah, and now he had Harper and a new baby on the way. *A baby.* A human being he had helped create. He couldn't quite wrap his mind around reality at the moment, but he told Harper exactly how he felt. "I'm so excited," Mitch said.

"Are you sure?"

"Of course." He paused and when he was just about to reveal to her something that she didn't know about him, he realized he had just assumed that Harper was excited as well. What if she wasn't? What if she had other thoughts? What if she didn't want him to have anything to do with the child? Of course not, he decided quickly, tucking that thought away. If she hadn't wanted him to know she wouldn't have shown up here, kissed him passionately, and then told him about the baby. "Are you?" he asked anyway.

She held a gigantic smile. "I am thrilled," she admitted. "At least now that I know you are okay with it. I was a nervous wreck the entire ride here, though."

"We'll figure it out," he promised. "One day at a time, we'll figure this out."

"You'll be around, right?"

"I'm not going to be a deadbeat dad like Donald," he guaranteed.

"What I really meant is—you'll be around—as in . . ." Harper wasn't sure how to piece these words together. "At the end of London's memoir, it said that you had cancer, too. I mean it's obvious that you made it longer than you expected, but Mitch, if you're dying I need to know. I'm so mad at my sister for not telling our family sooner about how serious her cancer had become." She was also still upset that London hadn't told them more about Mitch and about the engagement ring they'd found on her finger at the funeral home—the one that no one there seemed to know anything about. Of course now she knew the story from the memoir, exactly the way London wanted her to know it, she assumed. "So if you're dying, I need to know." Harper kept rambling, worrying. "I know I wasn't up front with you before, but like I said earlier, I want us to tell each other everything regardless of what we think might happen."

Mitch eventually butted in, interrupting Harper's fears. "I'm not dying," he admitted. "I was, or at least I was supposed to, but then God healed me," he admitted for the first time ever. This new news proved to him that God had to be real. Too many miracles had happened just to cast all of this off as coincidence. "I have absolutely no cancer cells in my body. The doctors say it's not possible, but they also say that their science is never incorrect. Go figure," he laughed. "They also said that I would never be able to have a biological child." He paused, letting reality sink in a little deeper. "I guess that makes me, and us, an anomaly."

Now Harper realized why Mitch's first reaction had been to ask if she was sure he was the father of the little baby that had begun to grow inside of her. "Mitch, I had no idea." She covered her mouth with her hands. All along she had been worried, but once again God had brought good out of what could have been a huge mistake. Harper hugged Mitch's neck, happy for him, happy for the both of them. "I think our entire relationship is an anomaly, but a good anomaly," she clarified. So was Mitch's acceptance of her showing up today. It had shocked her that he hadn't even shown one ounce of resentment toward her. She wasn't sure what she expected, especially once she told him about being pregnant, but it couldn't get any better than this.

"Me too," Mitch agreed, then he remembered something that he'd been wanting to tell Harper. "I hate to bring up this subject at such a time as this, but do you remember that day on the dock in Morehead City when I said, 'People who are not supposed to fall in love do fall in love sometimes'?"

"Yes, I do."

"Well, I kind of had a hunch that day that you might be London's sister."

"Are you saying that your words of wisdom had a double meaning?"

Mitch shrugged, holding a crooked smile. "I thought if I said it then maybe I wouldn't freak out if and when I actually found my hunch to be correct, but then I guess a part of me thought there was no possible way that you could be London's sister."

"For better or worse, I am," she said.

"My life is better because of both of you," he wanted her to know.

"Right back at you," Harper agreed. "And since you brought up your wise saying—which on the surface was about Tara and James—this reminds me that I have more news to tell you."

"We're having twins?" Mitch teased.

"Funny, but I hope not," she rebutted, glancing at her stomach as if she could actually tell any difference from the way it had looked a month ago.

"So what did you find out about Tara and your ex?"

"Well, that's kind of why my car is packed to the brim."

"Oh, yeah, I was planning to ask you about that." Mitch glanced toward the car, the sun now beaming off the dusty windshield. "But I figured I better wait until we ate lunch, patched things up between us, and talked about you being pregnant," he laughed. He loved how they found a way to keep a playful banter even in the midst of serious discussions.

"There are actually two things I want you to know."

"You're just filled with surprises, Ms. Adams."

She wondered if she would always remember the first time he called her that, and she had to admit that she liked the sound of her last name rolling off his lips. "First, I quit my job." Harper sighed then breathed in the taste of fresh salt air.

"I thought you loved your job," Mitch queried, his brow furrowed.

"I did." Harper pursed her lips, then started. "Here's the story in a nutshell: When I made it back to Silver Spring, I confronted Tara about James. She told me the whole story about how he'd been in a car accident . . ."

Mitch interrupted. "Is he okay?"

It was nice that Mitch cared enough to ask, but it kind of surprised Harper. "Yes, he's fine. Tara told me that James had contacted her trying to get ahold of me."

"So you're saying that I have some competition."

"Mitch, would you let me finish," she hissed, playfully. She watched him pretend to clam up. "Tara promised me that nothing was going on between them. Things between her and me went back to normal. We ran together, went out for dinner, talked about you." Harper could tell that he wanted to interject so badly as she wore a grin, but she put her finger over his lips, feeling his smile move ever so slightly against her skin. "Then I remembered that Tara, my best friend, hadn't invited me to her house one single time since James left me. What kind of friend does that, especially after all that I've been through?" Mitch responded by raising his eyebrows. "I followed her home from work one day," Harper admitted.

"And you saw her with James?" Mitch said through her finger.

"No." She shook her head as she continued. "So I stalked her for a few evenings, and sure enough, one night I caught the two of them making out."

"What did you do?"

"Nothing, at least not until the next morning. Then I walked into her office, told her I quit, and said that she knew why. At first, she tried to deny the affair, but then I backed her into a corner, and she confessed everything." Harper shook her head. She was so over it. "Mitch, she is the one James cheated on me with when he and I were still married. They've had a secret relationship going on this whole time."

Mitch listened as Harper blew off steam until Hannah met them on the porch and asked if they wanted to play with her. So they followed her to her bedroom and crawled around the floor like three kids for the next hour.

Life seemed to fall into place from there. Mitch and Harper had dragged all of their skeletons out of the closet. That evening they unpacked her car and moved her in next door. Mitch busted out laughing when Harper asked if he knew of any place to stay on the island. Then Harper followed suit when he said, *yes, I think Jack and Megan broke up.*

The two of them thought it would be best for Hannah if Harper lived next door for a little while. It would give them all some time to figure out how this new life would work.

In an attempt to avoid future confusion, they went ahead and explained to Hannah that Harper was London's sister. When they brought up the fact that Addison was her middle name and Harper was her first name, and that Hannah could call her either, they expected Hannah to be thoroughly baffled, but instead she became excited. She said that Harper sounded a lot more like Hannah, and she wanted to call her Harper.

The first night Hannah asked Harper to help Mitch put her to bed. He couldn't help but notice how the way Harper treated Hannah was even more attractive than her soft smile or the curves that filled out her jeans and the white polo she had been wearing since showing up on his porch today. He hadn't had the nerve to tell her that there was a splash of chocolate milk on her collar. Hannah asked if they would read *Goodnight Moon* two times. Once for every carton of chocolate milk she'd drank today. Mitch read the story first, then Hannah asked for water. While Mitch went to the kitchen, Harper began her turn reading. A few moments later, with a small cup in his hand, Mitch stopped just outside the doorframe. He let his body slide down the hallway wall, thinking about everything in his life that had changed today. Thinking about the baby.

Crouching near the floor, he began to run his finger across the groove in the hardwood slats as he listened to Harper read a bedtime story to the little girl he loved. Resting there, he felt himself falling in love, all over again, with the woman sitting on the bed next to Hannah.

When Harper ended the story, his ears perched as Hannah's soft voice lingered into the hallway. "Since London went to Heaven, will you be my mommy?" she asked sincerely.

Harper had no idea Mitch was just outside the door, holding on to every word. She answered the only way she knew how. "I will be anything your daddy will let me be." She paused for a moment and reached for the lamp, letting the darkness absorb her tears. In the hallway, Mitch did the same. "Did you know I gave this bear to London when she was about your age?" Harper asked, tugging at Snuggles, wedged in Hannah's arms as usual.

Mitch had yet to ask why Harper had taken Snuggles. Now he figured he wouldn't ever need to ask.

Hannah shook her head and Harper began stroking her thin blonde hair. She continued, sniffling as she shared the story, "I gave it to her when she was in the hospital. I wanted her to have a friend to sleep with because I couldn't be there with her at night. So I poured all of the money out of my piggy bank and bought Snuggles. I think she slept with him every night for the rest of her life; that's why he is a flat bear instead of a round bear," she smiled, as the light seeping in from the hallway began to brighten the room.

Hannah smiled, too. "Is it okay if I keep him?"

Harper wiped away a line of tears. "You bet." She kissed Hannah on the cheek and then heard Mitch's footsteps.

Mitch let Hannah take a swig of water from a small cup. Then he kissed her, told her how much he loved her, and said *goodnight*.

As soon as Mitch and Harper reached the hallway, he swept Harper into his arms. This time there was no thinking, no second-guessing, and in a matter of minutes the two of them found themselves wrapped in covers and connected by emotions greater than either of them.

— ～

On most days Harper wandered over for breakfast, and Mitch and Hannah would end up walking her back in the dark just before bedtime. On nights when Harper stayed past Hannah's bedtime—when consenting adults needed time to give in to desires—Mitch would walk out on the porch after their time together and watch her walk to her new house. Most nights he'd whistle or howl, and she'd shake her head. They spent many days on the beach and often fished at night on the pier where they'd first met. Just about every time their lines were dangling in the water, they'd spot a few sharks swimming around below. All of the bait, and the fish attracted by the bait, drew the sharks to the pier.

One evening, Harper ran into her old film crew taking video of people fishing while the sharks swam below. She introduced everyone to Mitch and Hannah, and they told her how much the staff at the office missed her. Of course, they'd heard the gossip about Tara and James, and one of the women had pulled her aside to tell her how sorry she was. Harper told her not to be, that her life here with Mitch and Hannah was way better. Before the crew left, they promised to send her a copy of the final footage prior to its airing on television. Hannah thought that was really neat, especially since they'd put her in a few of the fishing shots with her hot pink rod-and-reel.

Mitch held on to his promise to take Harper to a Morehead City Marlins baseball game. The three of them ate hot dogs and peanuts, drank too much caffeine and half way paid attention to *a bunch of men running around on grass and sand*—Hannah's description of the sport. They went several more times that summer. The first night they'd gone to a baseball game had been the week Harper showed back up in Emerald Isle. They went to celebrate her birthday. Earlier in the day, Mitch had given her the most wonderful gift: a European facial followed by a 45-minute full body massage, then came a manicure and a pedicure. Cotton balls separated her toes and a green mask cooled the skin on her face. *Life doesn't get much better than this,* she had realized, as she traveled from one treatment room to the next— all decorated with antiques and tapestries—each overlooking the Atlantic Ocean. After two hours of pampering, Mitch and Hannah had met her at the front door. Later that night, when they said a prayer and tucked Hannah into bed, Hannah pulled out a box from beneath one of her pillows. "I wrapped it myself," she disclosed with joy.

Tears of joy soon flooded Harper's eyes. She had no idea how Mitch and Hannah had found a bear exactly like Snuggles, minus the years of loving wear and tear, but that part didn't really matter, she figured. A bear just like London's was the most perfect gift anyone had ever given to her, and when Hannah told her that she'd bought it with the money in her piggy bank, *just like you did for London,* she hugged her for what felt like hours.

35

The rest of the summer flew by. Temperatures were typical for Emerald Isle. Hot. One more shark attack happened—a middle-aged woman had her calf bitten, but the shark didn't stick around and she ended up with just a little more than a scare—setting a record at seven shark attacks in one year on the North Carolina coast. When September rolled around, Mitch and Harper hoped they'd heard of the last shark attack in the area. There hadn't been one reported in a month and with summer break for most schools being over, the beaches were thinning out, especially on the weekdays. Saturdays and Sundays would stay busy as long as the weather remained warm. The evenings were prime for fishing on the pier and walking on the beach. When the sun dropped, the temperatures fell along with it and the constant cool breeze produced by the effects of the Atlantic Ocean made the night feel almost perfect. Mitch had been planning *this* Friday evening activity for a couple of weeks now although he'd only let Harper and Hannah in on the plans this weekend. It all started when the three of them walked down to the pier to enjoy a dinner on the dock at the table where Mitch and Harper had their first meal together back in early June. Hannah felt special that they'd brought her along. Mitch liked that he and Harper most always chose for Hannah to accompany them on their dates. Today marked three months to the day of when he and Harper met, which made this dinner even more special. Hannah basically ate hush puppies as her meal, and Mitch and Harper thought it would be nostalgic if they ordered the same dishes they'd had that first night, but with a twist, they decided. When the waitress brought out their plates, Harper passed Mitch her flounder and she ate his mahi-mahi. As they ate and talked about memories of their first summer together, the sun slowly sank below the endless rolling waves, casting a glimmering film on the surface of the water as far as the eye could see. It would have been a perfect photo opportunity, Mitch realized.

When all of the plates on the table were cleaned, the three of them grabbed their fishing gear—which they'd placed at the end of the restaurant seating area earlier—and headed down the pier to find a spot to nestle in for the rest of the evening. Built-in wooden benches facing the ocean lined either side of the long, large wooden structure. As with most Friday evenings, the pier was packed with a mixture of families and fishermen. During dinner, they'd watched folks reel in fish from afar, and they'd already heard talk of several sharks being spotted swimming around the pier. The last time they'd come out here to fish, Mitch had reeled in a small sand shark himself. You could always tell who hadn't fished a lot because those were the people who would begin to gather around anytime a baby shark began to flop around on the weathered boards beneath their feet. The true fishermen had seen plenty of sharks—small and large—so they just went on about their business. Some were there to catch fish that their family would eat for dinner and others just for the adventure. Mitch, Harper, and Hannah had kept a dozen or so fish this summer. Some they had grilled for dinner; others Harper fried in a skillet, but most of the time they would simply catch and release or use the smaller fish for bait. The first time Hannah witnessed Mitch slice a fish, she cried, "Why did you kill him, Daddy?" Mitch felt bad initially, but then after a few minutes of consoling her and explaining the purpose, she began to understand.

Mitch tapped Harper on the shoulder when he spotted Officer Pete Dunlap at the end of the pier, a prime fishing location, and the three of them walked the remaining twenty yards to speak to him and his family. His wife and kids were fishing alongside him. Mitch and Harper had gotten to know the family fairly well during the recent months. A couple of weeks after Harper's second arrival in Emerald Isle, she had started freelance writing for the local newspaper which just happened to be located near the police station. She'd even talked Mitch into submitting a photograph for each story she penned, and so far the results had been overwhelmingly positive. The first time she'd walked over to let Pete know she was back in town, his twins—a boy and a girl around Hannah's age—had been at the station with him. They'd set up a play date for the kids to meet, and since then they'd all gotten together a handful of times. On the rare occasion that Mitch and Harper had gone out on a date alone, they'd let Hannah stay with the Dunlap's. They felt safe with her there. She would have ordinarily stayed with Doc, but Doc had suddenly passed away of a heart attack in mid-July. It hadn't shocked Mitch when he got the phone call, but it hurt just the same as if he hadn't expected it. Hannah had taken it hard, but she'd seen so much death during her time in the children's cancer ward at Duke that in a way Mitch thought she might have been more prepared for the loss that he had been. Harper had been the one to pull the three of them together. She'd gone out of her way to make sure that they still found time to laugh on days when they didn't really want to. Doc had left a small fortune for Hannah. Enough for her to attend pretty much any college she wanted, buy a house, and then some. He'd left Mitch in charge of his estate and making sure

Hannah received the money in allotments throughout the years to come. He'd left his home overlooking the Atlantic Ocean to Mitch, with a request that he and Mitch had talked about in the past. He wanted it turned into a bed and breakfast specifically designed for kids with cancer. Once an application and review took place, the child and family would be invited for a one-week vacation at the beach at absolutely no cost. Meals would be covered. Travel expenses would be covered. Everything. Doc had purchased an enormous life insurance policy that ensured the home would have operational expenses too far into the future to even imagine. Mitch and Harper had been working to set up all the legalities with a lawyer that he and Doc had been meeting with off and on for the past year. The last time they'd sat at the long table in the attorney's office, Mitch made some changes to his own life insurance policy. After finding out about Harper's pregnancy, he made her his primary beneficiary just in case anything were to happen to him. He wanted to be certain that she and the baby were taken care of, just like Doc had done for Hannah. Mitch also made sure to keep Hannah included in his will, as well.

Mitch winked at Pete when he said that they could take over his family's fishing spot at the end of the pier. While they gathered their things, the adults talked, and the kids played nearby.

"Are y'all sure you don't want to stay out here and fish with us?" Harper asked.

"I think we're going to head where y'all just came from," Pete's wife suggested. "The kids are starving and Pete's getting grumpy because it's getting dark out and he hasn't eaten yet."

They all laughed.

Pete pointed to a rectangular sign posted at the end of the pier: *No Jumping or Diving.* "We've seen a group of hungry sharks circling the end of the pier every so often, so I don't recommend a swim tonight, Mitch," Pete said, his shoulders bouncing as he laughed.

It was always exciting to see the sharks from this vantage point, but it was kind of scary to think of all the people who had been swimming nearby earlier in the day, which was a reason that Harper had made sure to include in her documentary story that people should steer clear of swimming near fishing piers regardless of the time of day but especially in the evenings when more folks were casting out bait. Studies had shown that shark attacks often happened in these areas. Many of them were related to surfers that liked to catch waves near the pier for one reason or another.

As the Dunlap family disappeared into the crowd near the restaurant, Mitch baited all three of their lines and cast each of them out. Neither Harper nor Hannah liked to cast their own line when the pier was packed like it was tonight. They were each afraid they'd accidentally snag a body part on their back swing. It had taken Mitch many years to feel comfortable casting in a crowded environment, so he completely understood their reluctance.

Mitch slid the tackle box to the left of their bench, and Harper set the cooler on the other side. They'd brought snacks and drinks for later in the evening when dinner would wear off. Most nights that they came to fish they'd end up here until Hannah got sleepy. She'd even fallen asleep on the pier a couple of times. The sound of the waves crashing against the trunk of the pier seemed to have a calming effect on everyone. Tonight Mitch needed her, though, at least until one of them caught the first fish. He and Hannah had rehearsed a plan to surprise Harper. Mitch had been thinking about it all evening, and he was shocked that he hadn't had to cover up any hints that Hannah might let slip out as the moment drew closer. He watched impatiently as their poles stretched over the railing, high enough that he'd never been concerned about Hannah falling over and low enough that she could rest her forearms on the top board for a peek into the water below. Regardless, Mitch always made sure to keep a close eye on her. They all kept an eye out for sharks, but so far they hadn't caught a good glimpse of one although Harper thought she had seen a fin pop out of the water about thirty minutes after their arrival. The people fishing on either side of them had introduced themselves, and they'd all shared stories about fishing and sharks and life at the beach.

Eventually, Harper felt a tug on her line. This was the moment Mitch and Hannah had been waiting for. They both cheered her on as she began the fight with the creature below the ocean's surface. As usual, it felt huge. The pole tightened first then began to bend toward the water. Harper reeled. "I've hooked one," she said. Everyone nearby encouraged her to keep up her end of the battle. Ultimately, that's what fishing came down to, a fight between a fish on one end—desperate to escape—and a fisherman on the other. She could feel the spinner pulling tighter as the fish neared the surface, and Mitch grew anxious as he realized that Harper was about to win the war. Once the fish popped out of the water, the hard part was over. She reeled him up slowly as those around her acknowledged her catch. Harper had been standing in between Mitch and Hannah the entire time. Once she brought the fish to pier level, Mitch reached out and grabbed it.

"This might be a keeper," he suggested. "Like you," he said with a grin.

As usual, Mitch knelt down next to the bench, Hannah following suit to get a closer look as he pulled the hook from the fish's mouth. It was a striper, a little longer than his shoe. Harper took a step back, keeping a firm grasp on the pole.

"Look, Daddy, there is something is his mouth," Hannah exclaimed, excitedly.

Mitch and Hannah tilted their heads closer to the fish—flopping anxiously on the boards below Harper's feet.

"It's sparkly," Mitch announced, glancing up at Harper, a smile on her face and more beautiful than the sunset they'd watched together earlier.

"What is it?" she inquired, taking a seat on the bench to get a closer look. With Mitch and Hannah hovered over the fish, no one could see the object they were discussing.

Their fishing neighbors and a few other onlookers took a step closer. Mitch's left knee rotated on the splintery wood toward Harper. He took her left hand with his right hand.

In that moment Harper caught a glimpse of the object Mitch and Hannah had been talking about, round and shiny, but she instantly realized that it hadn't really been in the fish's mouth.

"Harper Adams," Mitch said sweetly and softly, his eyes locked on hers, the world around him fading into the distance. "Will you marry me?"

Harper's grin stretched from one side of the pier to the other. She could feel that the eyes of those in the crowd had shifted from the fish to her, but in the moment she found a way to drown out all the outside noise and focused on the man on one knee. Mitch was holding the most precious diamond ring she'd ever laid eyes on. It wasn't large or gaudy, it was simply perfect. The moment was perfect. The evening had been perfect. The way that Mitch and Hannah had planned this out was perfect. It suddenly all came together in Harper's mind as the world seemed to stop so that she could take a mental picture of this entire evening that would hopefully last a lifetime: dinner at the restaurant where she and Mitch first met, Pete and his family coincidentally giving up the perfect spot on the pier—that should have drawn a red flag, Hannah holding out on her and ever-so-cutely saying that there was something in the fish's mouth to draw her attention. The proposal was so original and so Mitch-like.

"Yes, Mitch Quinn," she answered. As soon as the words slipped out of her mouth she felt the ring begin to slip onto her finger. Like a true gentleman, he'd waited for her to answer before fully tempting her with the bait.

The crowd around them erupted in hoots and hollers and ap-
plause. Harper imagined how this evening would end when she
glanced to her left to find the Dunlap's now at the forefront of the
small crowd. She bet that Mitch had even thought to ask them to let
Hannah have a sleepover at their house. Knowing Pete, they'd probably been watching with binoculars from the other end of the pier,
waiting to scurry back down for the big moment, which would allow
her and Mitch to finish the night much the way they had their first
night together—making love beneath a beautiful Carolina moon in
the steamy outdoor shower behind the house that they would soon
be able to call their family home. The two of them, Hannah, and
the new baby that would be here in March.

Mitch hugged Harper tightly, then kissed her passionately. The
crowd erupted again. Once he released her soft lips, he shook Pete's
hand. "Thanks, buddy," he said.

Harper hugged Pete's wife's neck. "You knew," she smiled.

Mitch turned to hug Hannah.

Hannah . . .

Mitch rotated 360 degrees. *Where was Hannah?* He didn't see her
with the twins standing next to their parents. She wasn't sitting
on the bench with their stuff. He looked around at everyone's feet
thinking maybe she had bent down to get the fish that had been
forgotten in all of the excitement, but he didn't see her or the fish.

"Hannah," he called out, continuing to search the surrounding area frantically and then running to the railing, thinking the
worst. Could she have fallen in? In all the commotion could that
have happened without anyone seeing her? Maybe she had stood on
the bench to throw the fish back in—and someone had accidentally
bumped her—or she'd lost her balance and flipped over the railing?

Harper was the first to notice the expression on Mitch's face.
Once she realized that Mitch was looking for Hannah, she began to
search the crowd, too. Pete noticed the fear in Mitch's voice, and he

was just about to run to the other end of the pier, set up a parameter, when another voice called out.

"She's over here."

Mitch turned. Harper turned. Everyone turned. The night air grew silent, eerily silent. The voice hadn't been one of a Good Samaritan that had found the little girl who had suddenly become lost in the crowd. It was one that caused chill bumps to climb Mitch's arms and send fear into the center of Harper's heart.

36

"**H**annah is *my* daughter," Donald exclaimed as if everyone in the crowd needed to know that information up front.

Those near him backed away. Mitch and Harper suddenly realized why—Donald was holding a knife to his own daughter's throat. Mitch could sense the fear in Hannah's innocent blue eyes bleeding with clear terror, and so overwhelmed that she hadn't even been able to scream. The cat didn't have her tongue, though, the devil did.

"Let her go," Mitch demanded.

"Not a chance."

Officer Dunlap stepped closer. "Donald, you don't want to harm your own daughter."

"You're right," he agreed. "But I want her to go with me, not them," he insisted, pointing the large butcher knife in Mitch's and Harper's direction.

"Just let her go so we can talk about this," Mitch pleaded.

Pete had a pistol tucked into a small holster inside the pocket of his shorts. He thought about pulling it, but he feared it would only make the tension grow. First, he wanted to try to talk Donald down. He didn't like the fact that he was standing on one of the benches, leaned up against the railing. One wrong move and he and Hannah could topple overboard.

"My dad is dead and I'm the only family she has left," Donald exclaimed. "She needs me."

Mitch had expected a run in with Donald at Doc's funeral, and he'd even asked Pete to be there just in case, but Donald hadn't even shown up; at the time, Mitch wondered if he even knew his dad had passed. "Donald, we can work something out," Mitch lied. He would say anything to convince Donald to release the blade from his daughter's throat. It was so close that Mitch was expecting to see blood at any moment. If only he could get a few feet closer without Donald freaking out, he thought, he might have a chance to disarm him. He wasn't sure the chance would be worth what could happen, one mistake and her throat could be slit. He hated this. Hated that he'd lost sight of Hannah in the first place. Hated that it had happened in the midst of what was supposed to be one of the happiest moments of his life, their life. Now the moment had become filled with fear and a completely different type of anticipation than what he'd expected.

"You're not just going to give her to me, I know that," Donald said. "That's why I've come here to take her with me."

"Where do you want to take her, Donald?" Pete asked, calmly.

Harper's ring finger trembled right along with the rest of them. She hadn't been able to speak a word. She'd locked eyes with Hannah the moment she'd heard Donald's voice and she hadn't let go since. Hannah had been looking all over the place, but mainly she'd been looking right back at her. Harper tried her best not to show the fear that had temporarily paralyzed her body.

"I'm taking her to a place that only she and I can go," he assured them, shouting.

"Let's talk about this," Officer Pete suggested. "Just lower the knife so your daughter can relax. You're scaring her."

"I'm the one in charge here."

Those words hit Harper like a brick. They were eerily similar to the words Donald had spoken to her when he'd held her against the door in Mitch's hallway. He had that same look in his eyes, too, like he could kill someone at any moment. She just couldn't fathom that he would hurt his own daughter. Why? How? But here he was with a knife pressed to her throat.

"Okay, so tell us what you want," Pete suggested. In training, he'd always been advised to let a man in this position give his demands and then work from there. He needed Donald to at least think he would have an opportunity to get away.

"I only want one thing. I want to take my daughter with me."

"Over my dead body," Mitch promised. He'd heard too many horror stories about what happened when people like Donald escaped a situation like this with an innocent little girl. Even though he found himself questioning whether Donald would bring physical harm to his own daughter, he wasn't willing to take that chance.

"You want to go with us, too?" Donald asked Mitch.

Mitch furrowed his brow. He'd been slowly inching closer each time Donald's eyes shifted to Officer Dunlap, who himself had methodically moved to his right to create a perimeter. There was no way for Donald to get past the two of them.

Pete knew all about Mitch's particular set of skills. He'd heard the story about the night in the bar when Harper had first come into town. One of his off-duty deputies had witnessed it firsthand, yet in this particular instance, he'd been praying that Mitch wouldn't make the first move. He hoped that Donald would lower his guard eventually and let Hannah escape his grasp. From there, he was pretty sure the two of them could keep Donald from harming anyone else. In that moment, he knew he would draw his gun, and if Mitch didn't get to Donald first, Donald would have two choices: do exactly as told or he wouldn't walk off this pier tonight.

"Yes, I'll go with you," Mitch offered. "Take me instead of Hannah. Put that knife to my throat." Mitch knew he would only need about two seconds to turn that knife around. What would happen next he wasn't sure; he'd been trained to avoid violence at all costs. Simply control the situation, but he didn't want to have to worry about Donald ever doing this again. He didn't want to show up at the school to pick up Hannah one afternoon and find out someone else had.

"Where we're going, you'll have to follow," Donald said with a creepy grin. "We'll find out how bad you want to come."

Officer Dunlap chimed in again. "Where would you like to go, Donald? I'll make sure you get there."

"We don't need your help getting to where we're going," Donald said, kissing the top of Hannah's head. "I love you, baby," he whispered. "I've always loved you."

Mitch didn't like the way he was talking. Donald had something up his sleeve, and he couldn't quite figure it out.

Harper noticed a trickle running down Hannah's leg from beneath her shorts where a wet spot began to blot. She hated this. It was so unfair for an innocent little girl to be put in such an awful situation. She turned to Mitch, feeling deep down in her gut that he was about to do something. She could see it in his eyes, sense it in her mind. She knew he had seen the drops falling from Hannah's shorts; he was observant like that, and a man like Mitch couldn't stand by and let another man harm a little girl like Hannah. His little girl. His world.

"You like to swim with sharks, Mitch?" Donald asked.

He's planning to jump with her, Mitch suddenly realized. "Don't do it, Donald. She's just a little girl. She has a bright future." Mitch glanced at the water beneath the pier, and sure enough a group of sharks were circling.

"A future without her real daddy isn't bright. She'd only end up hating you for taking her away from me." Donald slid his free arm around Hannah's chest, just under the knife. A moment later, blood was dripping from the blade.

Officer Dunlap reached into his pocket and aimed his firearm at Donald's head. "This isn't going to end well for you, Donald," he said, realizing the same plan that Mitch had just caught onto.

Blood began to ooze from Donald's arm. "Sharks love blood, Mitch." He paused, glancing down at the water slapping up against the large round legs of the pier. "A little bit of mine . . . ," he said.

Then Donald raised Hannah up closer to his face. Pete gritted his teeth. He realized he'd just lost any chance he had at a fatal shot to the temple. He could shoot Donald's leg, but as long as the knife remained up against Hannah's jugular, it was a risk he wasn't willing to take.

". . . a little bit of Hannah's," Donald added, scraping the knife slowly across the soft skin on her forearm.

Mitch took two steps closer. He was within lunging distance, now all he needed was for Donald to wave the knife in his direction. That was his plan. If he could get Donald to take the knife off Hannah for even a split second, he could get his hand wrapped around Donald's wrist or at least the knife. He didn't care if he got cut, he'd live. Hopefully.

Not one single soul on the pier had spoken a word other than Mitch, Pete, and Donald. Some of the families had scurried away with their children. A couple dozen adults and teenagers were within the sound of the three voices they'd been listening to for the past five minutes.

"If you come a step closer, I'm going to cut her throat, too," Donald hissed. Blood had already surfaced on her arm, Mitch noticed as he felt anger building within the walls of his body.

"Why don't you be a man and cut *my* throat?" Mitch challenged.

His words struck rage within Donald, and that was the moment Mitch had been waiting for. The instant Donald swung the knife in his direction he catapulted his entire body toward the handle Donald was holding. He had one goal and one goal only—get his hands on that knife so that his little girl wouldn't suffer one more cut.

The moment Pete saw Mitch leave his feet he holstered his gun and moved in quickly. He watched Mitch's fingers wrap around the blade of the knife, watched the other hand grab tightly onto Donald's wrist. Donald flailed his arms harshly causing Mitch's body to shift. Mitch's ribs slammed up against the top rail of the pier, but he didn't loosen his grip on the blade. Hannah was still wrapped in Donald's other arm, and in one motion everyone on the pier watched Donald fling her small body over the rail. She screamed, and Mitch made a second lunge, trying to grab Hannah while holding tightly onto the knife. He hadn't felt any pain yet. That would come later, he knew. Blood was pouring all over the place as Donald and Mitch's bodies also toppled over the railing. He'd been unable to reach Hannah, and now they were all headed toward the waves below.

Pete had moved fast but not fast enough. He'd reached for Hannah, too, but he'd merely touched the sole of her shoe as she went airborne. Then he'd tried to grab Donald's jacket, but it was too late. Pete knew he had failed, twice. The entire time he and Mitch had been trying to talk Donald down, he'd been thinking of how he'd walked right past Donald earlier. The guy had seemed out of place—a dark hooded jacket, staring out to sea with no fishing pole, sitting alone—but his mind had been on the plan, the proposal, and he had ignored the warning sign.

The first splash was small but the hardest to swallow. Harper peered over the rail, wanting to help but not knowing how. The three of them were twenty-five feet below in dangerous waters.

Hannah's body had disappeared beneath the dark water as the spray from the larger splashes caused by Mitch and Donald erupted. The waves were slamming up against the end of the pier. Fishing lines were haphazardly cast all around the area where they'd all landed. The large spotlights that outlined the railing of the pier made the surface of the water visible. The railing was now filled with people trying to get a view of what was going on beneath them. If there was one good sign, it was that the sharks had seemed to scatter at the sound of the impact. Maybe they had swam away. Maybe they had ducked further into the ocean. Harper wasn't sure. She'd just prayed they wouldn't attack Mitch or Hannah.

Pete began to take off his shoes. Harper was so focused on hopes of locating Mitch and Hannah's heads as soon as they popped out of the water that she didn't see the shark fins headed back in the direction of the splashes. Others began to scream out, "There are sharks down there!" Some pointed. Some stood in awe, their mouths agape.

Mitch had felt his hand losing grip of Donald as they fell through the air. There were too many variables for him to hold on. The force in which they'd left the dock had taken them in slightly different directions. It would probably turn out to be a good thing; his one focus, once in the water, needed to be on finding Hannah. Once he'd felt impact, he knew his body weight and the speed of the fall would hold him beneath the water for several seconds. Once he reached the bottom of his descent, he yanked off his shoes and swam viciously toward the surface. He knew that time wasn't on his side. Hannah had hit the water hard before him. He'd seen her out of the corner of his eye and he had a good idea where her body would surface. Even if she didn't swim to the top like he had, buoyancy would force her body upward. There were other obstacles to consider. The current would be strong and waves that would bring a smile to a surfer's face were crashing all around and could easily toss her light body into one of the beams that held the pier. She wouldn't survive long, but neither would he, not with blood oozing from his hand and God knows how many sharks lurking below the murky water. Even if he hadn't seen the group of sharks just before joining them in their habitat, he knew they could smell blood from a relatively long distance. Knowing they were nearby, he realized he had to reach Hannah before a shark and before Donald.

"Mitch," he heard Harper call out. "Hannah is right there." Harper had seen Hannah's head emerge just before Mitch, but by the time she'd been able to get his attention, Hannah had sunk out of sight again.

Mitch swam sharply in the direction Harper had pointed him. Others were motioning along with her. Pete jumped from the railing and landed about twenty feet from Mitch. Mitch spotted Hannah, her arms flailing. He was close enough to hear her choking on salt water, but not close enough to stop swimming and reach for her yet. The undertow was carrying her toward the pier when Mitch heard the splash made by Pete. He wished Pete had stayed up on the dock. There were already too many people in the water, but Pete was the one who yelled out to Mitch, "Watch out," just as Mitch reached for Hannah. Mitch actually felt the wet cotton on her shirt just as two hands violently grabbed his shoulders and forced his entire body beneath the surface. Salt water flooded his mouth, and he found himself choking as he fought to regain control of his own body. Beneath the water, the struggle resumed. Donald wrapped his arms tightly around Mitch's chest from behind. Gravity didn't work quite the same way in the ocean, but Mitch was able to twist Donald's wrist much like he had the man at the bar at the other end of the pier a few months ago. He was able to contort his body enough under water so that he was facing Donald when they surfaced. If just the two of them were down there together, he would put him in a choke hold and swim back to shore with him, unconcerned as to whether Donald would still be breathing once they made it, but he didn't have time for that. He had to get to Hannah.

"I'm coming, Mitch," Pete called out, swimming as fast as he could in the direction of the struggle, but not making much leeway amongst the white caps.

Mitch grabbed Donald by the head with both hands and head-butted him square in the nose. Mitch could actually taste the blood—spitting everywhere—as he turned to swim for Hannah.

Up above, Harper and everyone else were screaming, trying to warn Mitch about the shark that was less than ten feet from him and lurking in his direction. The others had seemed to disappear again.

Mitch could hear the voices, but he couldn't hear what anyone was saying. All he could hear was a ringing inside of his head. He even felt dizzy from the blow he'd dealt Donald. He had a good idea that Donald was unconscious, but he didn't care. In that moment, he hoped he would drown or become shark bait.

Finally, Mitch spotted Hannah again, and he knew this was his last chance. He saw three of her; his vision had gone blurry, and salt was burning his eyes. He gave every ounce of energy he had left to make it through the waves to her. She'd surfaced near one of the large poles connected to the pier. When he reached her, he noticed that she was barely conscious. He knew she'd swallowed a lot of water, probably a lot more than he had, and he knew he had to get her to the ladder that stretched from the water to the top of the dock. What he didn't know is that he was about to find out what it felt like to be bitten by a shark. All of the bait and blood had drawn the interest of the largest one in the bunch. When Mitch grabbed ahold of Hannah, he squeezed her tightly and flipped onto his back to swim toward the ladder. He'd climbed it a hundred times when he was a kid. He imagined climbing it in just moments with her in his arms. "I've got you, Hannah," he ensured. "You're safe now."

As Mitch rapidly kicked his legs with Hannah nestled tightly against his chest, he tilted his neck backward to find the ladder from this unusual vantage point. When his eyes locked onto the first rung, he saw a foot. He glanced up and spotted Harper pointing and screaming. Mitch looked up at her then toward his legs, kicking to keep Hannah and himself afloat. That's when he spotted the shark's fin. *Don't panic*, he told himself. He never saw its eyes, but he felt its teeth grab hold of his foot. He kicked violently with both feet stretching at the same time with his arms to hand Hannah up to Harper like a quarterback handing a football off to the running back just as he was being tackled.

Harper reached as far as possible with her right arm, holding onto one of the ladder rungs with her left. She pulled Hannah from Mitch, from the water, just as she watched the shark pull Mitch beneath the waves. Red blood instantly slapped against their clothing, quickly covering the surface of the water.

Hannah was choking, then all of a sudden, she wasn't breathing. Harper looked up. She wasn't sure if she had the strength to hoist herself and Hannah up this ladder to safety. Thankfully, when she had turned to climb, she spotted the fisherman that had been sitting beside them coming down the ladder. He grabbed Hannah and wedged her between his body and the ladder and one step at a time lifted her to safety.

Harper looked for Mitch, but she didn't see him anywhere. She only saw Pete, and she realized he was doing the same, out in the water, vulnerable. Just like her, Pete had watched everything happen. Donald was nowhere in sight either. Harper wasn't sure if he'd drowned, swam away, or been bitten by a shark, too. Pete swam around looking for Mitch until he couldn't swim anymore. Two more men had climbed down the ladder, and eventually they convinced Harper to climb back up. Her strength to hang on to the rungs had dissipated. She knew she had to climb up without Mitch, but she hated leaving him down there. The men helped her, and Pete had to follow. He'd lost his strength, and another shark had chased him to the pier.

The waves continued to slap against the pier, but no one heard them. Fishing lines continued to sway in the wind, but no one at the other end was fishing. The sound of the ocean hadn't changed, but Harper knew her life had. She watched helplessly as a middle-aged woman performed CPR on Hannah, her hands pushing with pressure on Hannah's little chest. Hannah's eyes were rolled back. She was as still as the moon in the clear sky, as cold as the breeze on her soaking wet body. She seemed to lie there motionless for minutes, but Harper knew it couldn't have been that long. She held her own breath as she prayed that Hannah could find one more. She also found herself praying for Mitch. People atop the pier were looking in the water for him. Others had run to the shore and were searching the shoreline. Some had even waded out into the ocean, knowing that sharks were out at the end of the pier, maybe closer. But Harper hadn't seen any of this, she'd just been waiting for Hannah to breathe.

The lady hovering over Hannah continued to pump her chest. "Come on," she said. "Come back," she urged.

Harper thought she had heard someone nearby say that the woman was a nurse. The moment that salt water erupted from Hannah's mouth, Harper decided instead that the lady was an angel. It spewed everywhere. The woman sat Hannah up, and she continued to cough up water.

For the first time since Mitch had slid the engagement ring onto her finger, Harper felt a tear roll down her cheek. Somehow she had been brave—or maybe too scared to cry until this point. Knowing that Hannah would be okay echoed a sigh of relief throughout her body.

"I'm right here," Harper comforted.

Hannah studied her face, then glanced around at all of the strangers watching her, pulling for her to survive. She felt confused. She knew she had been in the ocean, but she couldn't really remember exactly what happened. "Where's Daddy—Mitch?" she clarified.

Harper nearly swallowed her lips. She didn't know how to respond.

37

Life takes all kinds of twists and turns. People overcome all types of bumps and bruises along the way, but Harper knew that all of the loss she and Hannah had endured wasn't fair. No person should have to ride a roller coaster as frightening as the one they'd experienced. First, they'd both lost London—a sister, a friend, an honorary mother to Hannah. Then Harper lost James. Even though this loss didn't sting as much as it once had, it still hurt. Rejection and betrayal seem to cut differently although just as sharply as tragedy and death, Harper realized. Hannah lost Doc. Harper wished she had been able to get to know Hannah's grandfather better as an adult, and she was thankful for the few times they'd spent together since she came back to Emerald Isle. He seemed to have his heart in all the right places. He'd left a legacy that would last well beyond her years, but from what Harper had learned from Mitch, she was pretty sure he would have given it all up for his son to have turned out differently.

Now Harper and Hannah would have to figure out how to live life without their hero. A man who saved each of their lives in one way or another. A man who'd sacrificed it all to protect the people he loved. He deserved a medal. A plaque. A statue. Something to signify what people should strive to be like on this side of Heaven.

The funeral was nearly unbearable. Harper wore a black dress to cover a heart that felt the same color, but there were moments when she knew why her heart now beat. Like in the clothing store shopping for a dress she didn't even want—Hannah had been right there by her side holding her hand. In fact, she'd been clinging to her since they walked off the pier hand in hand that eerie September evening. One of the best and worst nights of Harper's life. The Coast Guard had searched for days but only found one body. Hannah asked for a matching black dress and at the funeral they looked just like mother and daughter standing over an empty casket, a mere symbol of a life well lived. Fate had brought the two of them to that intersection. Harper initially had no idea what would happen to Hannah now that Doc, Mitch and her biological father weren't around, but she knew what she had to do, what she wanted to do. Officer Pete Dunlap had agreed to let her take Hannah home the night after the calamity at the pier. He also promised to vouch for her being the best candidate to provide a nurturing, safe, and happy home for Hannah. Pete even went with Harper to the attorney's office where they found out that Mitch had left everything in his will to her, Hannah, and the baby. He had even included a line that stated if anything were to happen to him he wanted Harper to have custody of Hannah. After the meeting, Pete brought up the day that he and Harper first met when she came to the station to pick up her car. They laughed about it briefly, and she learned something new. Something that meant way more now than it would have then. Mitch had been the one to pay the tow bill for her car that day. Always the gentleman, she reminisced.

There were only two families that attended Donald Thorpe's funeral, just one day before Mitch Quinn's: Harper and Hannah and Officer Pete's family; the Dunlap's had only come to support

Harper and Hannah. Initially, Harper hadn't been sure whether they should attend, but she didn't want to look back five or ten years from now and regret not taking Hannah to her biological father's funeral. Harper felt sad that his life had turned out the way it had. At one point he'd been a good kid with a bright future, but a few poor decisions had taken him down a road that led to disaster. The fact that no one he'd encountered in all of the years in his life cared enough to show up at his funeral bothered Harper. In a way, she hated him for what he'd done to the family they would have had, but she still found a soft spot in her heart for him.

Every week, she and Hannah would place flowers at four grave sites in the local cemetery, shaded by massive oak trees with moss dangling from the branches. They'd pluck a few sporadic weeds, say a prayer at each stone, and usually one or both of them would end up crying. Walking through the dusty path that led around the graveyard didn't really get easier, it just became a little more normal as time passed. London and Mitch's stones were side by side. It just seemed right. Hannah liked to bring Snuggles with her, and Harper let her talk her into bringing Snuggles, Jr—the name Hannah picked out for Harper's bear—each time as well. They'd been searching for Snuggles III, the first present that they'd give the new baby, who was growing healthily beneath the small bump in Harper's tummy.

It wasn't fair that neither she nor London had been able to marry Mitch Quinn, but Harper couldn't help but think that maybe this was the way it was all supposed to turn out. She'd often laughed at the thought of sharing him with her sister for eternity. He had enough good in him here on Earth for the both of them, so maybe the same would be true in Heaven. Although she figured relationships there were much different, somehow it would all work out just like it had on Earth. She hoped London had been waiting for Mitch, hoped she'd welcomed him to his new home with a smile and a cancer-free body. If anyone deserved to be there with London, it was Mitch.

Life slowly inched in a better direction. Harper made the decision to carry out Doc's request to open the bed and breakfast. She and Hannah visited each time a new family came to town. Three photos lined the wall just inside the front door: one of Doc with a crowd of children around him in the children's ward at Duke as he read a story to them—photo credit to Mitch Quinn; one of London and Hannah eating ice cream by a water fountain in Emerald Isle—photo credit to Mitch Quinn; and one of Hannah on Mitch's shoulders gazing out at the Atlantic Ocean—selfie photo credit to Hannah Quinn. Hannah felt special when she realized that she was in all three of the photos since she was sitting on Doc's lap in the group photo.

When they would greet the new guests, Harper would give the parents a copy of London's memoir, *Mitch & Me*. It had sold over ten thousand copies already after Harper found a publisher that fell in love with the story. The proceeds went entirely to the "The London House"—the name Doc had chosen for the bed and breakfast. Hannah would give each child a Snuggles bear. Once they'd found the online shop where Mitch had tracked down Snuggles, Jr., Harper ordered every bear they had in stock. Hannah would spend time with the kids suffering from cancer and tell them her story and all about the original Snuggles, and so far she'd been able to bring a smile to the face of every single child she'd met there.

Hannah started school, as had been planned, and she loved her teacher. She made lots of new friends at school, but her best friends were the Dunlap twins, who always sat beside her in class. They came over for sleepovers regularly and they played well together.

Harper and Hannah hadn't been back to the pier, but they would always be reminded of it since they could see it as soon as they walked across the small sand dunes between the house and the beach. Harper didn't know if she would ever walk the pier again, but she'd grown fond of the idea that it would always remind her of Mitch Quinn. Maybe the pier was his statue, she'd decided—strong and sturdy, built to withstand storms, but not invincible.

THE END

A Note from the Author

Thank you for reading *Losing London*! I am honored that you invested your time in this novel. If you haven't yet read my debut novel, *A Bridge Apart*, I hope you will soon. If you enjoyed the story you just experienced, I hope you will please consider helping me spread the novel to others, in the following ways:

-Write an online review at Amazon.com, goodreads.com, bn.com, bamm.com.

-Recommend this book to friends at your workplace, book club, church, school, or social groups.

-Visit my website: www.Joey-Jones.com. "Like" Facebook.com/ JoeyJonesWriter (post a comment about the novel). "Follow" me at Twitter.com/JoeyJonesWriter (#LosingLondonNovel). "Pin" on Pinterest. Write a blog post.

-Pick up a copy for someone you know who you think would enjoy the story.

-Subscribe to my Email Newsletter for insider information on upcoming novels, behind-the-scenes looks, promotions, charities and other exciting news.

Sincerely,
Joey Jones

About the Author

Joey Jones fell in love with creative writing at a young age and decided in his early twenties that he wanted to write a novel. His debut novel, *A Bridge Apart,* was released years later, in September 2015. In the meantime, his day job was in the marketing field. He holds a Bachelor of Arts in Business Communications from the University of Maryland University College, where he earned a 3.8 GPA.

He lives in North Carolina with his family. In his spare time, he enjoys spending time with his loved ones, playing sports, reading, and serving others. His favorite meal is a New York Style Pizza with a Mt. Dew, and his favorite movies are romantic comedies.

Joey Jones is currently writing his third novel.

Book Club/Group Discussion Questions

1. Were you immediately engaged in the novel?
2. What emotions did you experience as you read the book?
3. Which character is your favorite? Why?
4. What do you like most about the story as a whole?
5. What is your favorite part/scene in the novel?
6. Are there any particular passages from the book that stand out to you?
7. As you read, what are some of the things that you thought might happen, but didn't?
8. Is there anything you would have liked to see turn out differently?
9. Is the ending satisfying? If so, why? If not, why not...and how would you change it?
10. Why might the author have chosen to tell the story the way he did?
11. If you could ask the author a question, what would you ask?
12. What author(s) would you compare to Joey Jones?
13. Have you ever read or heard a story anything like this one?
14. Would you read this novel again?

760
5860

Made in the USA
Middletown, DE
25 February 2017